D0458808

Night of the Living Dust Bunnies

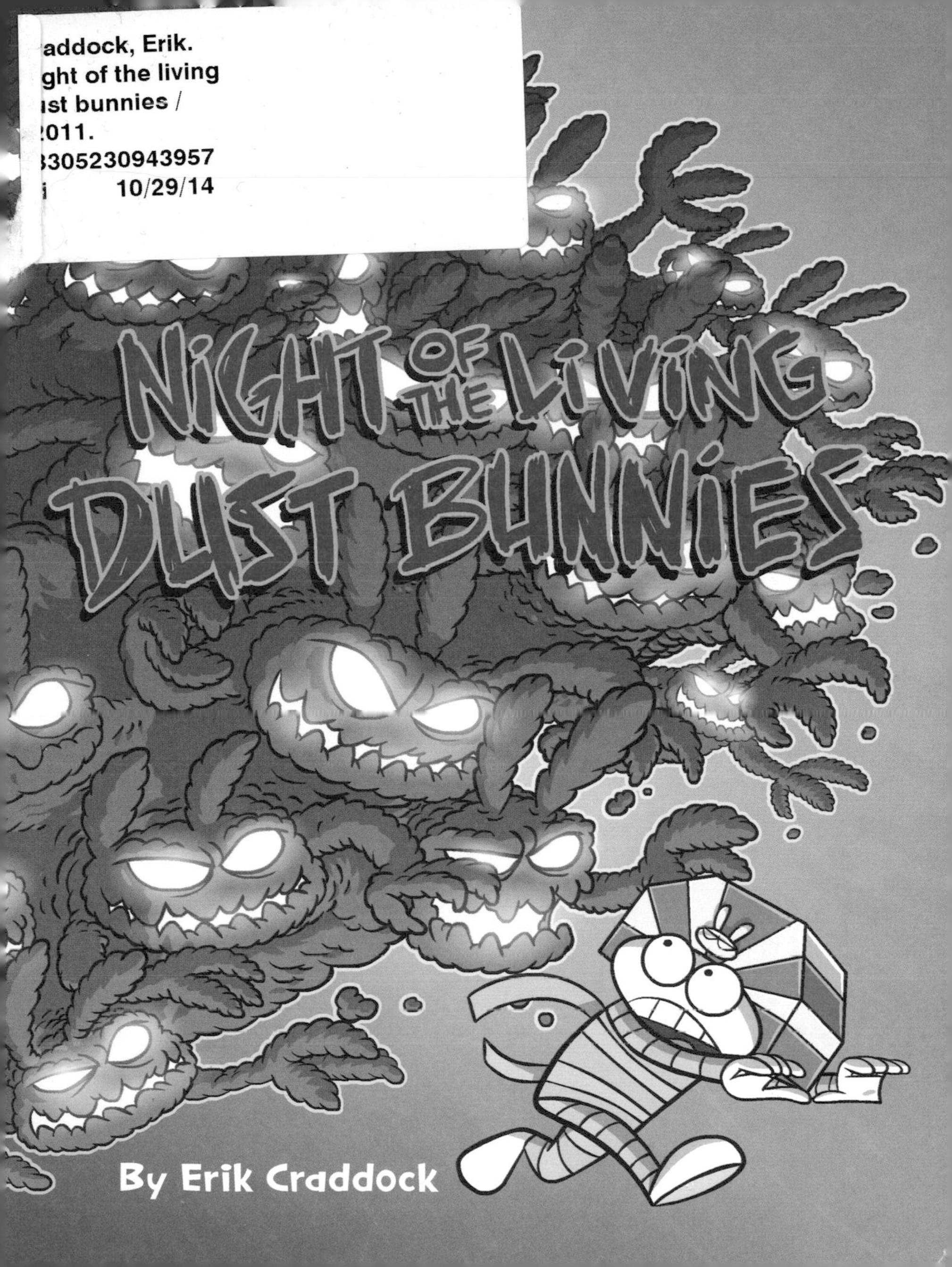

By Erik Craddock

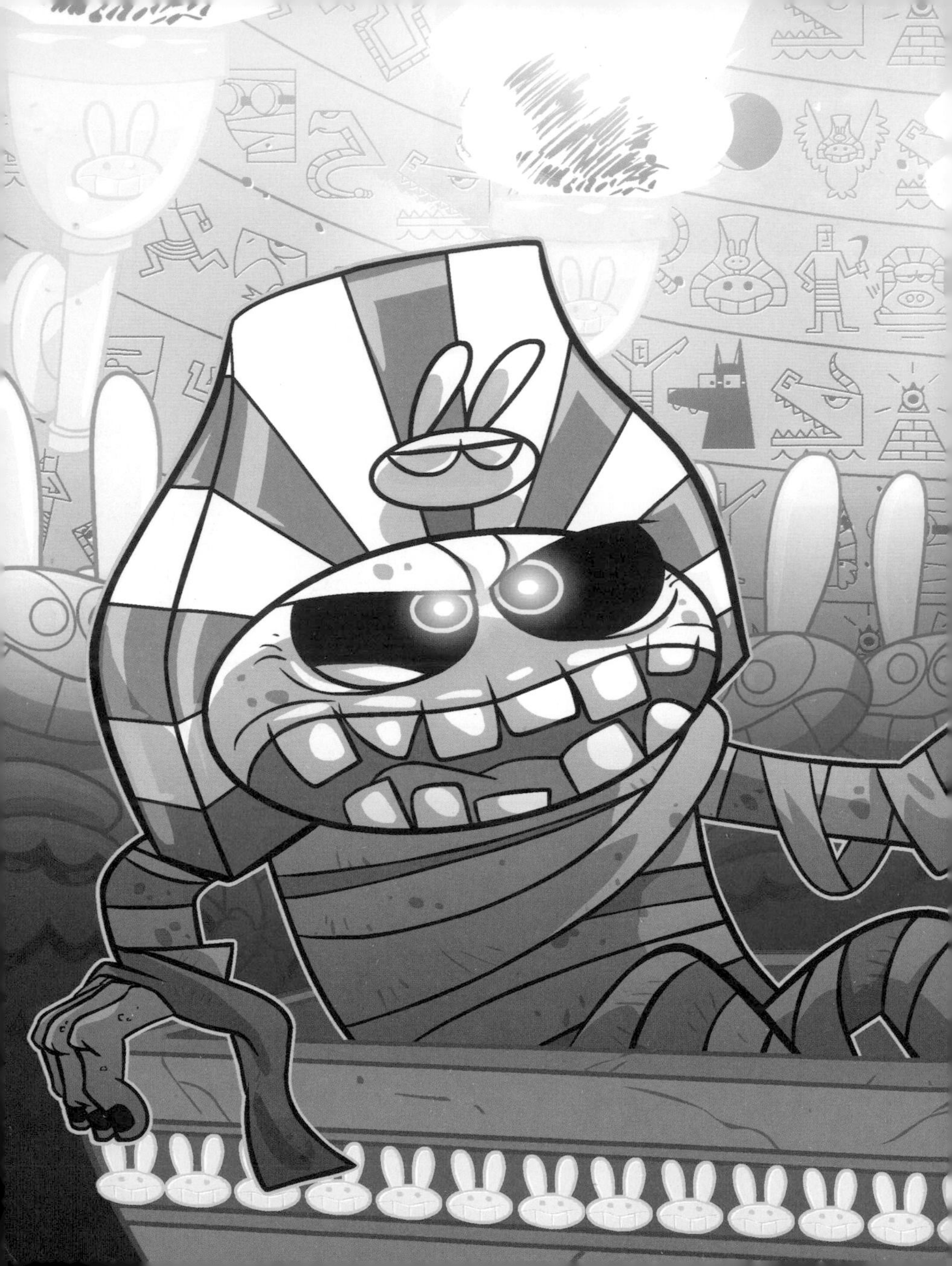

This is a work of fiction. Names, characters, places, and incidents either are the product of the author's imagination or are used fictitiously. Any resemblance to actual persons, living or dead, events, or locales is entirely coincidental.

Copyright © 2011 by Erik Craddock.

All rights reserved. Published in the United States by Random House Children's Books, a division of Random House, Inc., New York.
Random House and the colophon are registered trademarks of Random House, Inc.

Visit us on the Web! www.randomhouse.com/kids

Educators and librarians, for a variety of teaching tools, visit us at www.randomhouse.com/teachers
stonerabbit.com

Library of Congress Cataloging-in-Publication Data
Craddock, Erik.
Night of the living dust bunnies / by Erik Craddock.
p. cm.
Summary: While Stone Rabbit, Andy Wolf, and Henri Tortoise are
trick-or-treating, zombie dust bunnies are taking over their town.
ISBN 978-0-375-86724-8 (pbk.) — ISBN 978-0-375-96724-5 (lib. bdg.)
1. Graphic novels. [1. Graphic novels. 2. Halloween—Fiction. 3. Zombies—Fiction.
4. Dust—Fiction. 5. Rabbits—Fiction. 6. Animals—Fiction. 7. Humorous stories.] I. Title.
PZ7.7.C73Nh 2011 [Fic]—dc22 2010023489

MANUFACTURED IN MALAYSIA   10 9 8 7 6 5 4 3 2   First Edition

Random House Children's Books supports the First Amendment and celebrates the right to read.

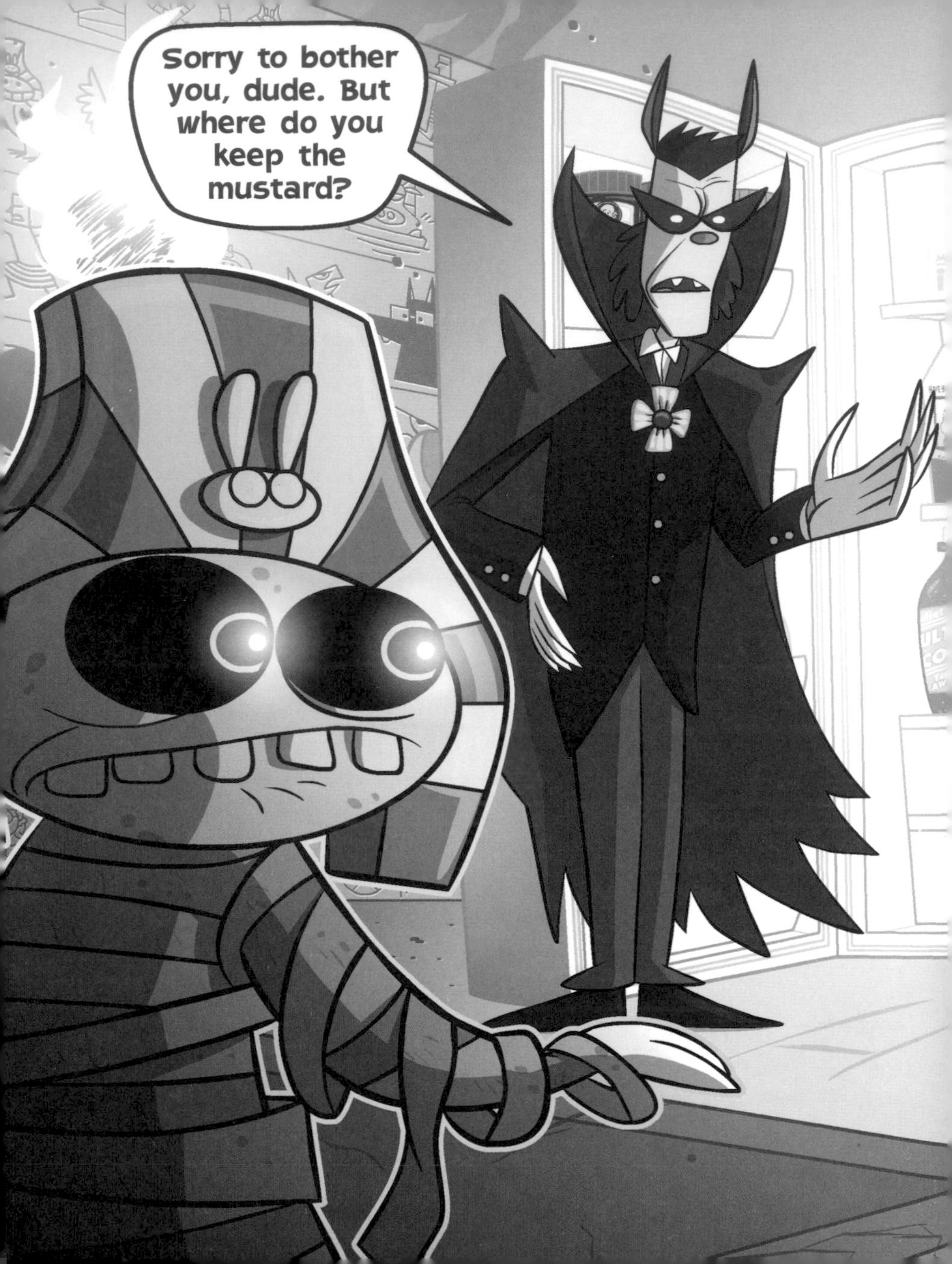
Sorry to bother you, dude. But where do you keep the mustard?

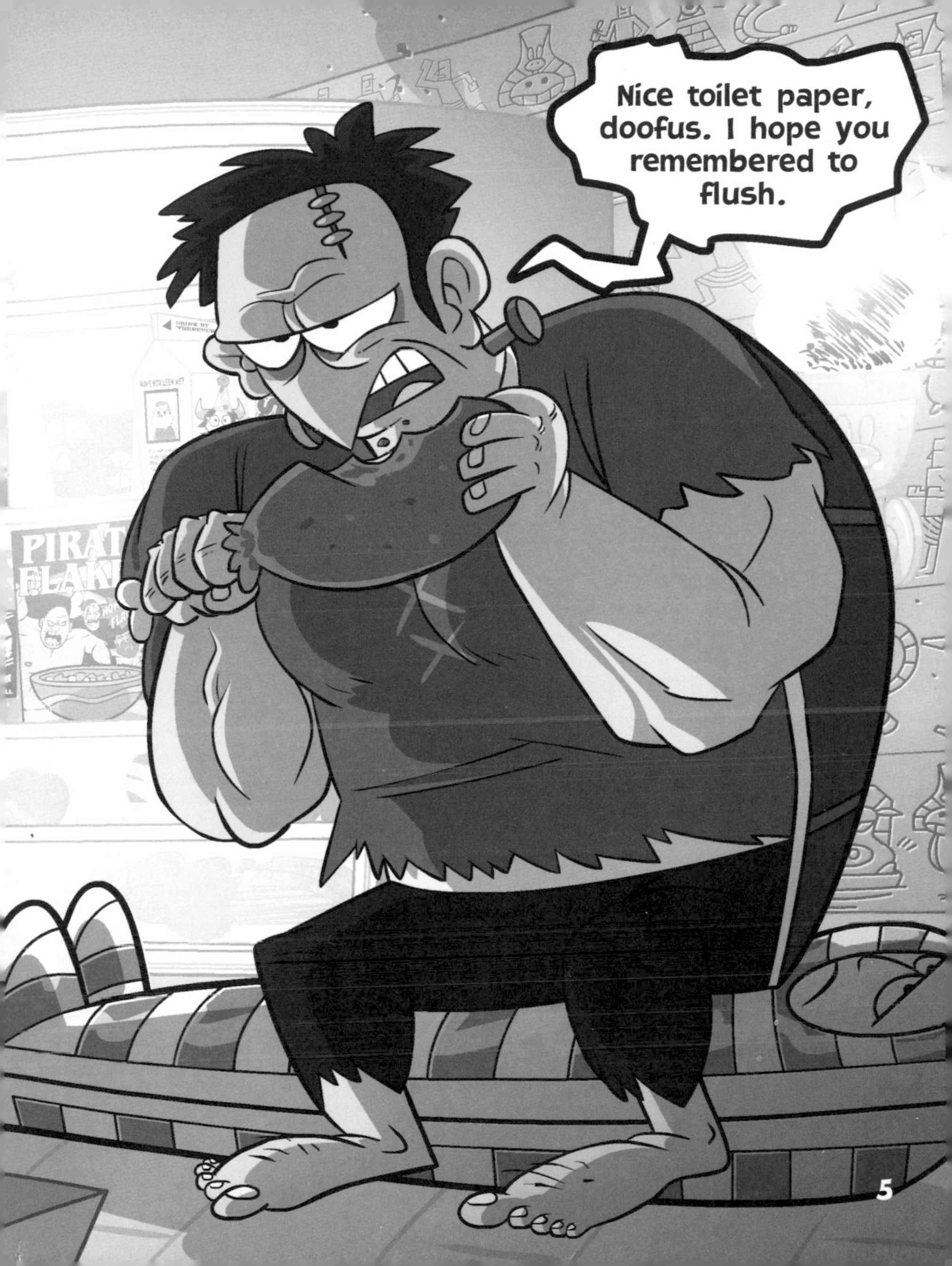
Nice toilet paper, doofus. I hope you remembered to flush.
PIRAT FLAK

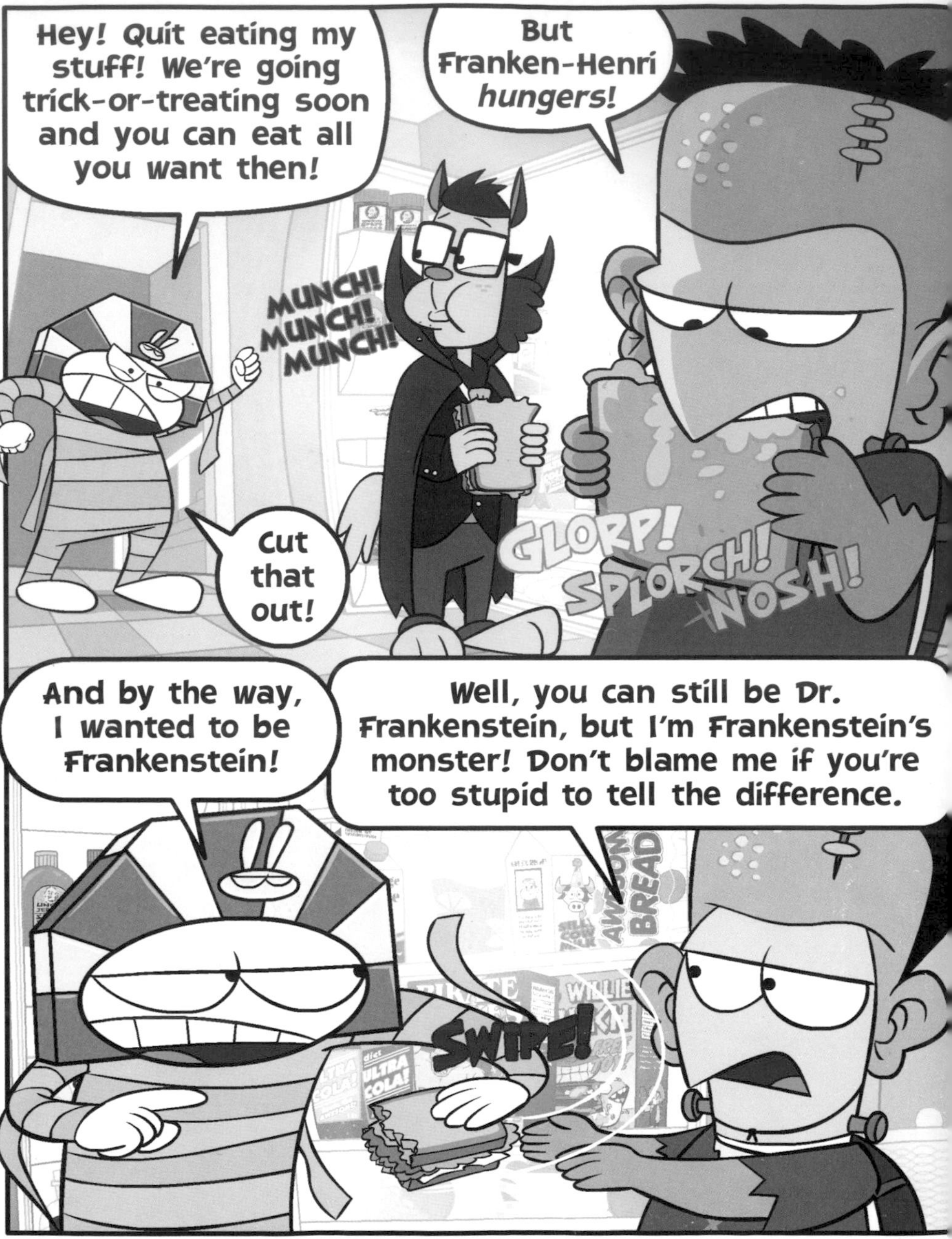
Hey! Quit eating my stuff! We're going trick-or-treating soon and you can eat all you want then!
But Franken-Henri *hungers!*
MUNCH! MUNCH! MUNCH!
Cut that out!
GLORP! SPLORCH! NOSH!
And by the way, I wanted to be Frankenstein!
Well, you can still be Dr. Frankenstein, but I'm Frankenstein's monster! Don't blame me if you're too stupid to tell the difference.
SWIPE!

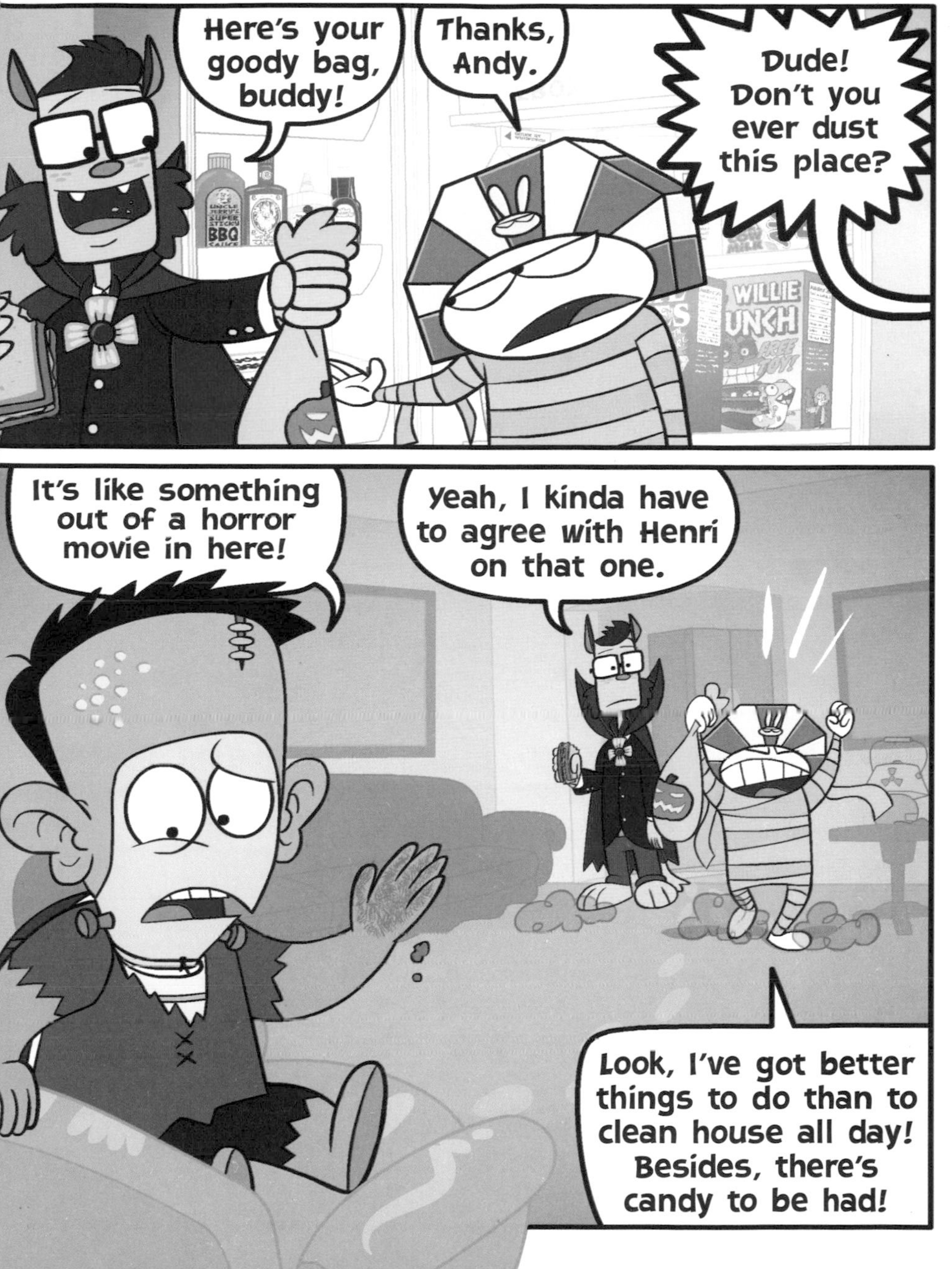
Here's your goody bag, buddy!
Thanks, Andy.
Dude! Don't you ever dust this place?
UNCLE JERRY'S SUPER STICKY BBQ SAUCE
WILLIE UNCH
FREE TOY!
It's like something out of a horror movie in here!
Yeah, I kinda have to agree with Henri on that one.
Look, I've got better things to do than to clean house all day! Besides, there's candy to be had!

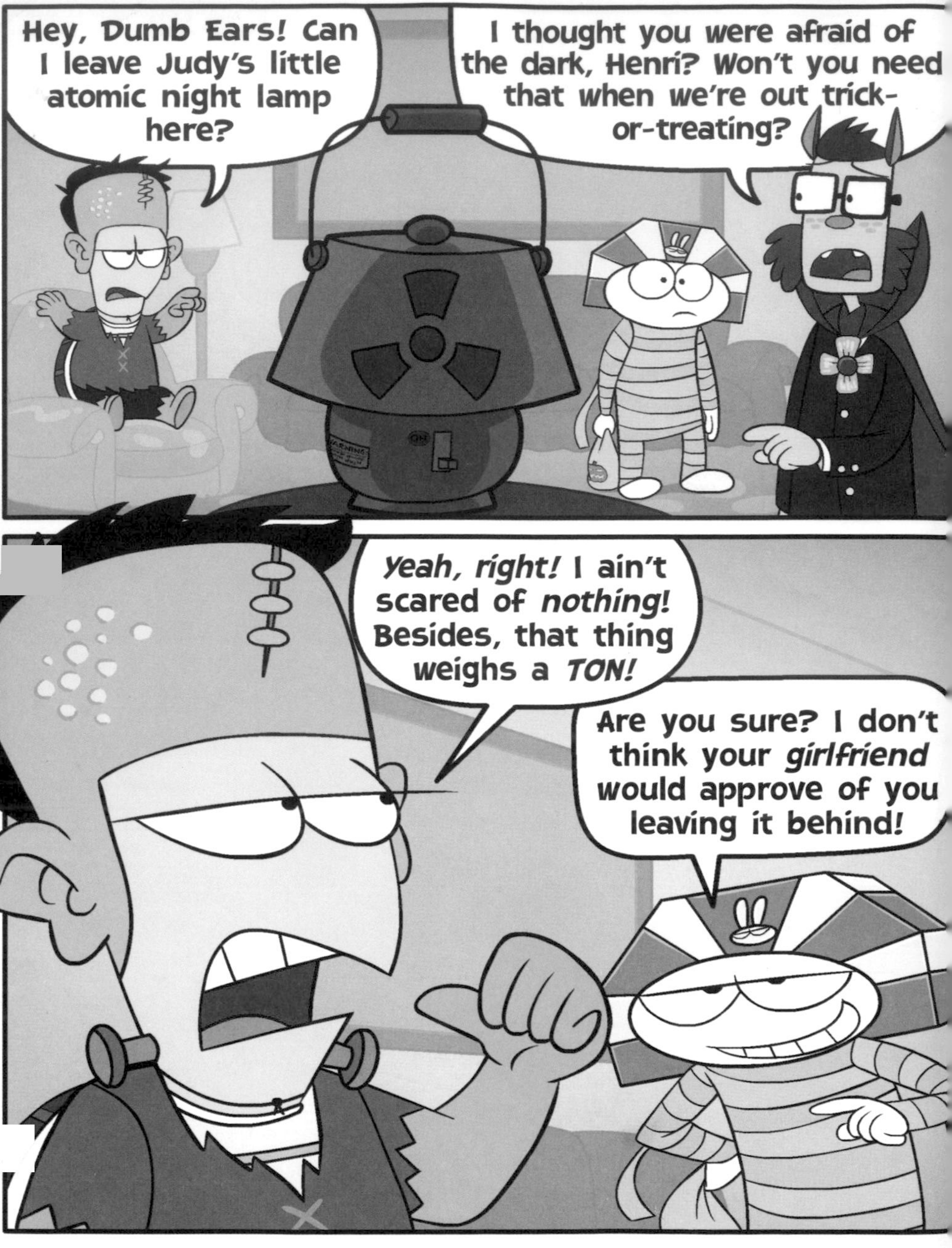
Hey, Dumb Ears! Can I leave Judy's little atomic night lamp here?
I thought you were afraid of the dark, Henri? Won't you need that when we're out trick-or-treating?
Yeah, right! I ain't scared of *nothing!* Besides, that thing weighs a *TON!*
Are you sure? I don't think your *girlfriend* would approve of you leaving it behind!

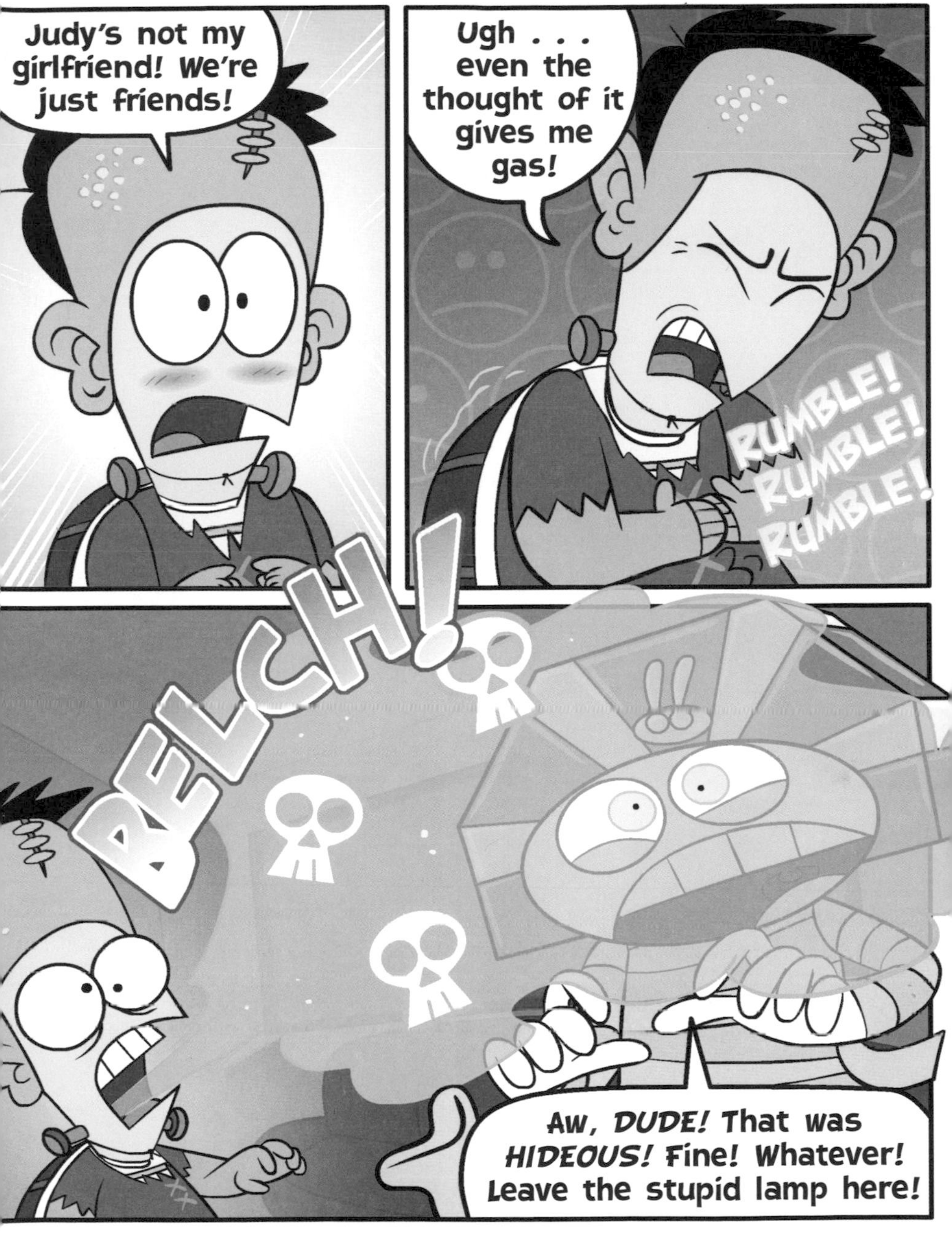
Judy's not my girlfriend! We're just friends!
Ugh . . . even the thought of it gives me gas!
RUMBLE! RUMBLE! RUMBLE!
BELCH!
Aw, DUDE! That was HIDEOUS! Fine! Whatever! Leave the stupid lamp here!

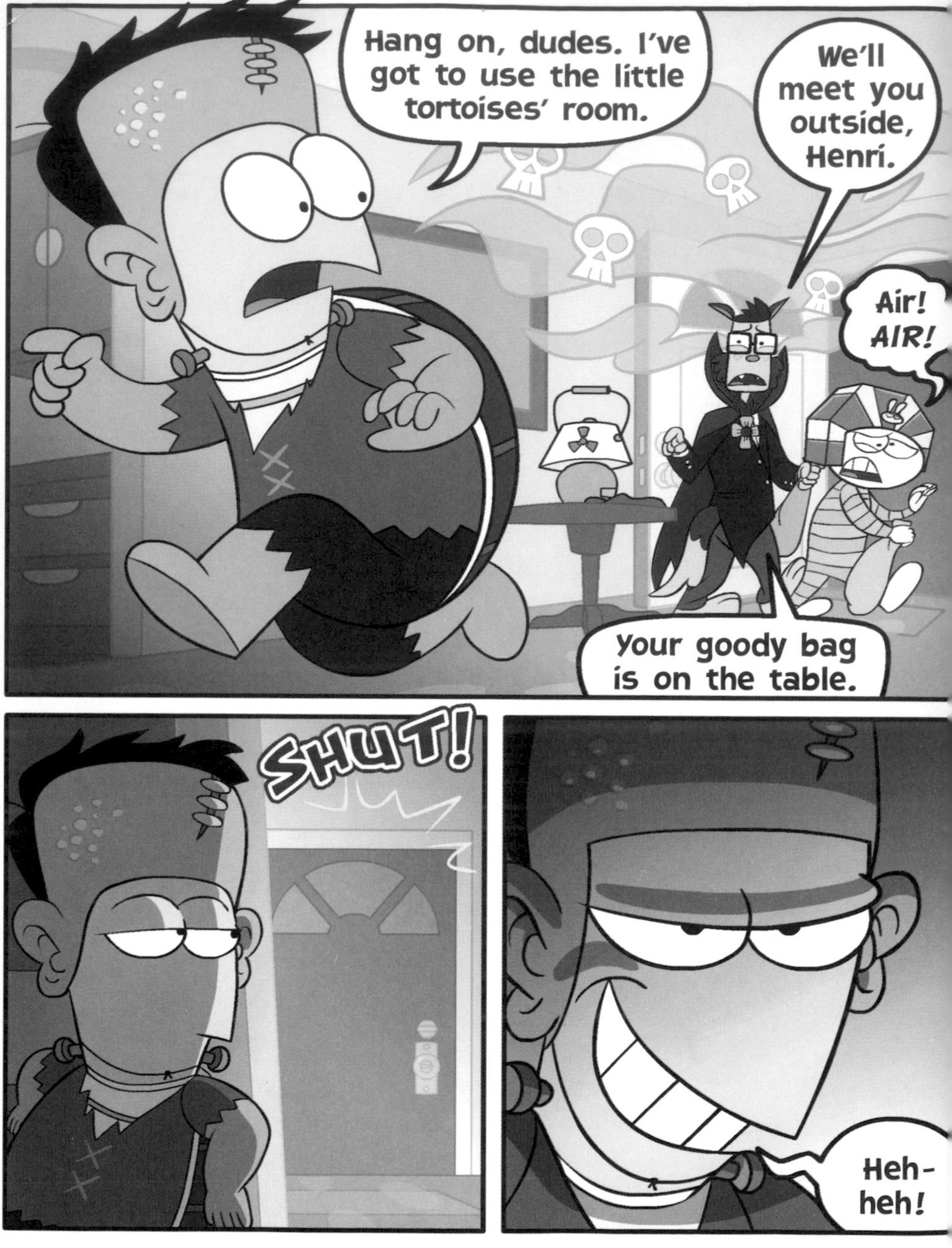
Hang on, dudes. I've got to use the little tortoises' room.
We'll meet you outside, Henri.
Air! AIR!
Your goody bag is on the table.
SHUT!
Heh-heh!

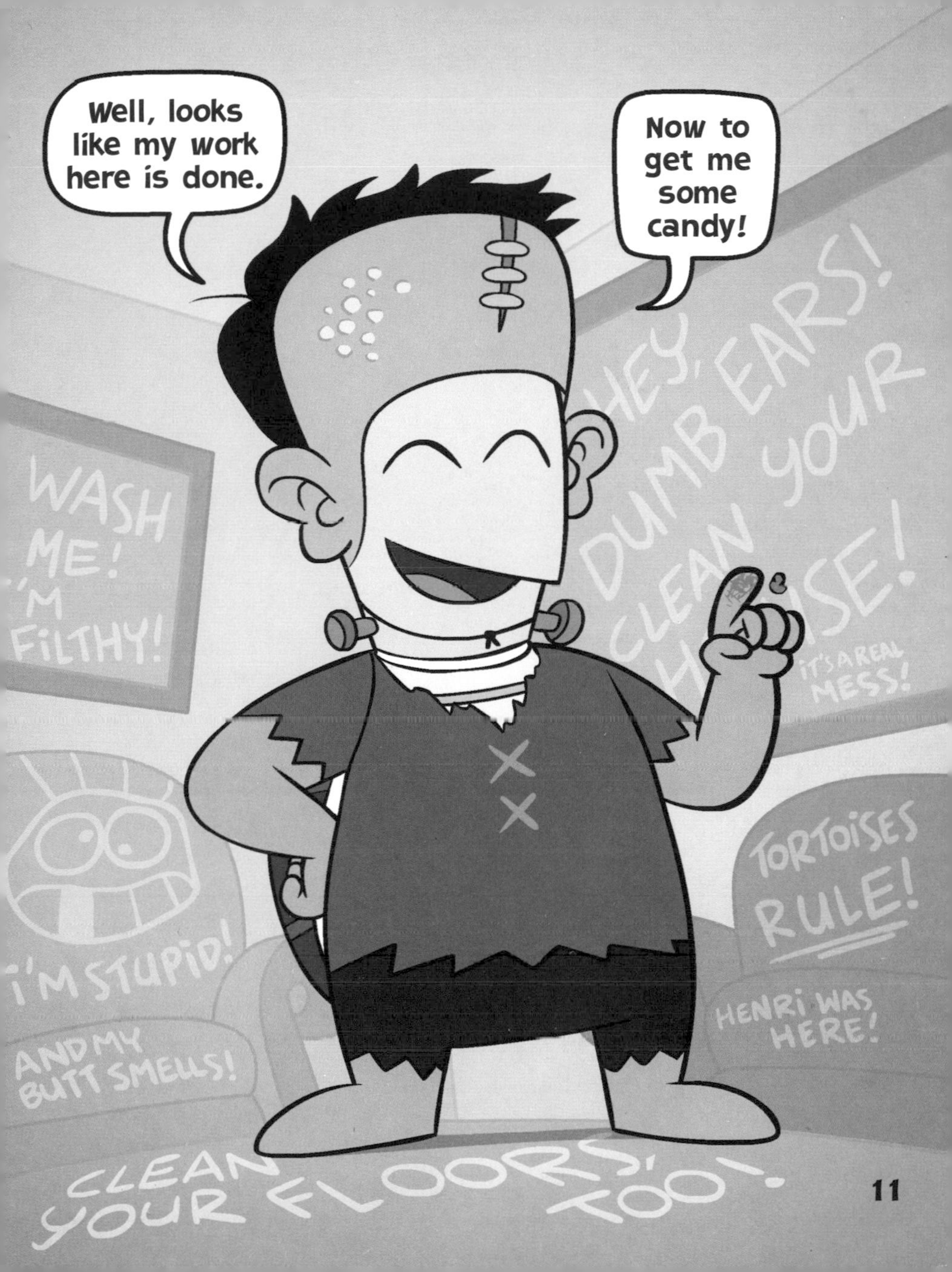
Well, looks like my work here is done.
Now to get me some candy!
WASH ME! I'M FILTHY!
HEY, DUMB EARS! CLEAN YOUR HOUSE!
IT'S A REAL MESS!
TORTOISES RULE!
I'M STUPID!
AND MY BUTT SMELLS!
HENRI WAS HERE!
CLEAN YOUR FLOORS, TOO!

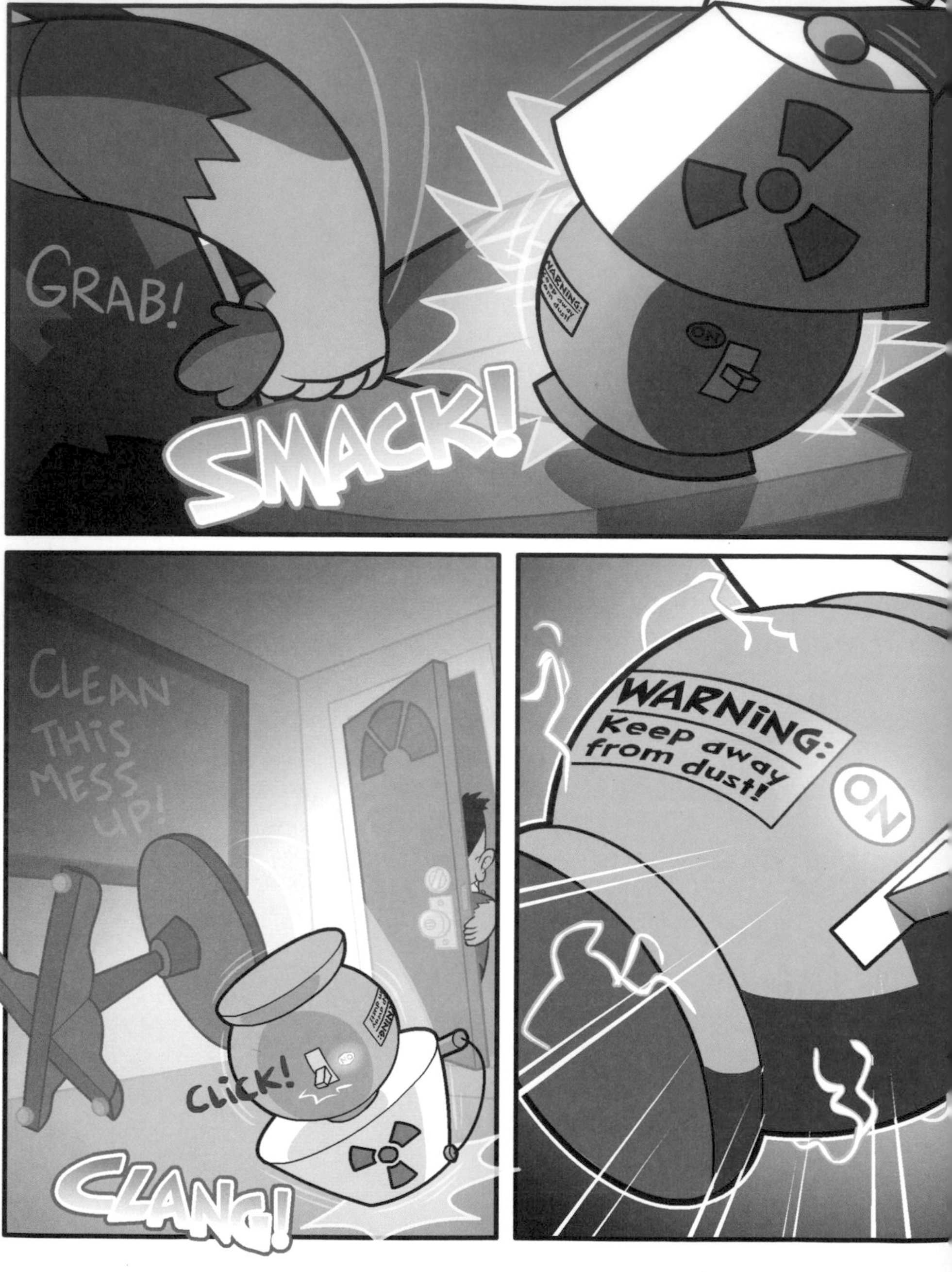
GRAB!
WARNING: Keep away from dust!
ON
SMACK!
CLEAN THIS MESS UP!
CLICK!
CLANG!
WARNING: Keep away from dust!
ON

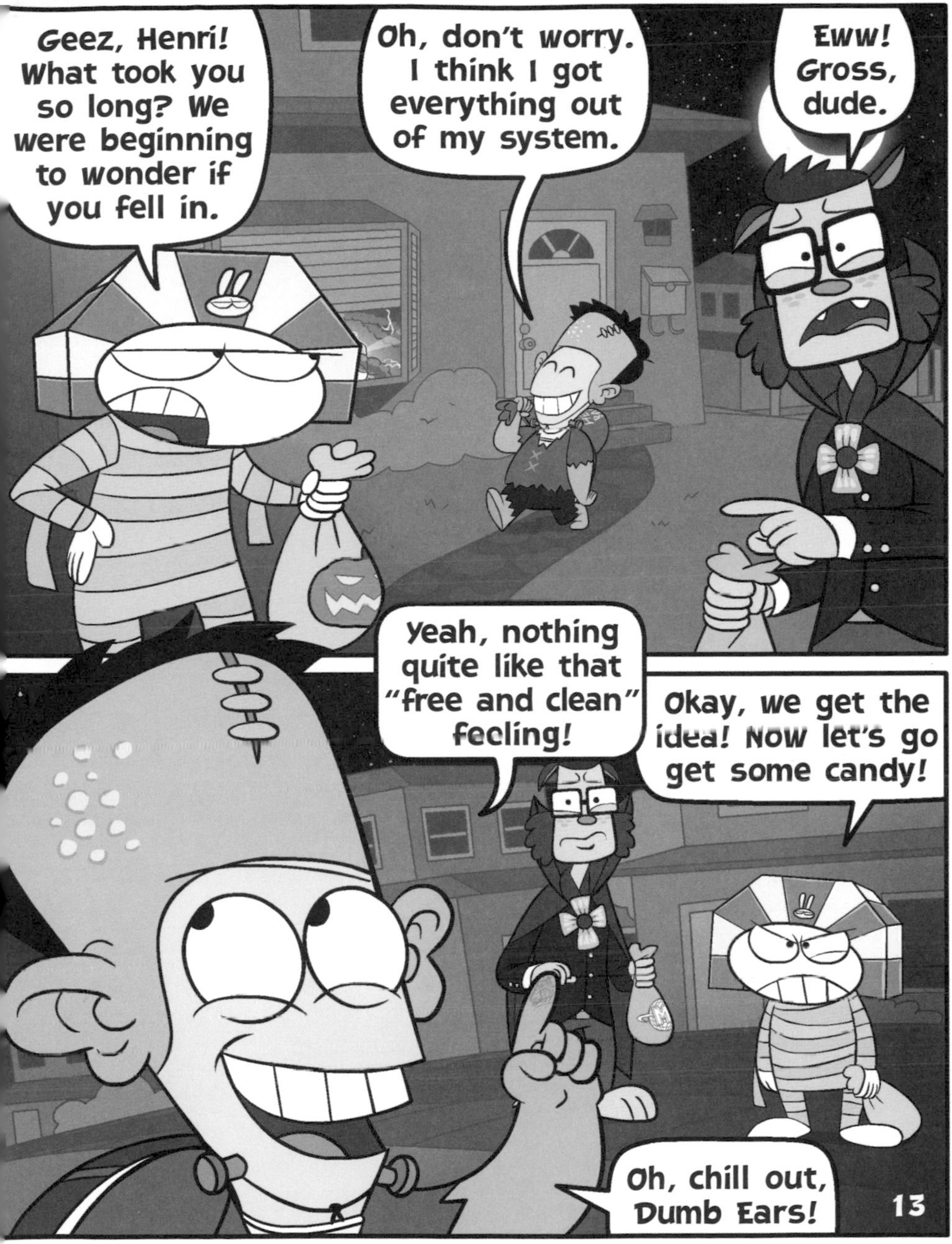
Geez, Henri! What took you so long? We were beginning to wonder if you fell in.
Oh, don't worry. I think I got everything out of my system.
Eww! Gross, dude.
Yeah, nothing quite like that "free and clean" feeling!
Okay, we get the idea! Now let's go get some candy!
Oh, chill out, Dumb Ears!

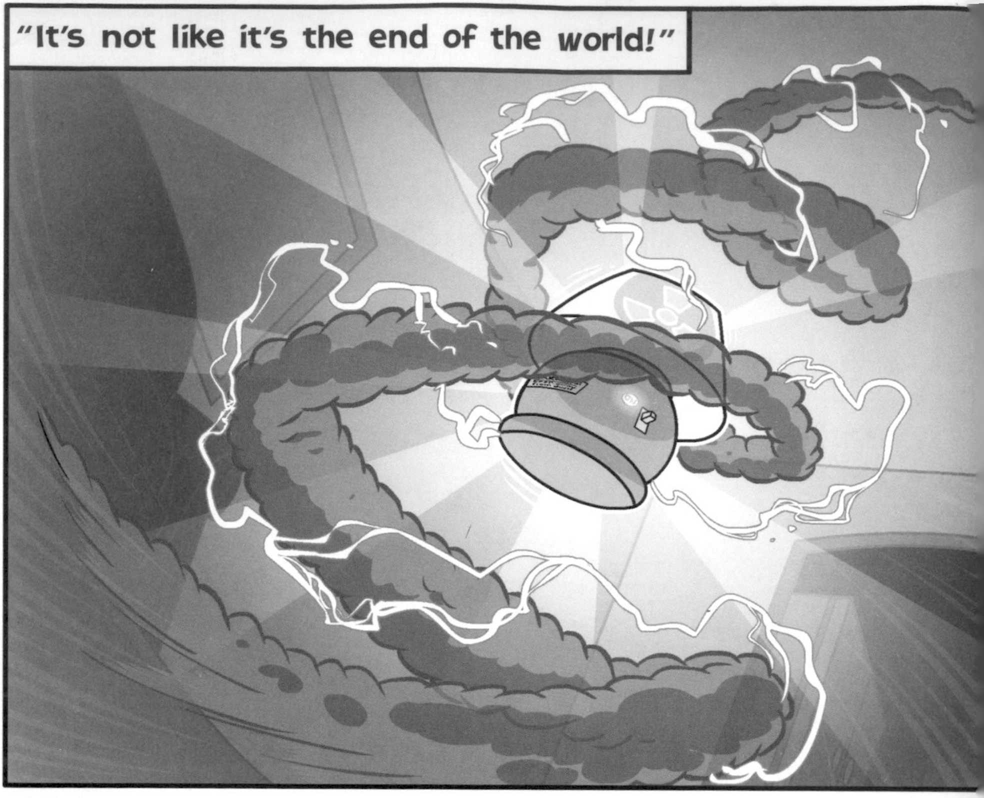
"It's not like it's the end of the world!"

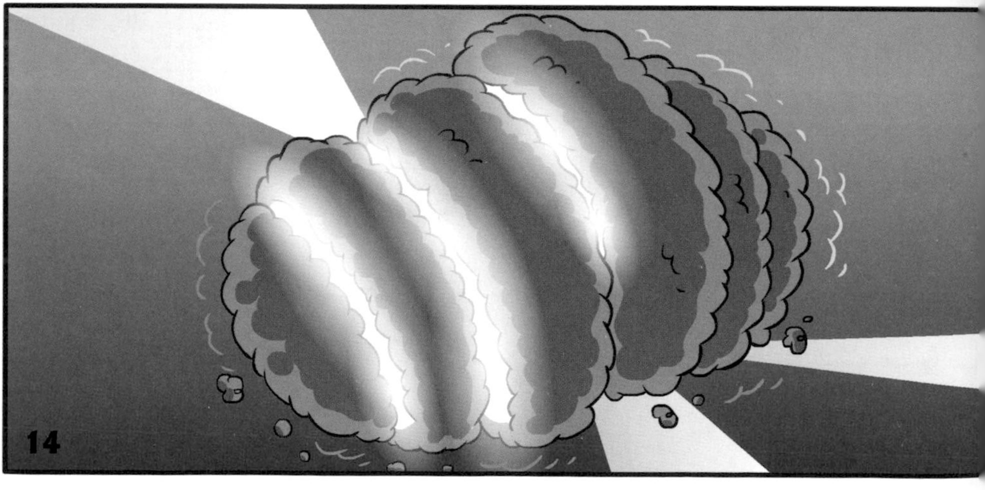

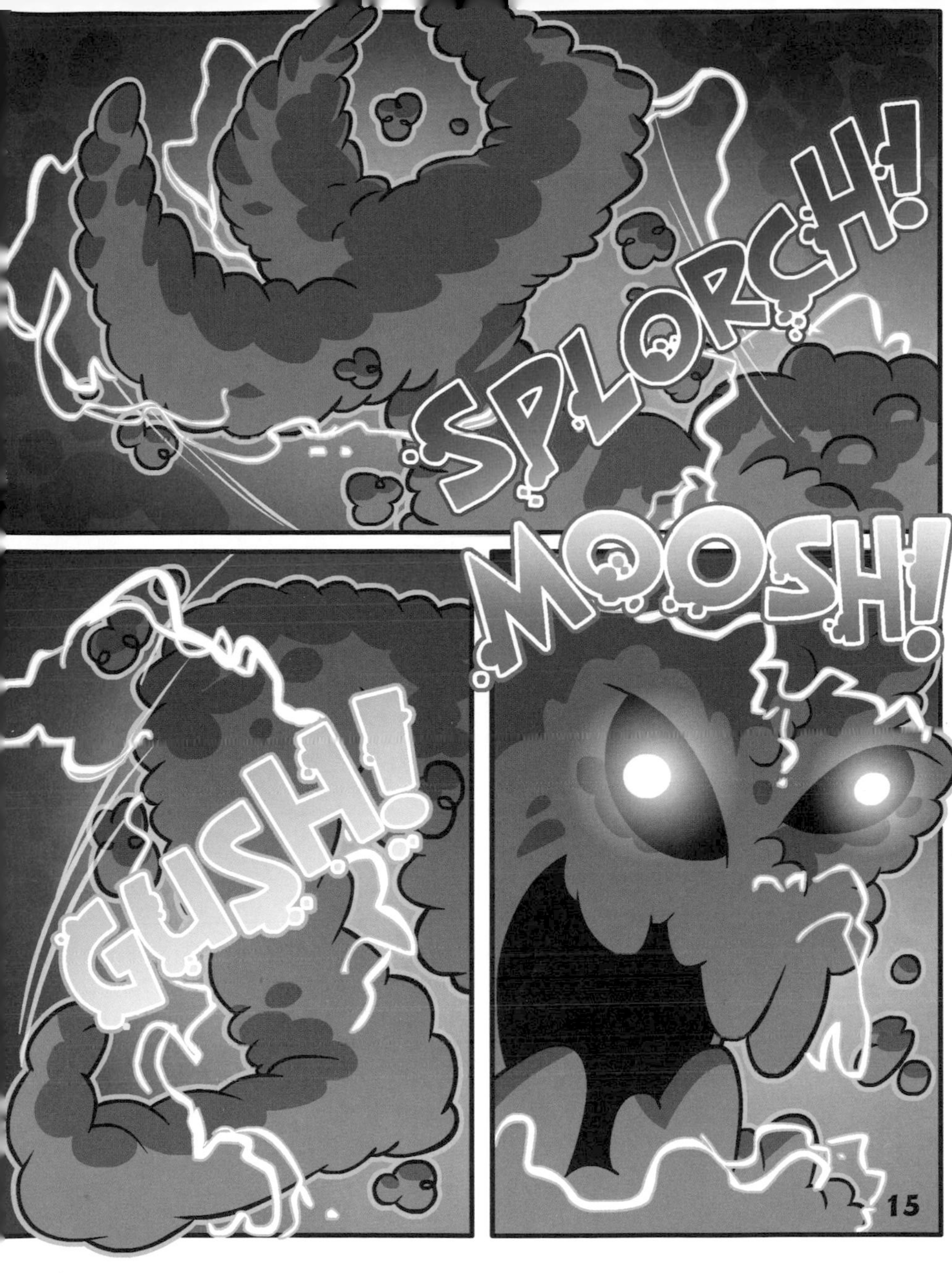
SPLORCH!
GUSH!
MOOSH!

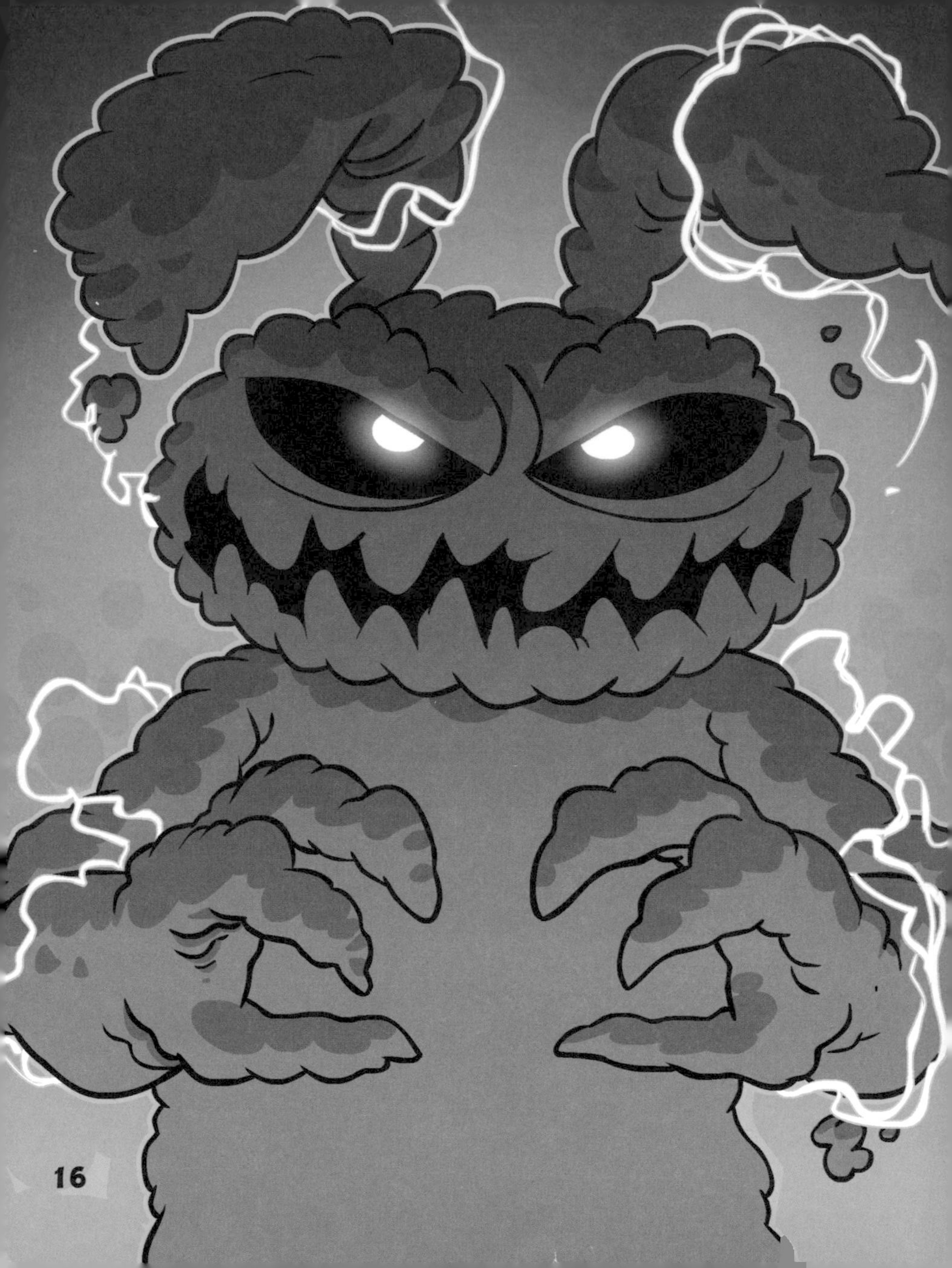

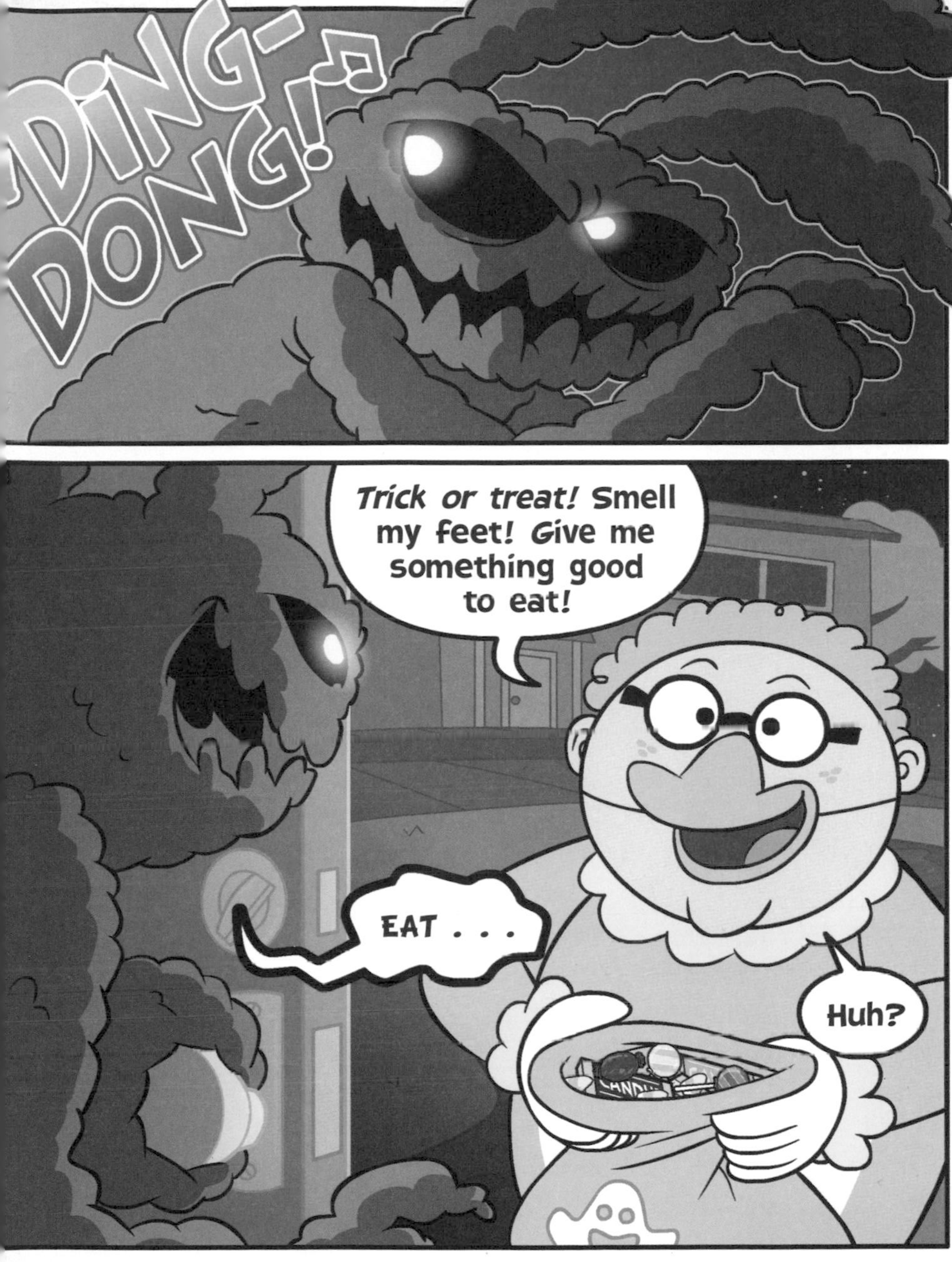
DING-DONG!
Trick or treat! Smell my feet! Give me something good to eat!
EAT . . .
Huh?

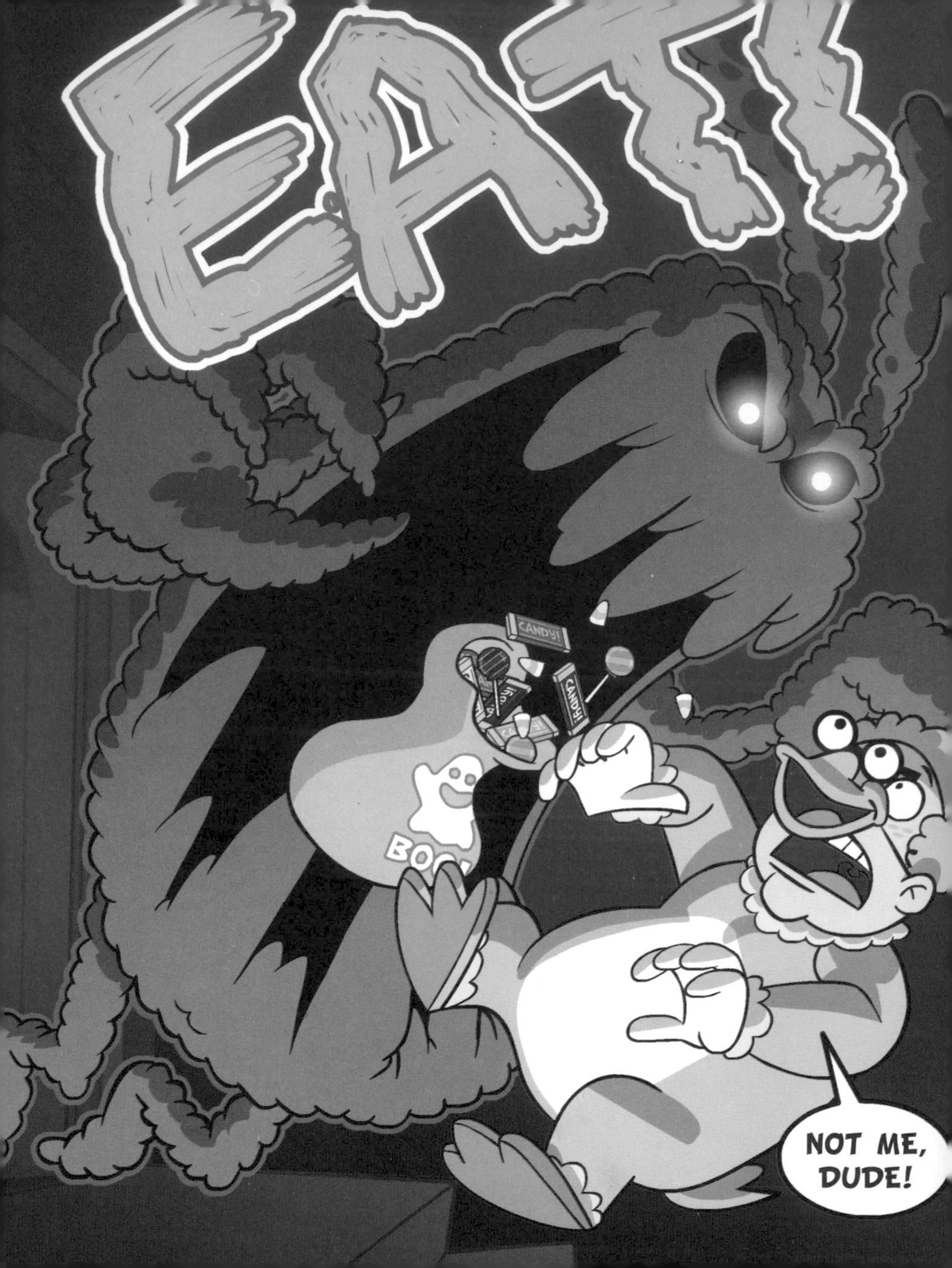
EAT!
CANDY!
CANDY!
CANDY!
BOO
NOT ME,
DUDE!

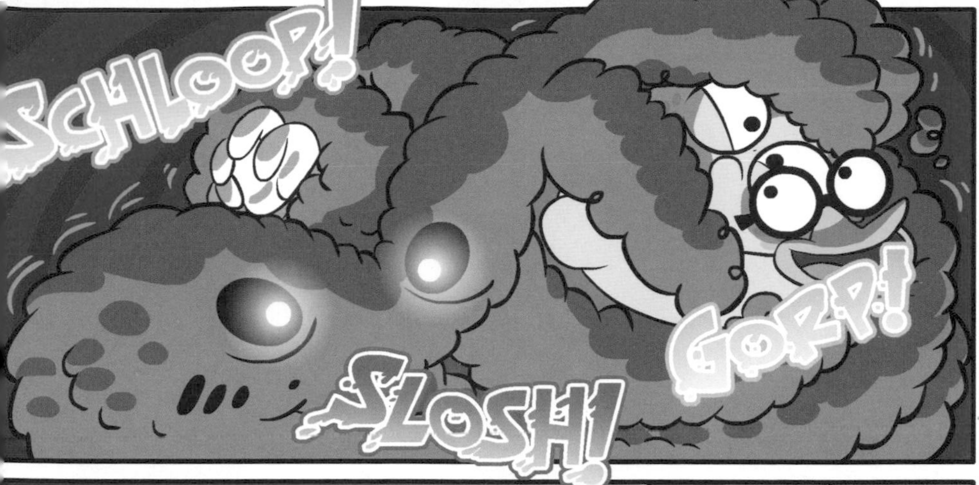
SCHLOOP!
SLOSH!
GORP!
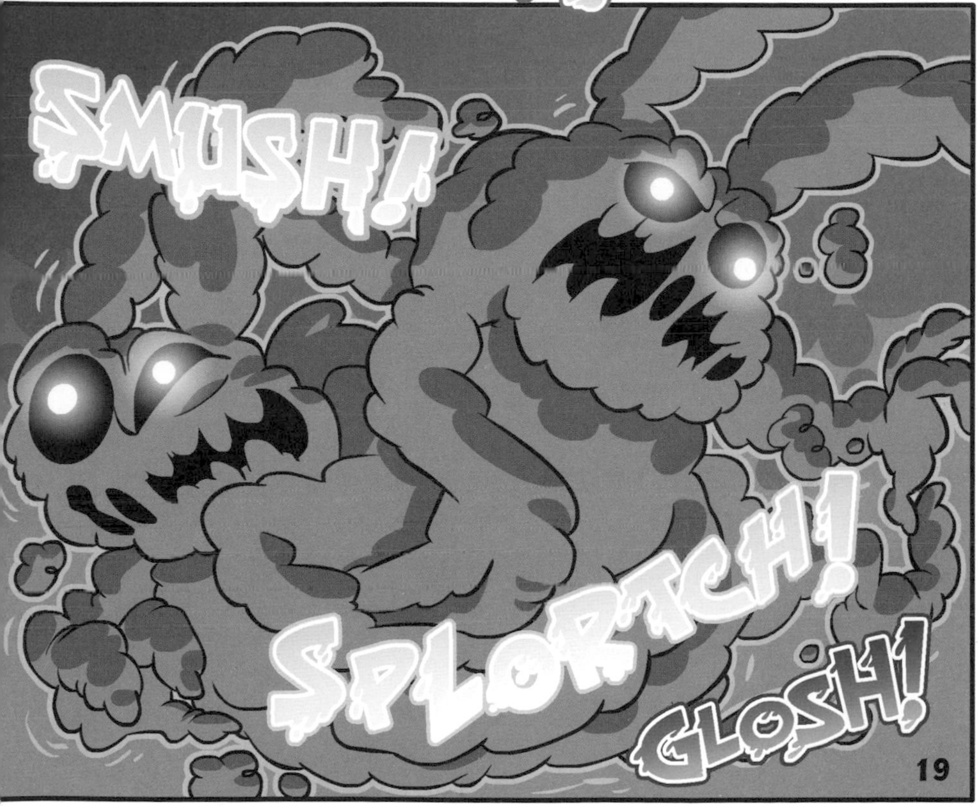
SMUSH!
SPLORTCH!
GLOSH!

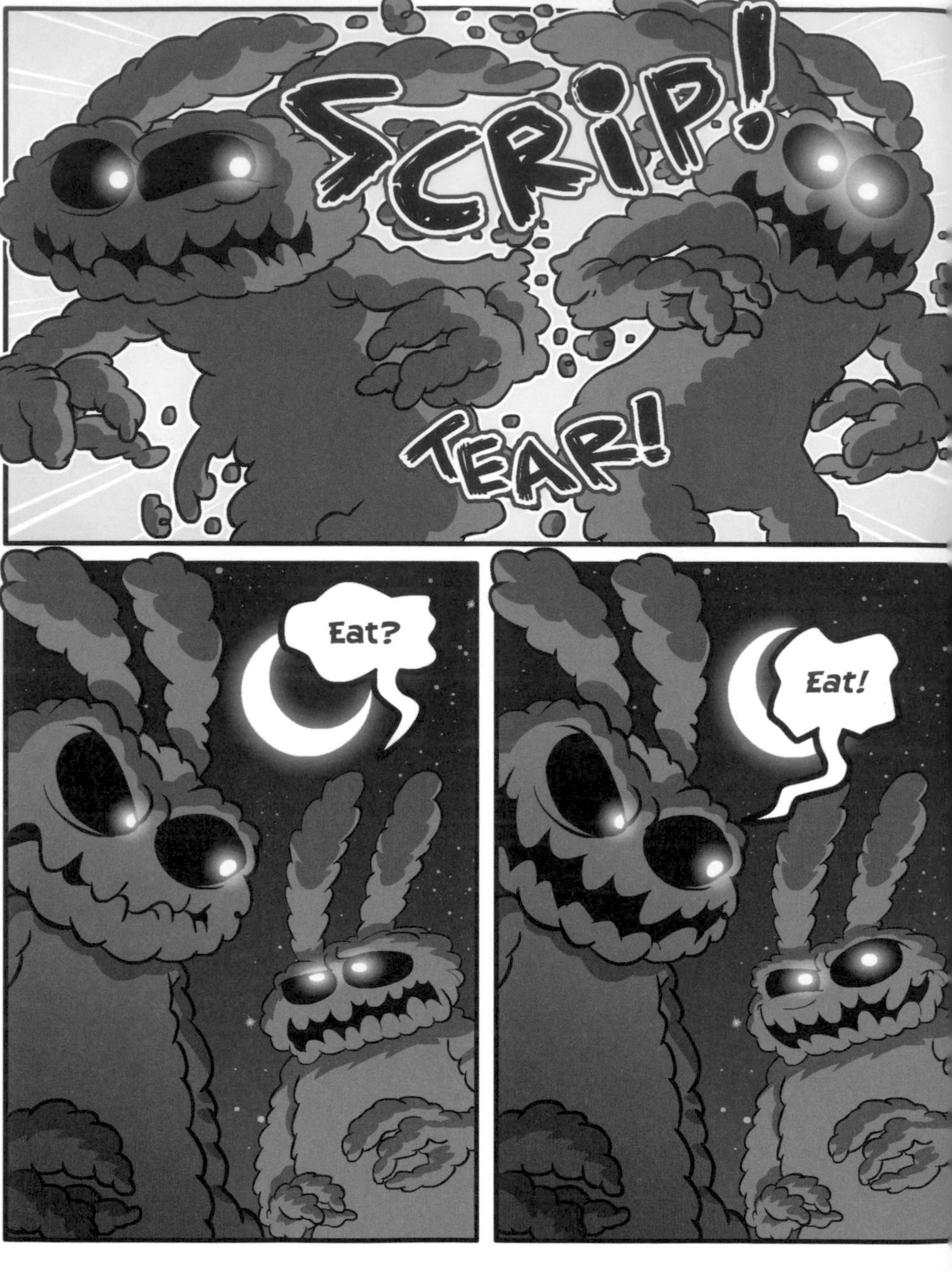
SCRIP!
TEAR!
Eat?
Eat!

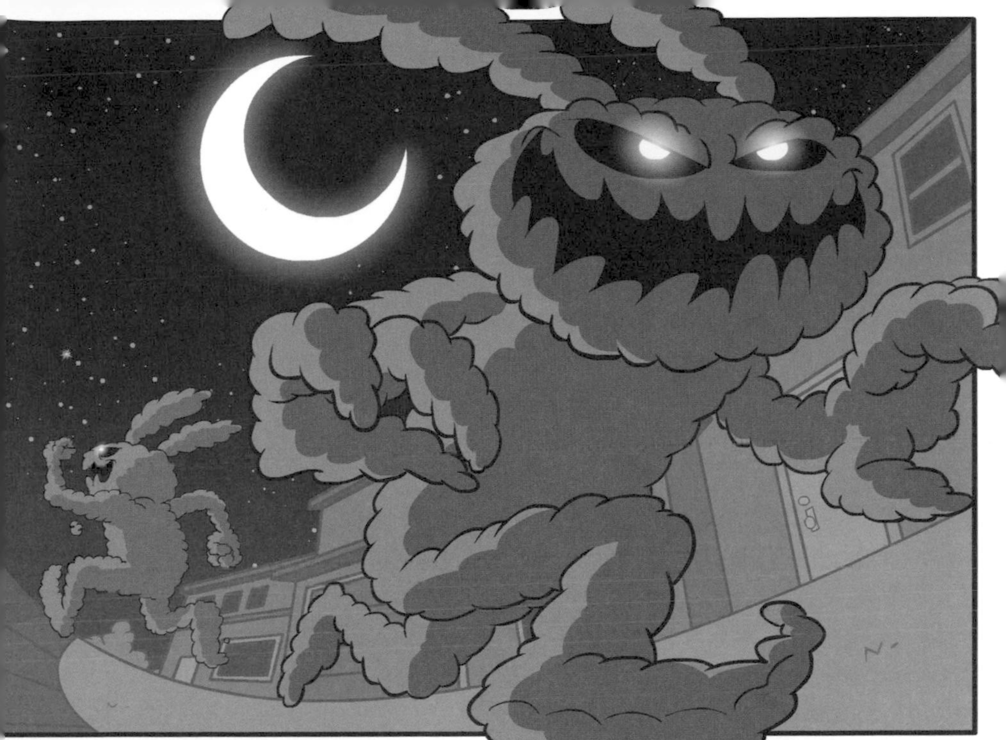

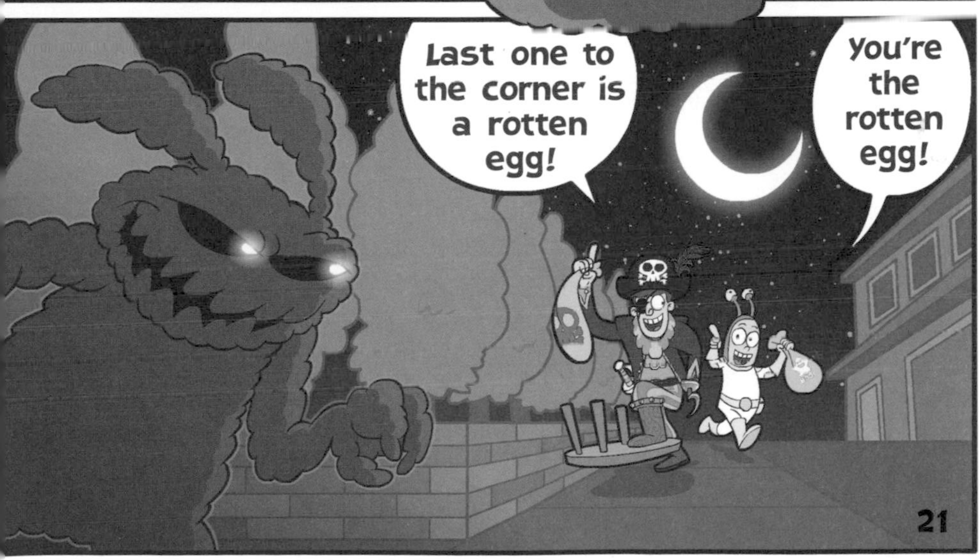
Last one to the corner is a rotten egg!
You're the rotten egg!

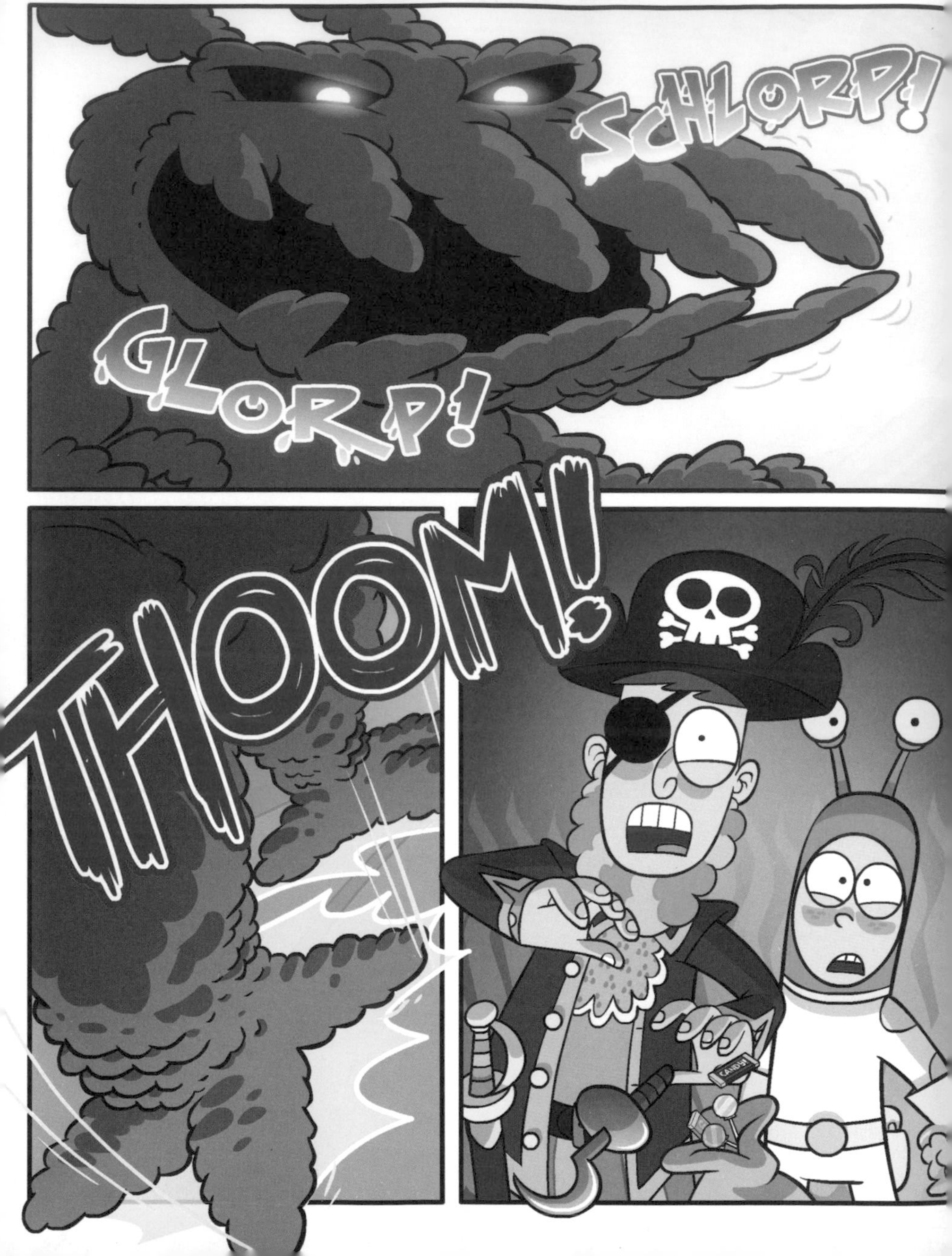
SCHLORP!
GLORP!
THOOM!
CANDY

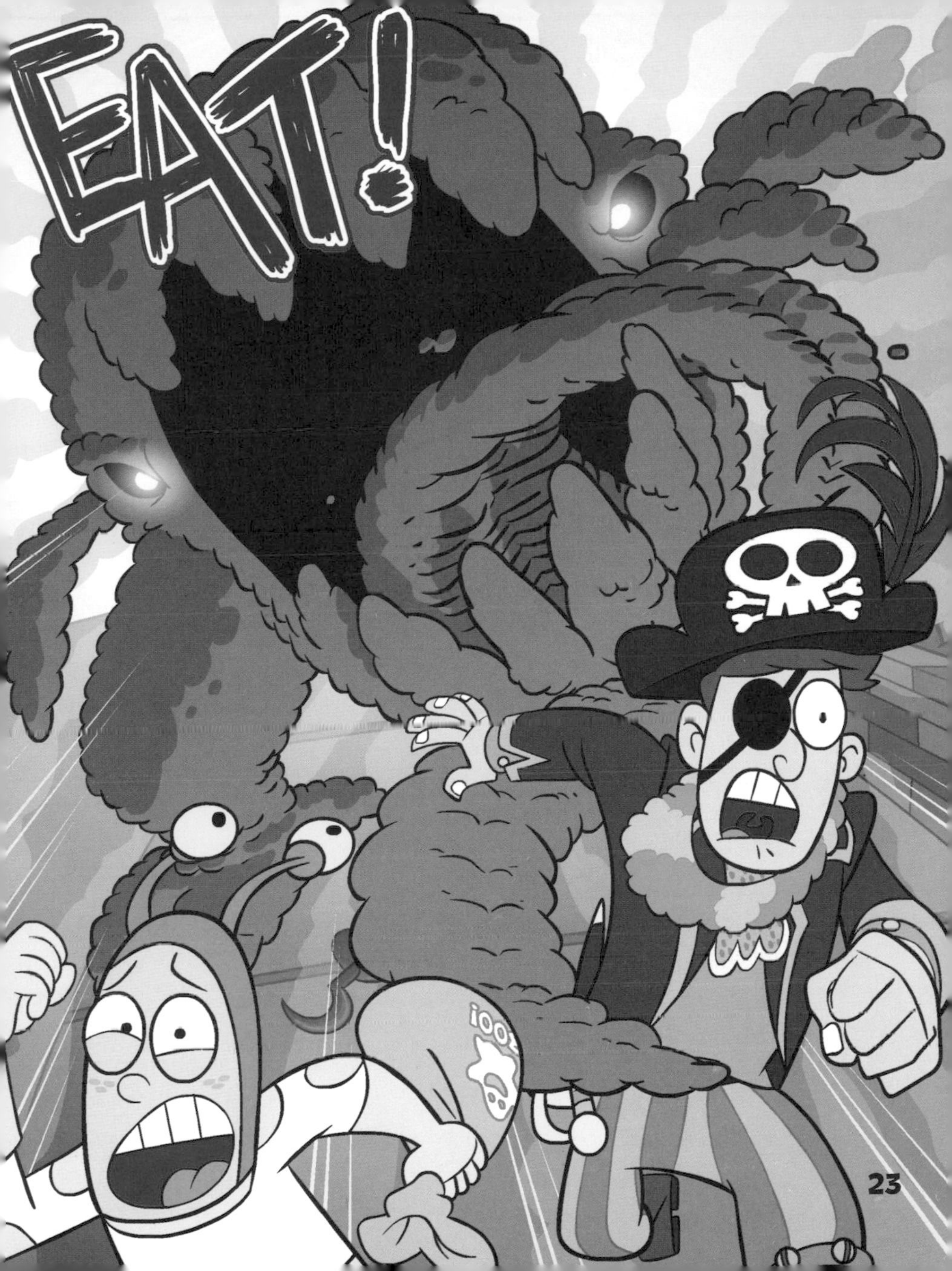
EAT!

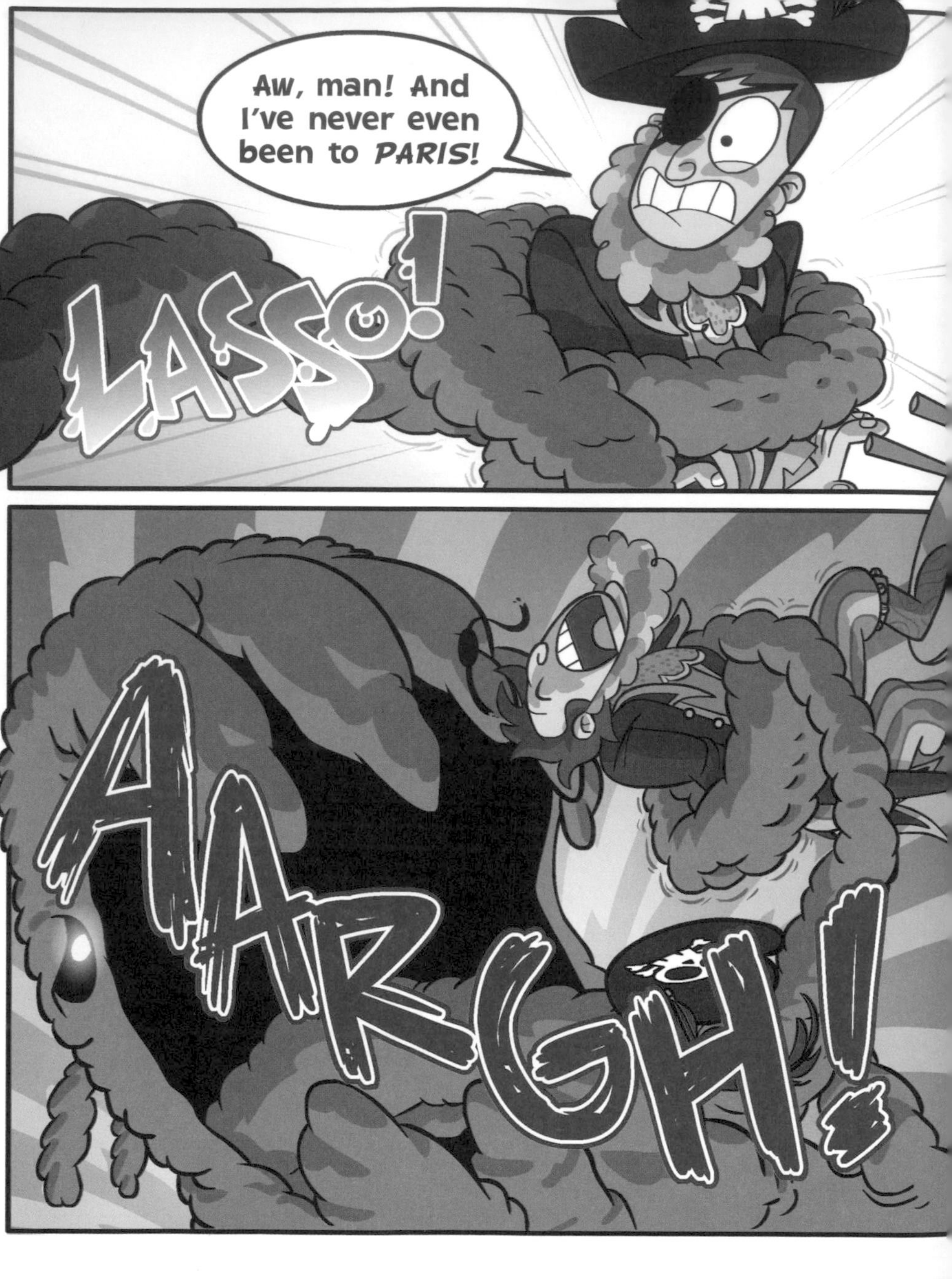
Aw, man! And I've never even been to PARIS!
LASSO!
AARGH!

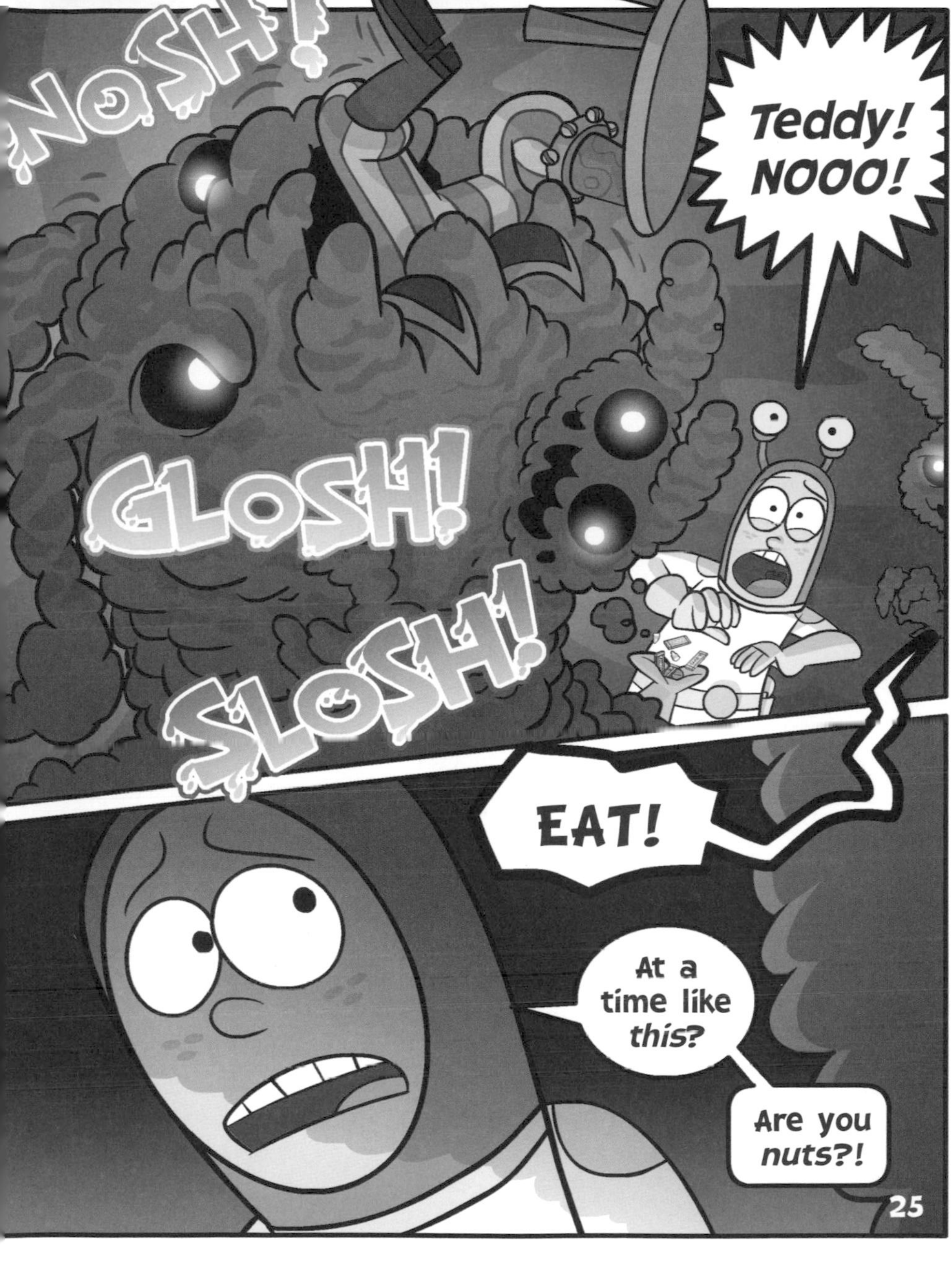
NOSH!
Teddy! NOOO!
GLOSH!
SLOSH!
EAT!
At a time like *this*?
Are you *nuts*?!

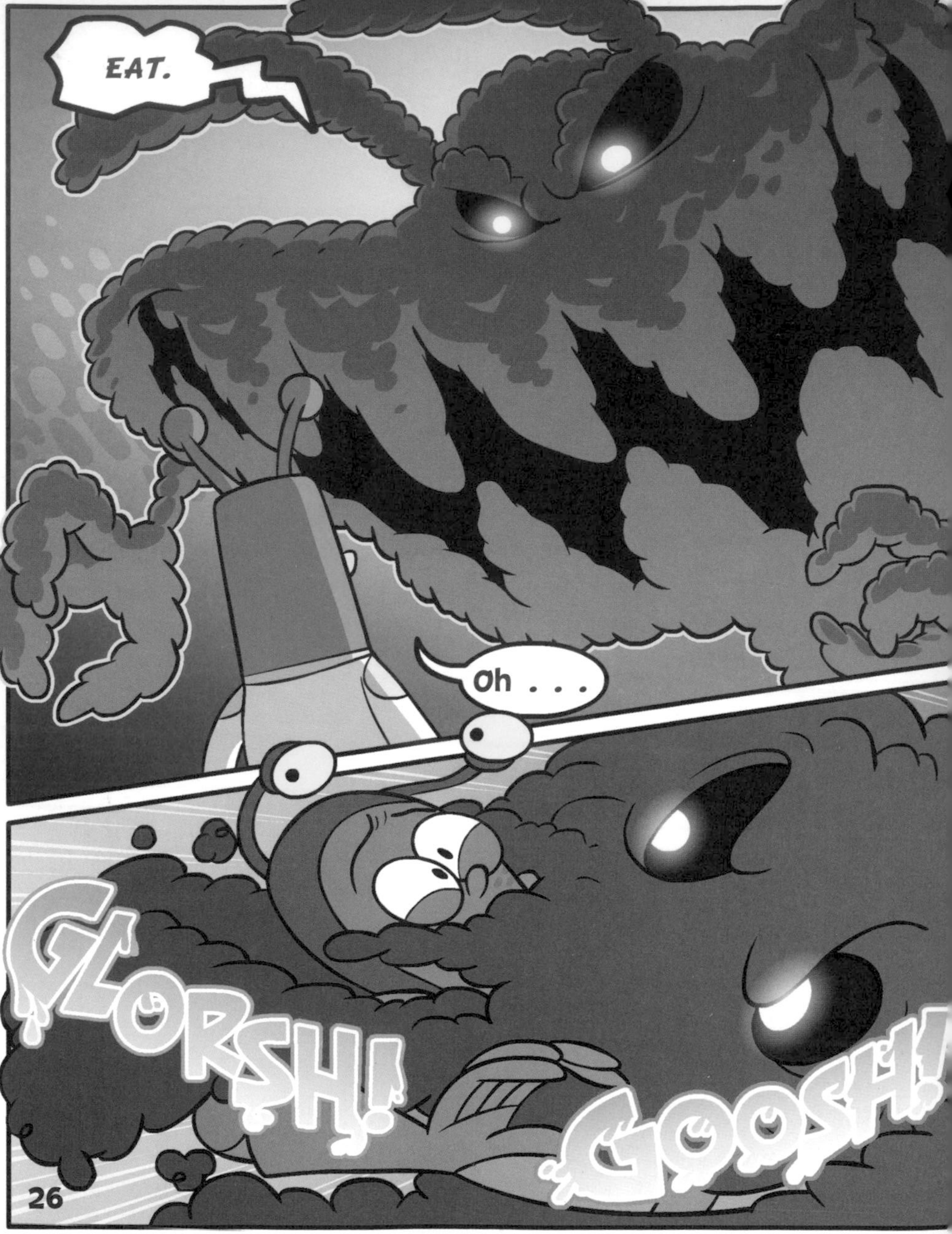
EAT.
Oh . . .
GLORSH!
GOOSH!

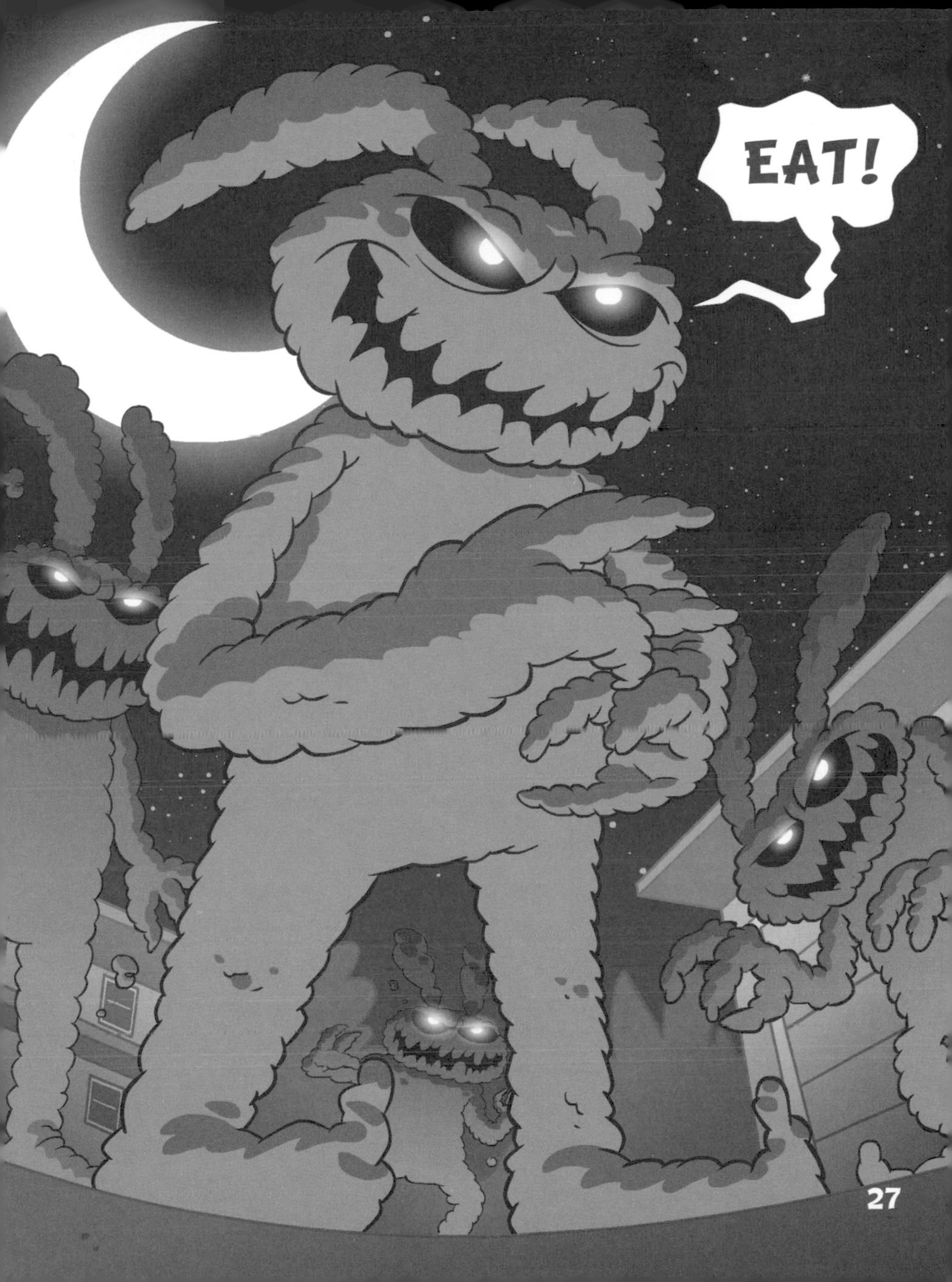
EAT!

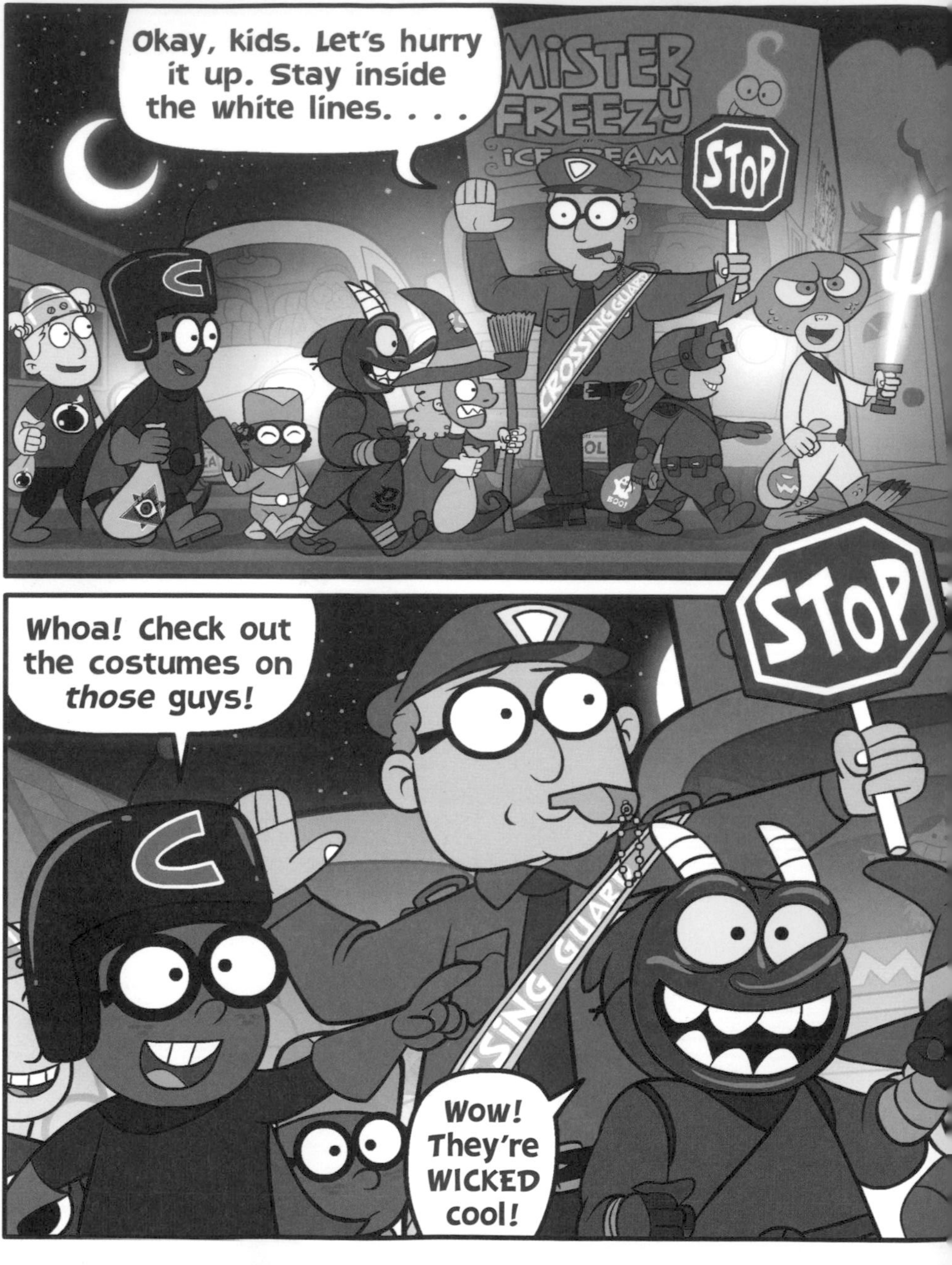
Okay, kids. Let's hurry it up. Stay inside the white lines. . . .
MISTER FREEZY
STOP
CROSSING GUARD
STOP
Whoa! Check out the costumes on *those* guys!
Wow! They're WICKED cool!

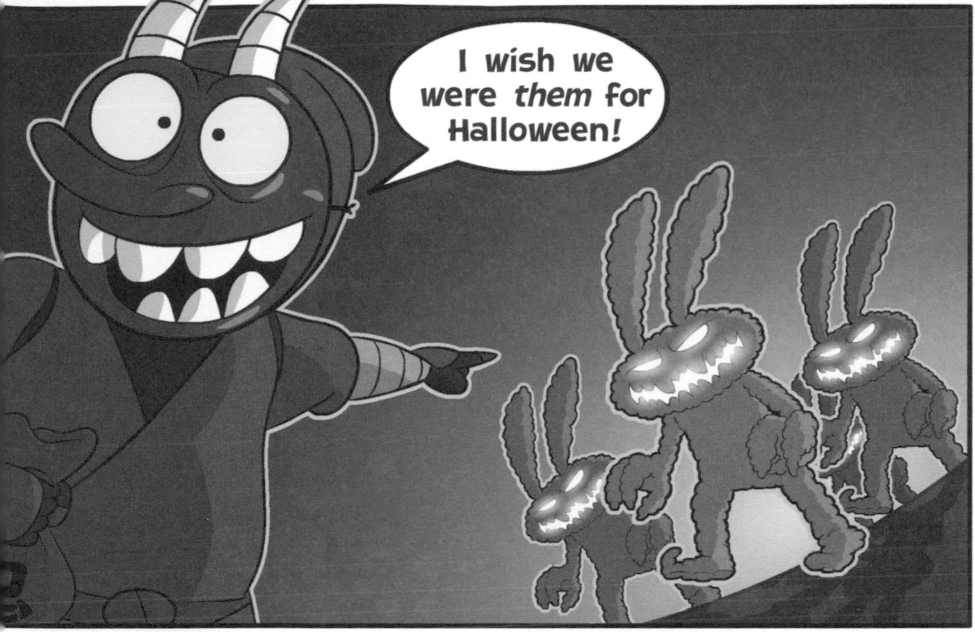
I wish we were *them* for Halloween!
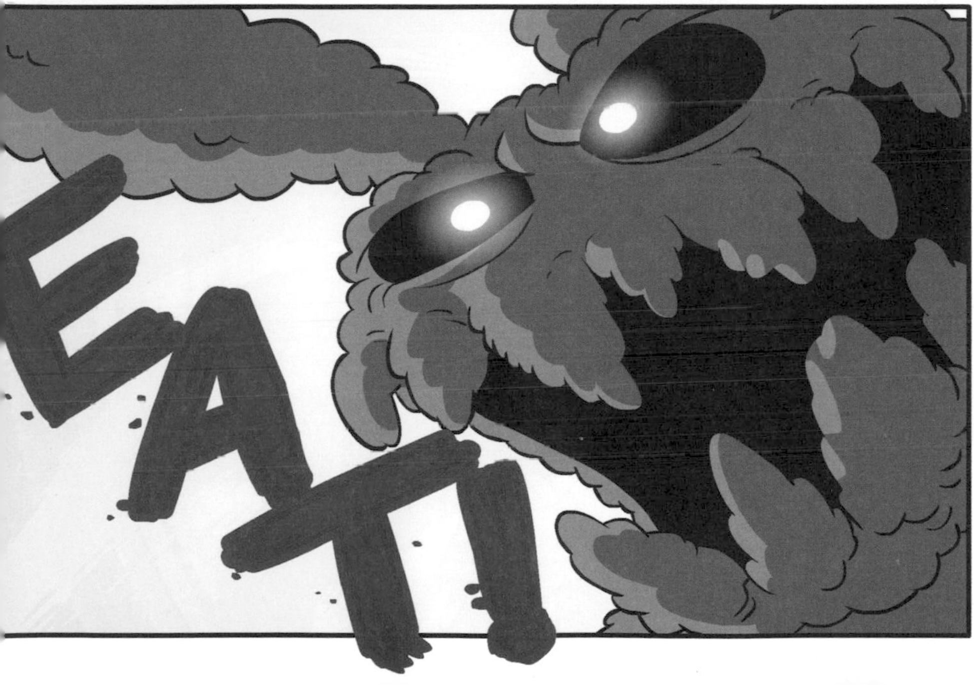
EAT!

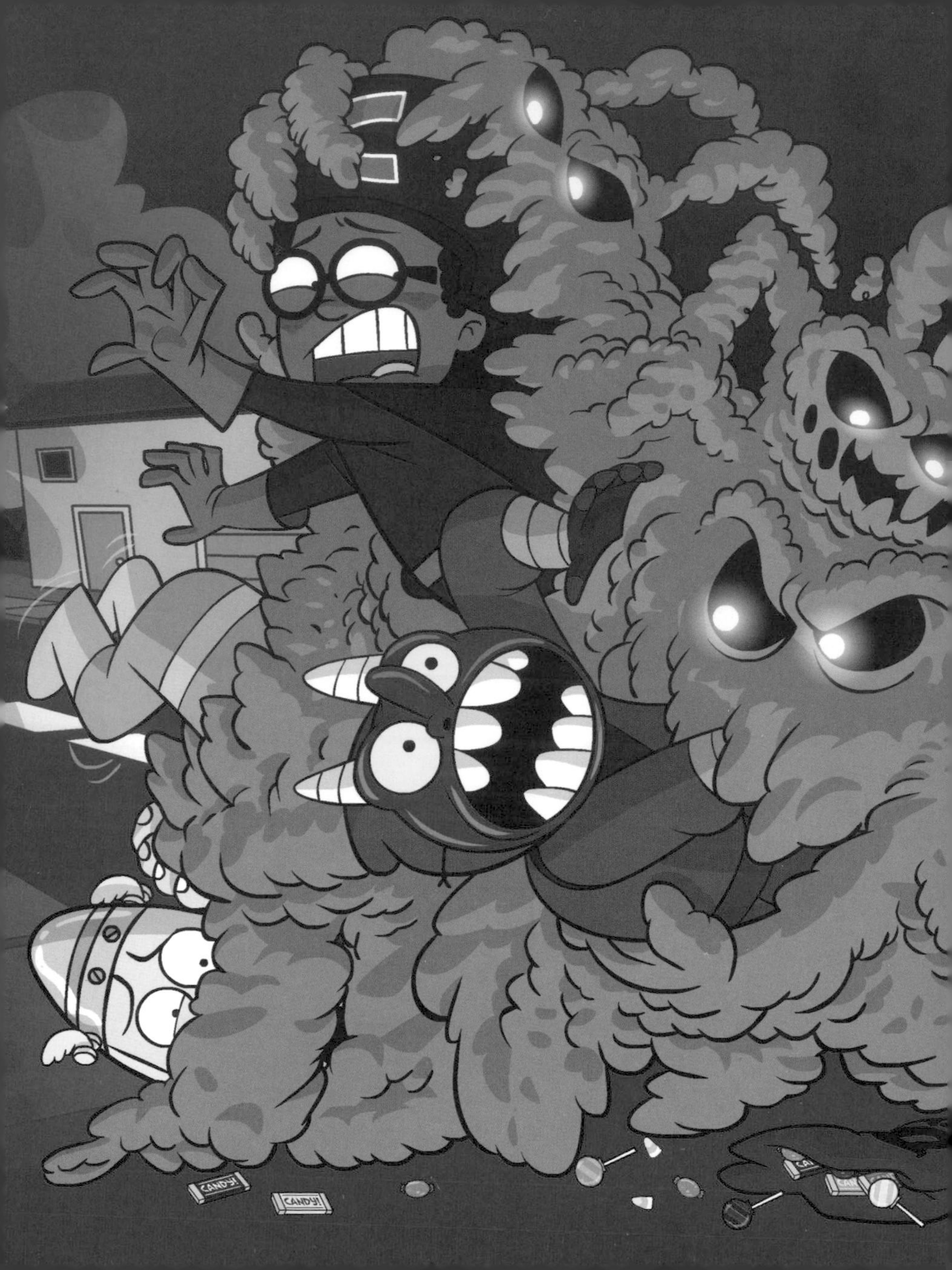
CANDY!
CANDY!

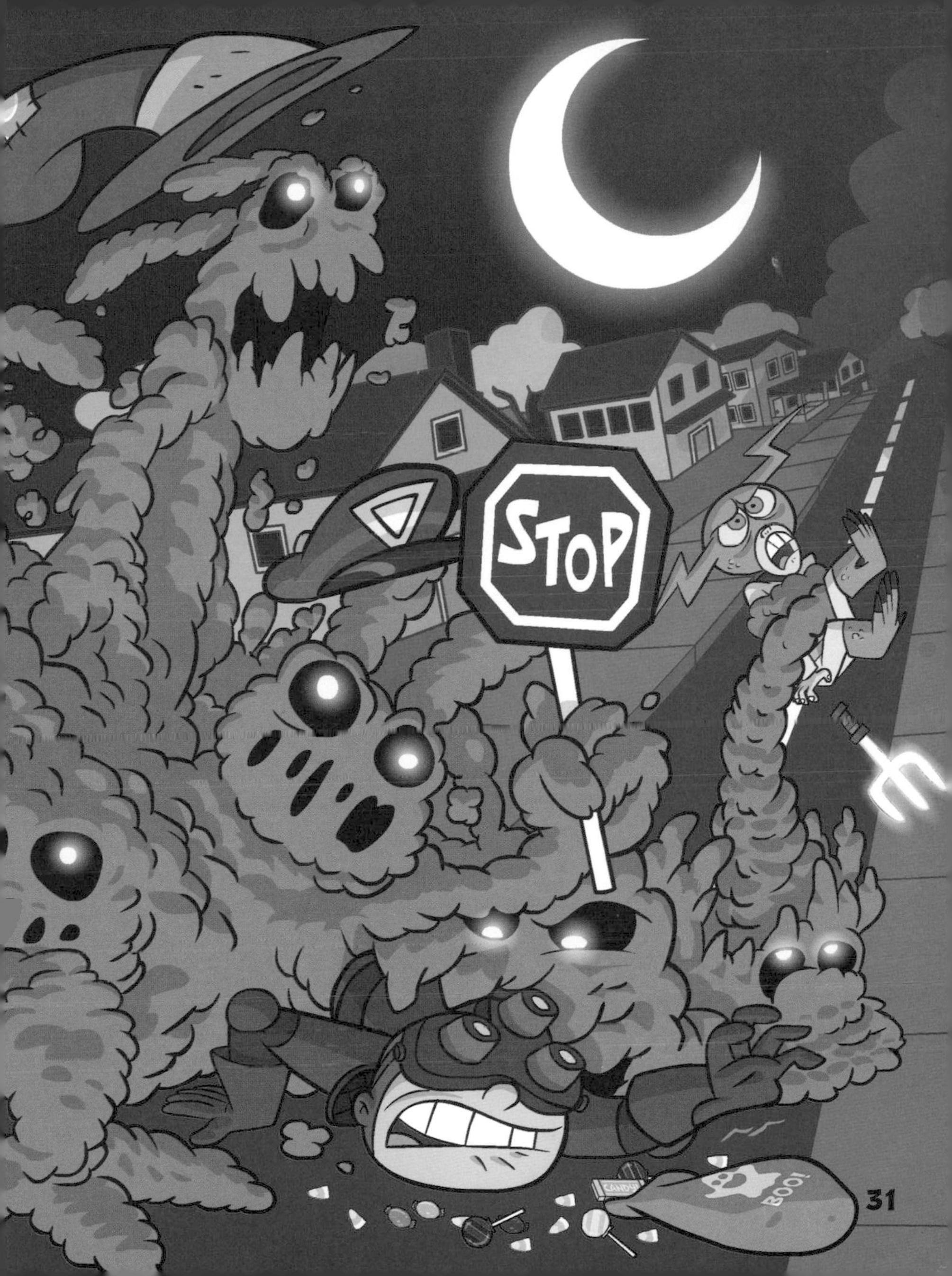
STOP
CANDY
BOO!

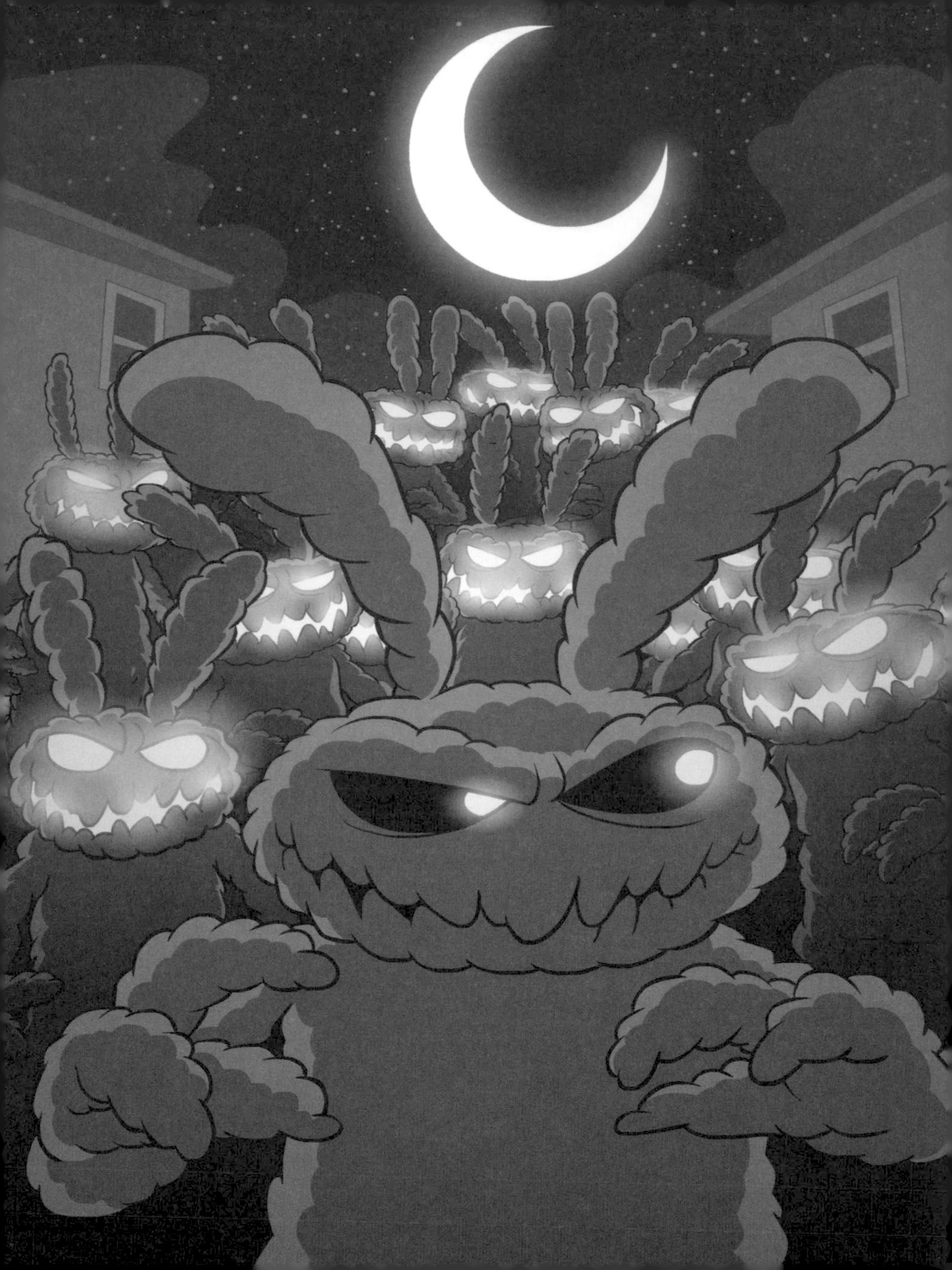

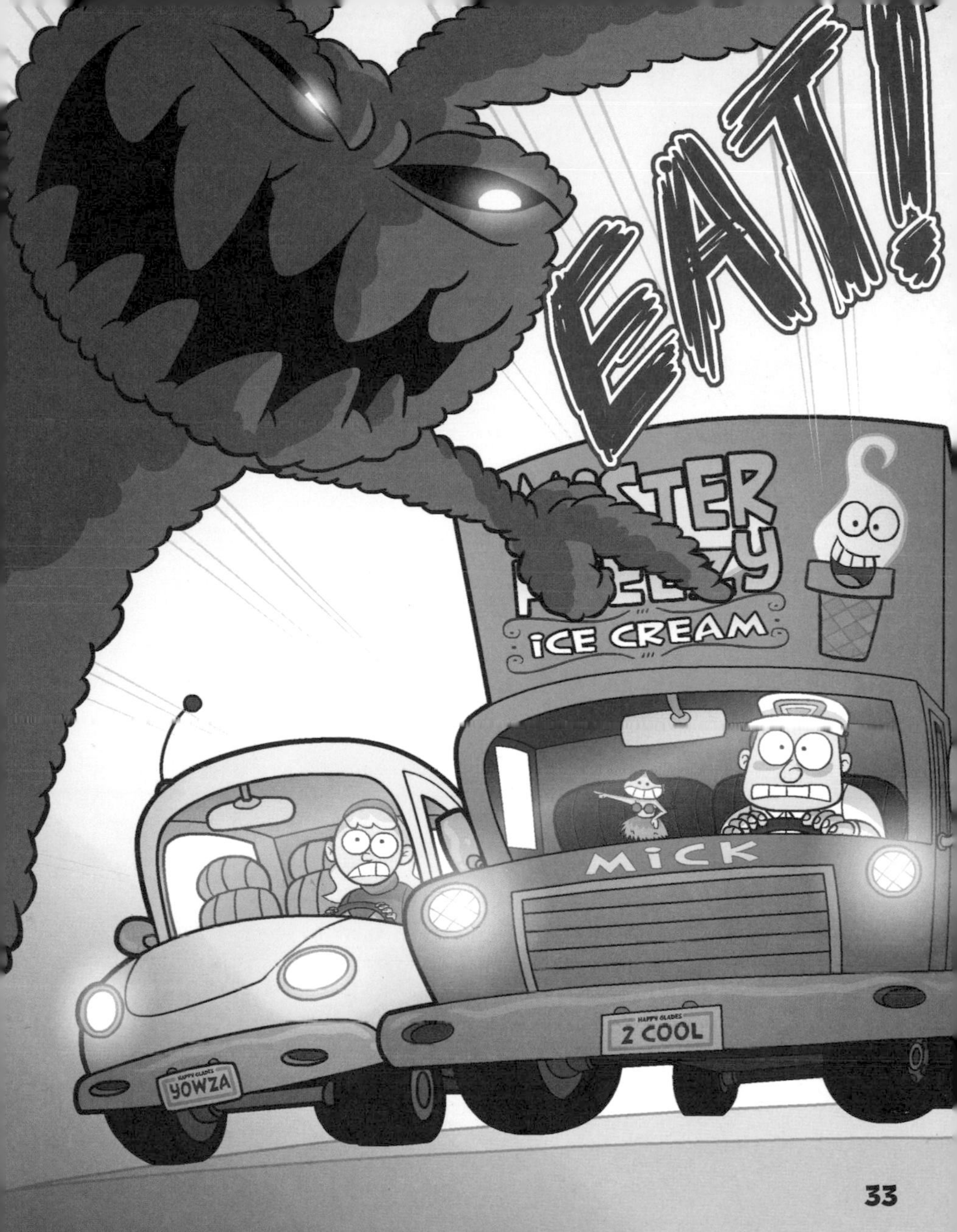
EAT!
ICE CREAM
MICK
YOWZA
2 COOL

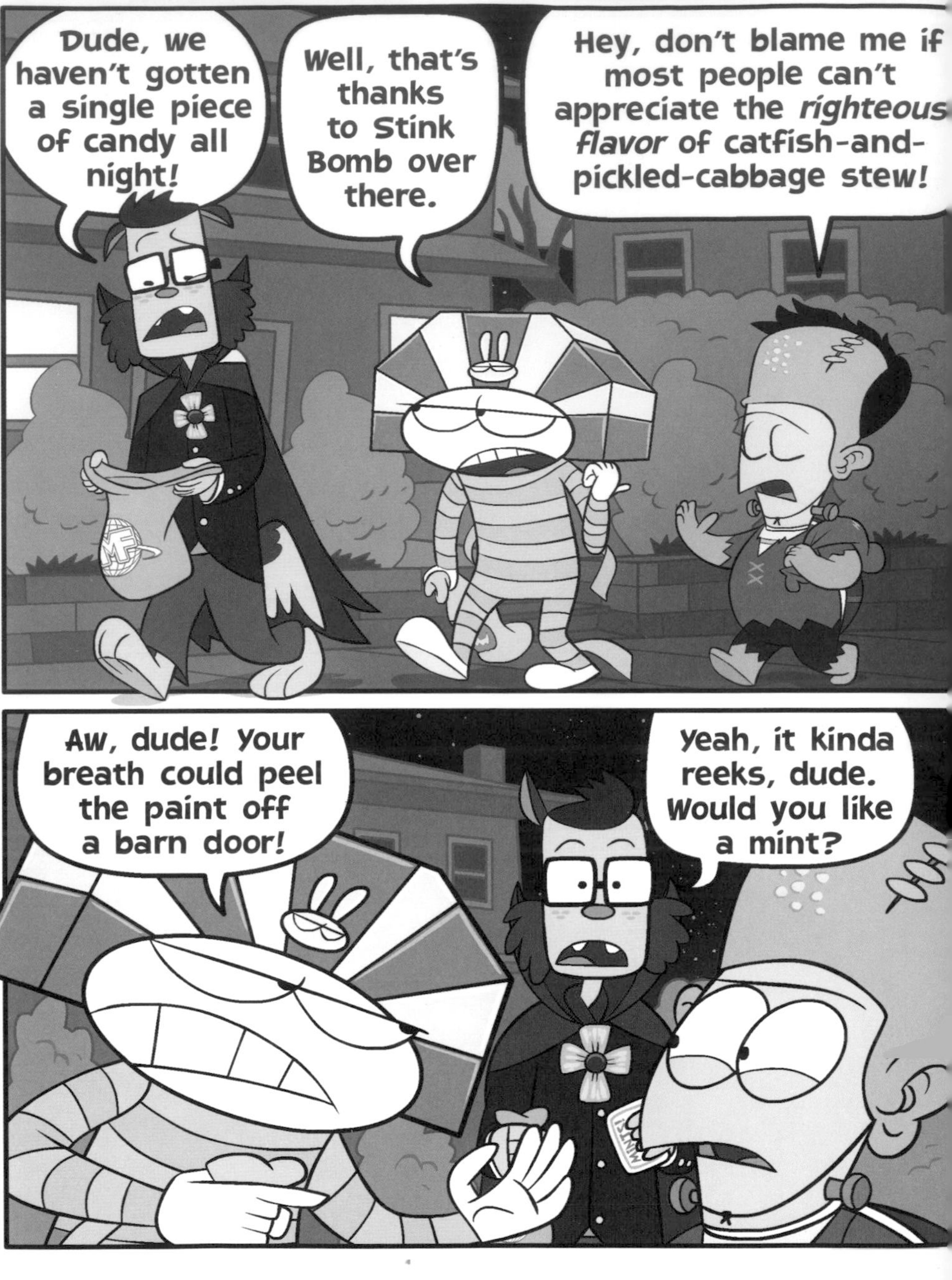
Dude, we haven't gotten a single piece of candy all night!
Well, that's thanks to Stink Bomb over there.
Hey, don't blame me if most people can't appreciate the *righteous flavor* of catfish-and-pickled-cabbage stew!
Aw, dude! Your breath could peel the paint off a barn door!
Yeah, it kinda reeks, dude. Would you like a mint?

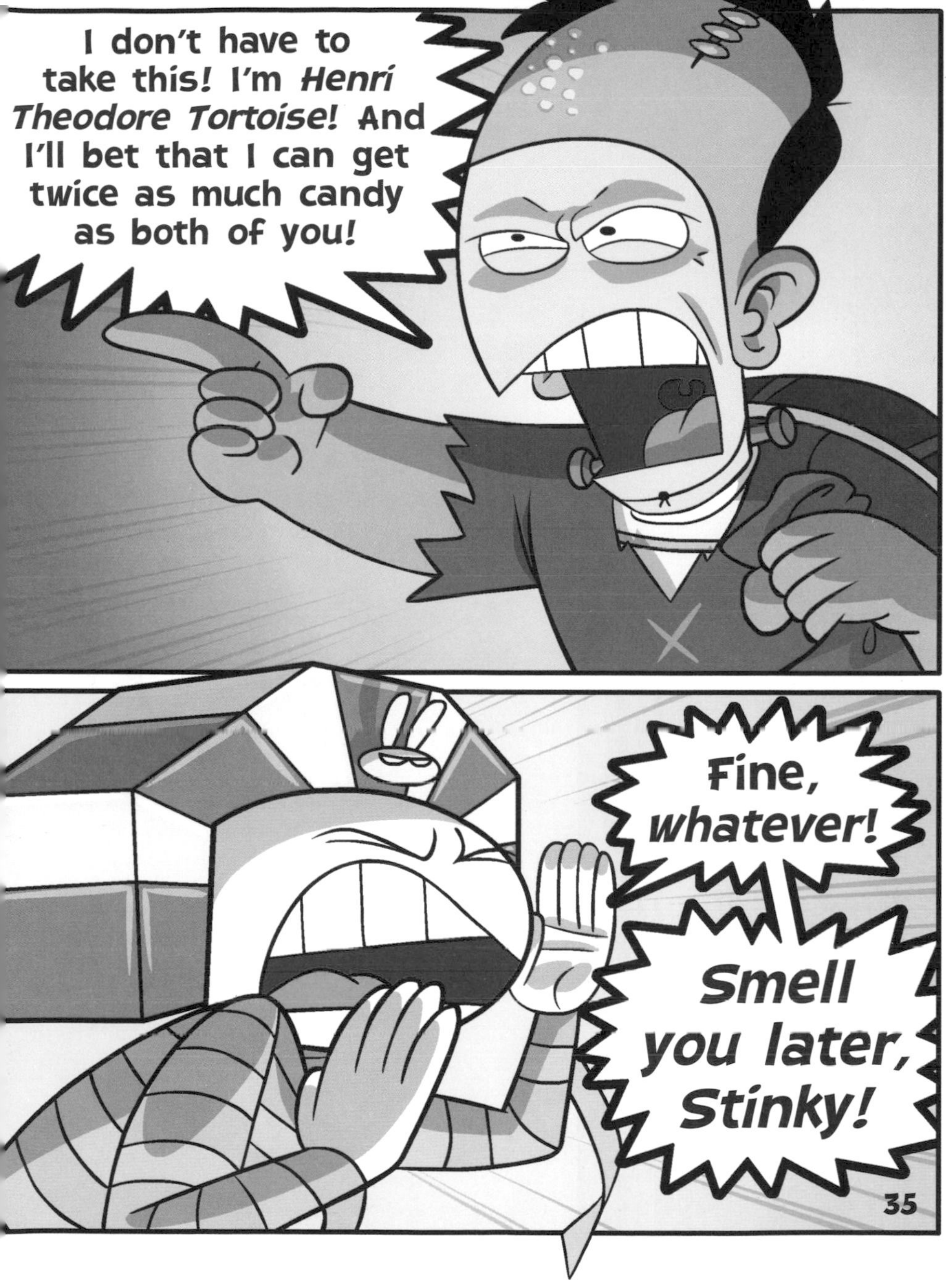
I don't have to take this! I'm *Henri Theodore Tortoise!* And I'll bet that I can get twice as much candy as both of you!
Fine, whatever!
Smell you later, Stinky!

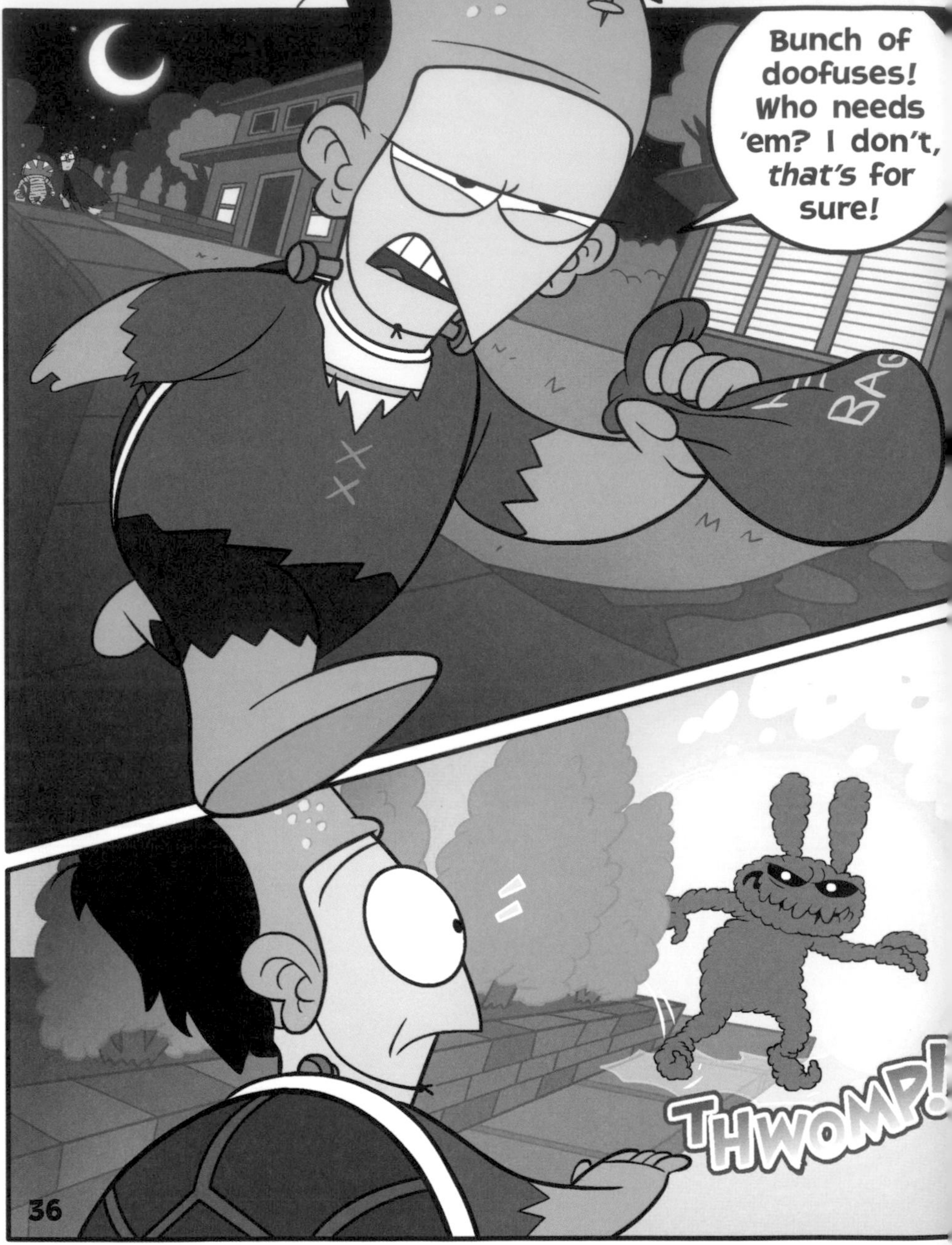
Bunch of doofuses! Who needs 'em? I don't, *that's* for sure!
THWOMP!

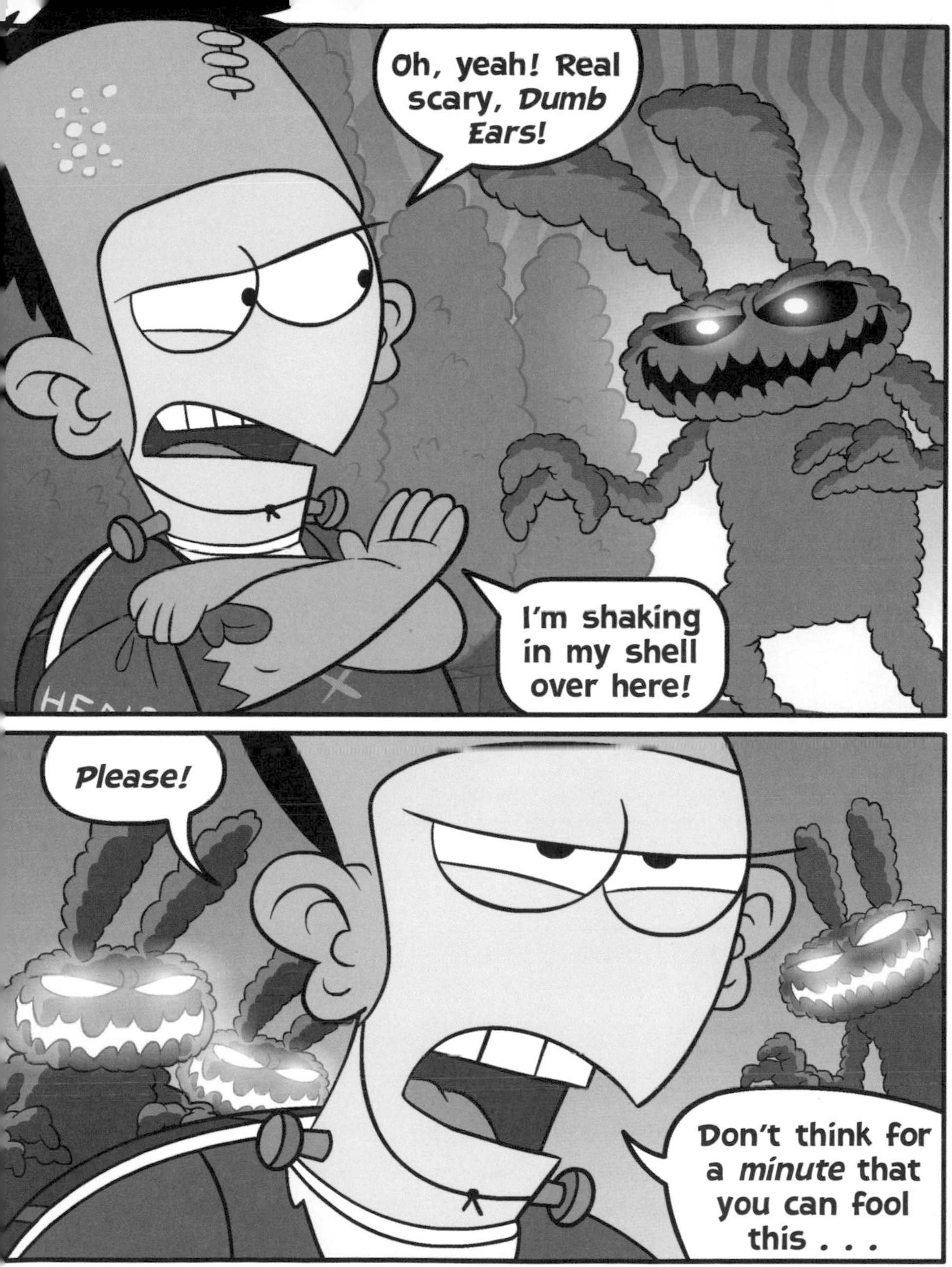
Oh, yeah! Real scary, *Dumb* Ears!
I'm shaking in my shell over here!
Please!
Don't think for a *minute* that you can fool this . . .

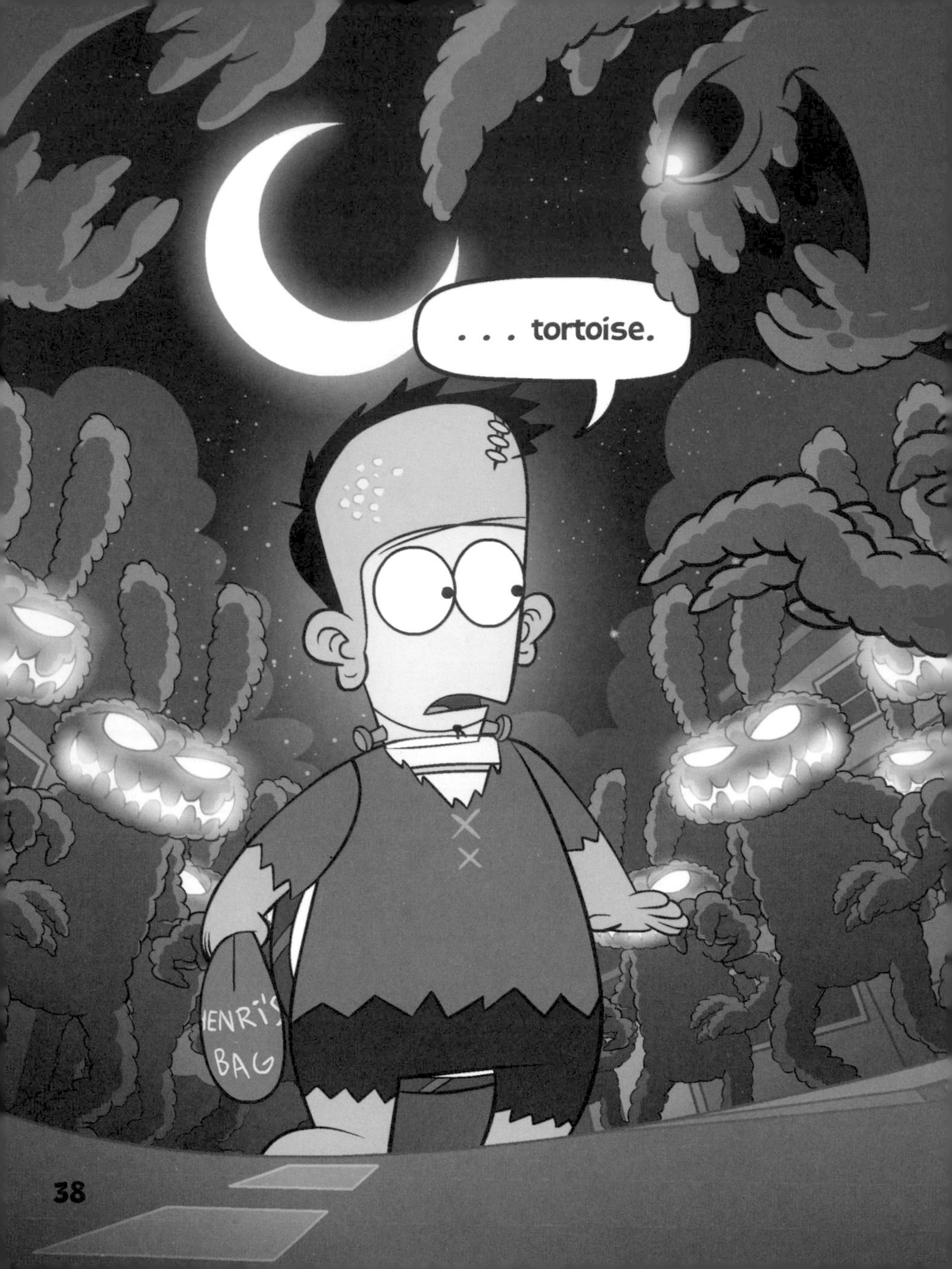
. . . tortoise.
HENRI'S BAG

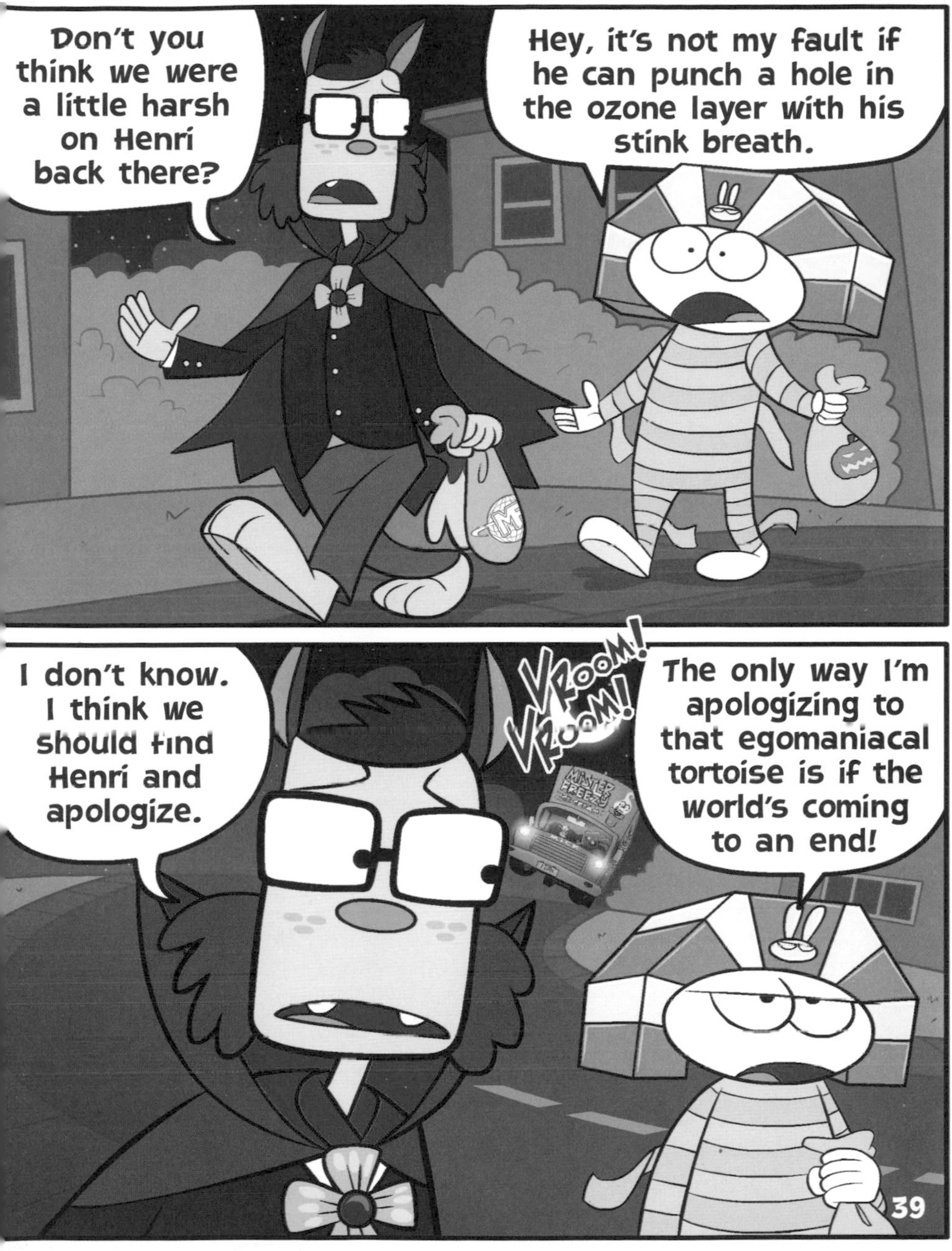
Don't you think we were a little harsh on Henri back there?
Hey, it's not my fault if he can punch a hole in the ozone layer with his stink breath.
I don't know. I think we should find Henri and apologize.
VROOM! VROOM!
The only way I'm apologizing to that egomaniacal tortoise is if the world's coming to an end!

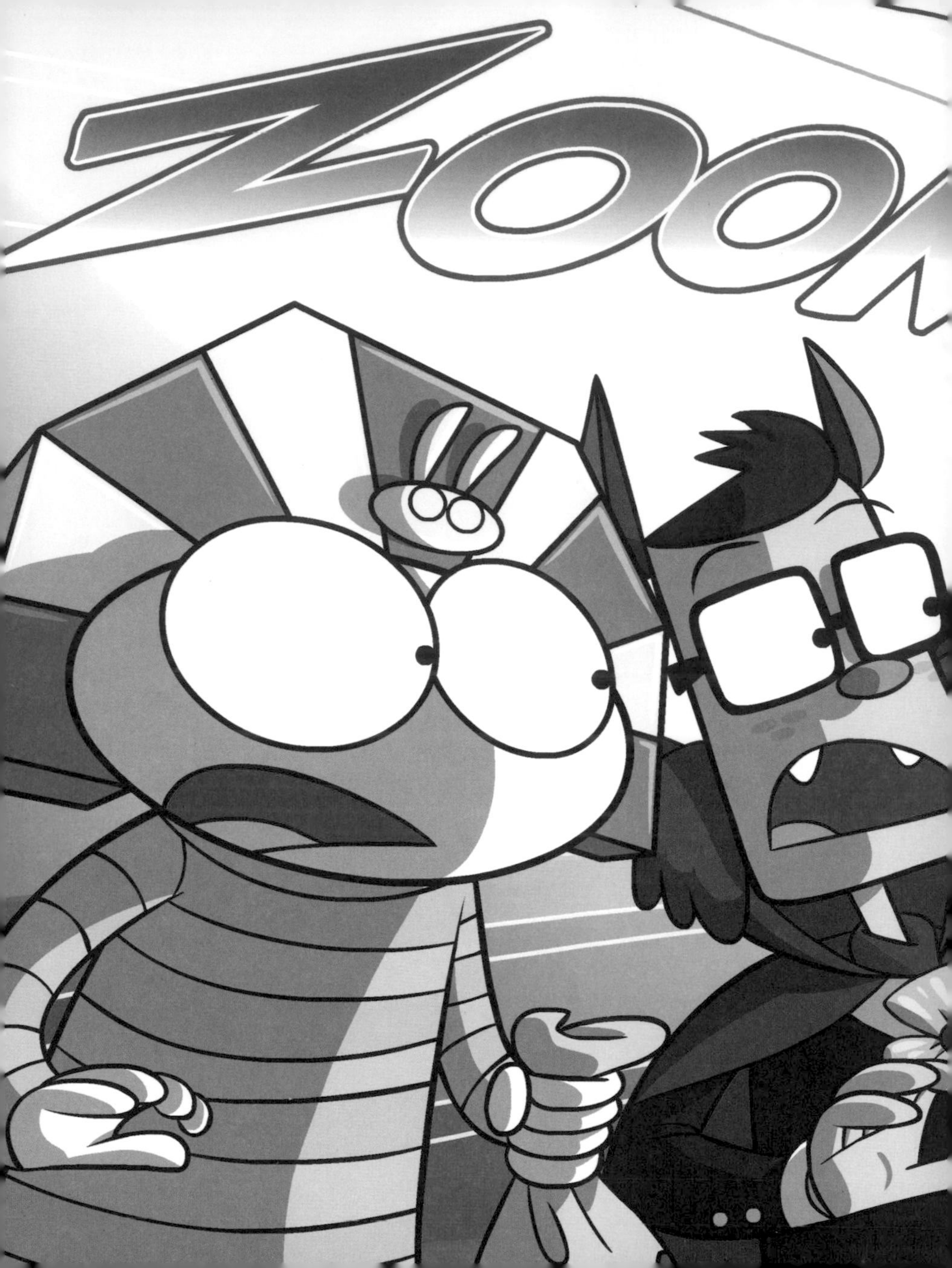
ZOO

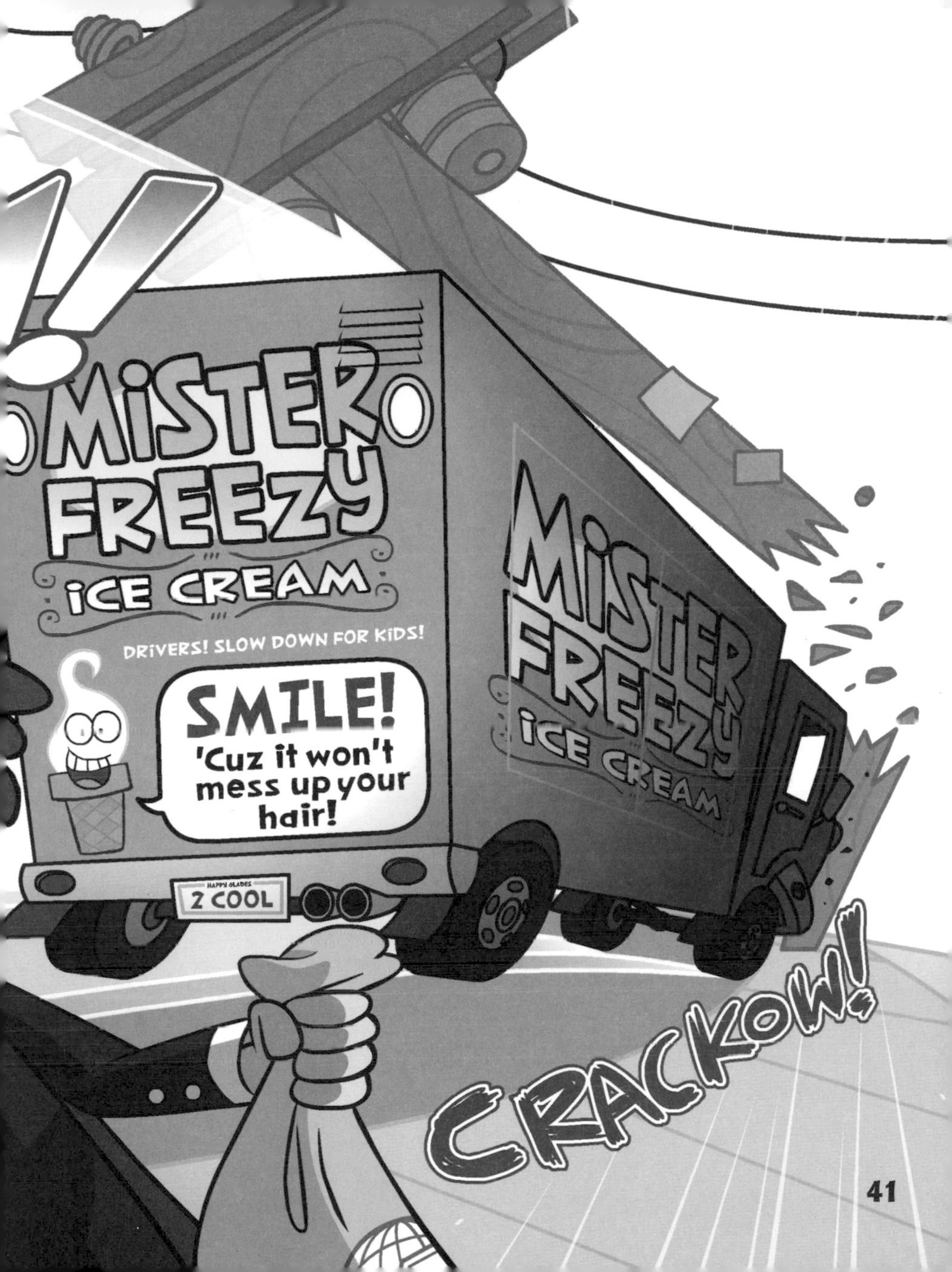
MISTER FREEZY
ICE CREAM
DRIVERS! SLOW DOWN FOR KIDS!
SMILE! 'Cuz it won't mess up your hair!
HAPPY GLADES
2 COOL
MISTER FREEZY
ICE CREAM
CRACKOW!

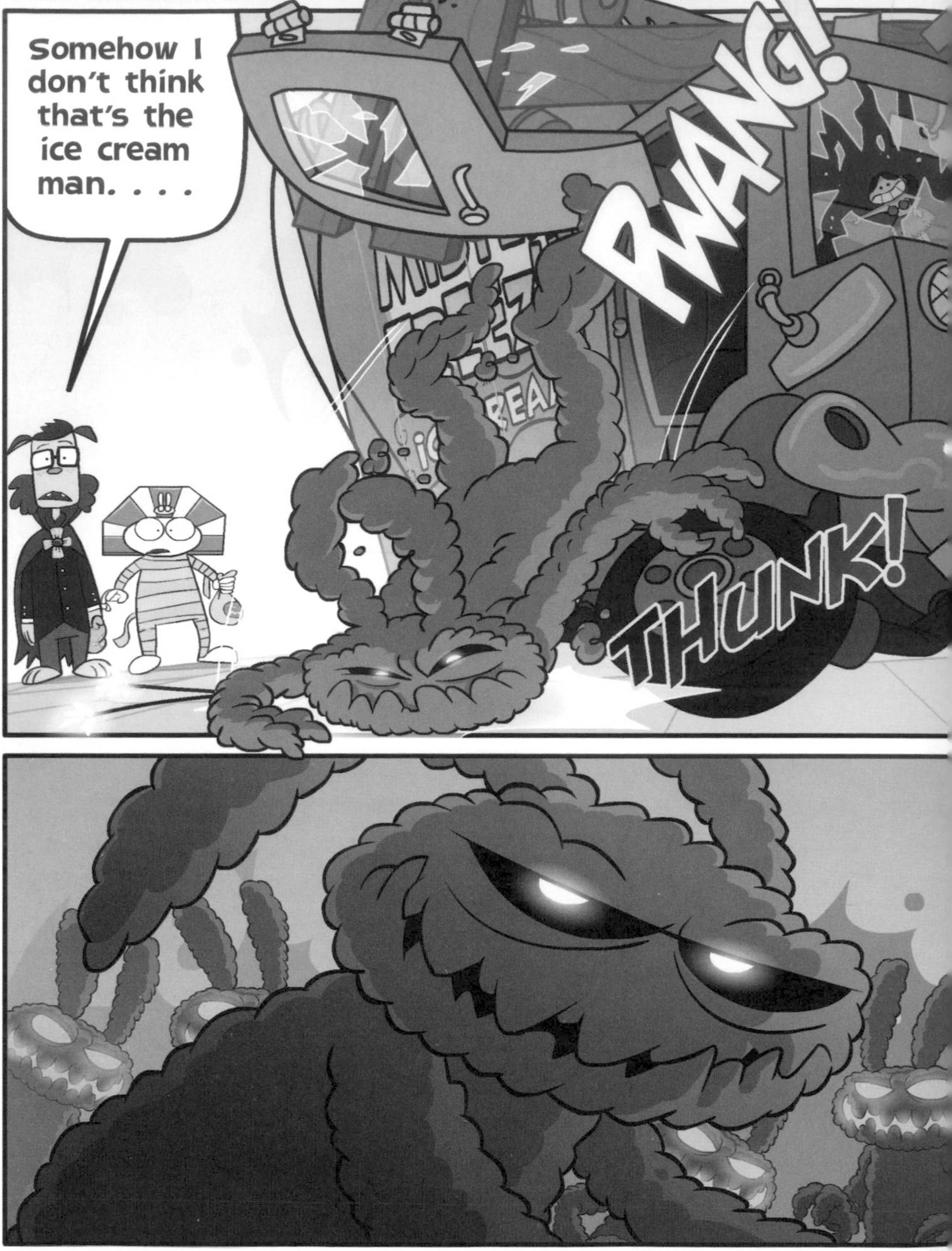
Somehow I don't think that's the ice cream man. . . .
RWANG!
THUNK!

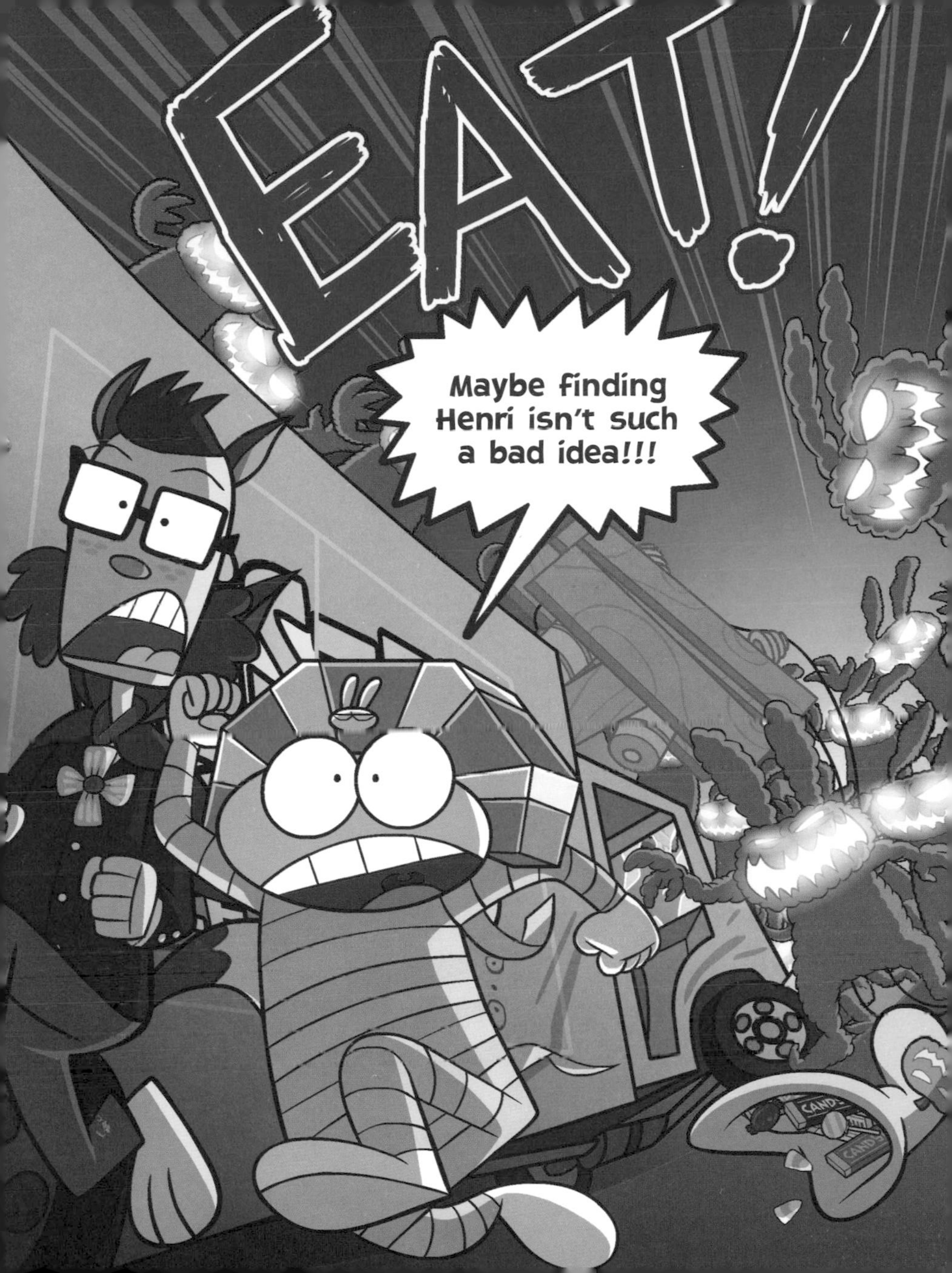
EAT!
Maybe finding Henri isn't such a bad idea!!!
CANDY
CANDY

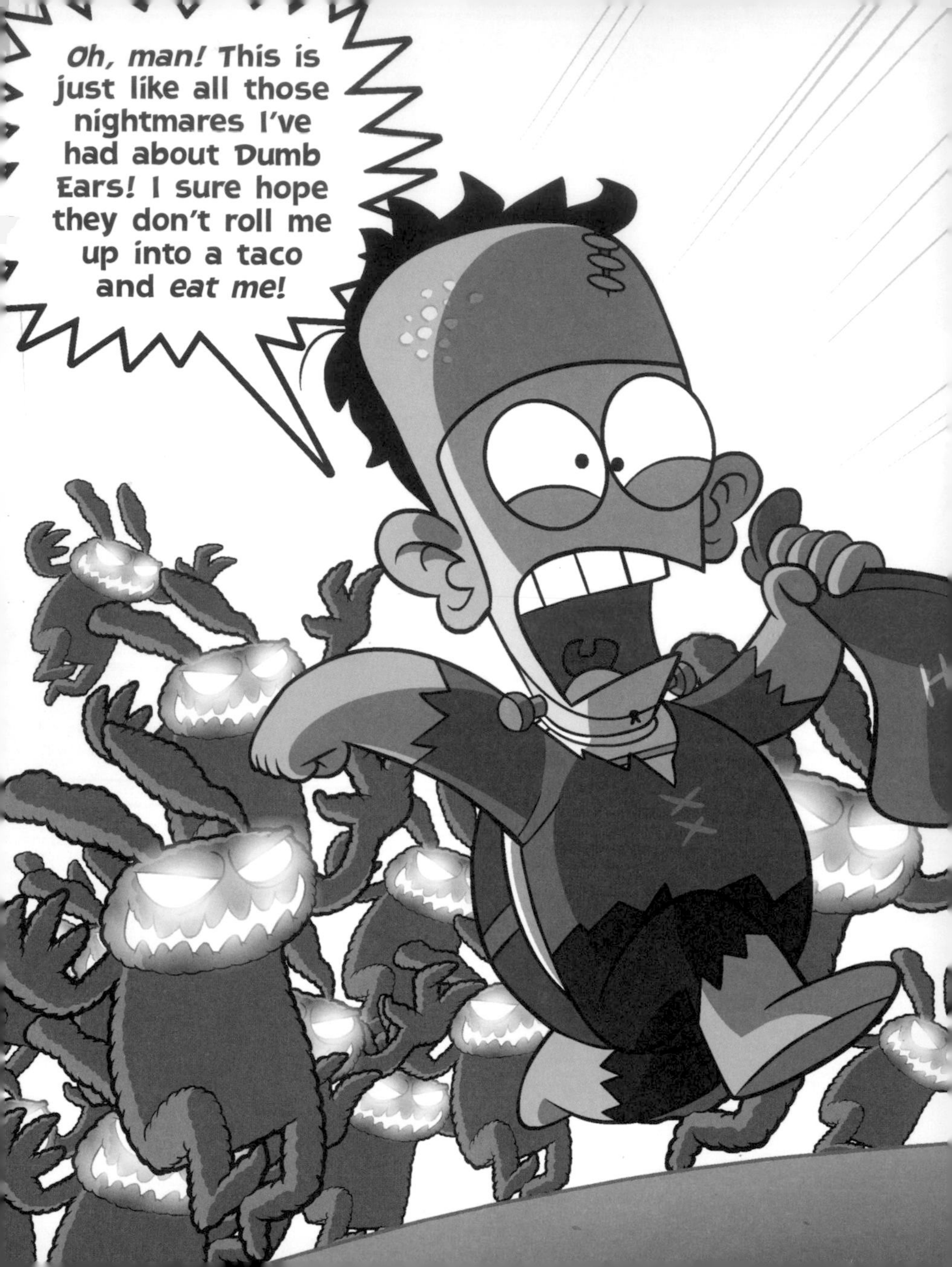
Oh, man! This is just like all those nightmares I've had about Dumb Ears! I sure hope they don't roll me up into a taco and *eat me!*

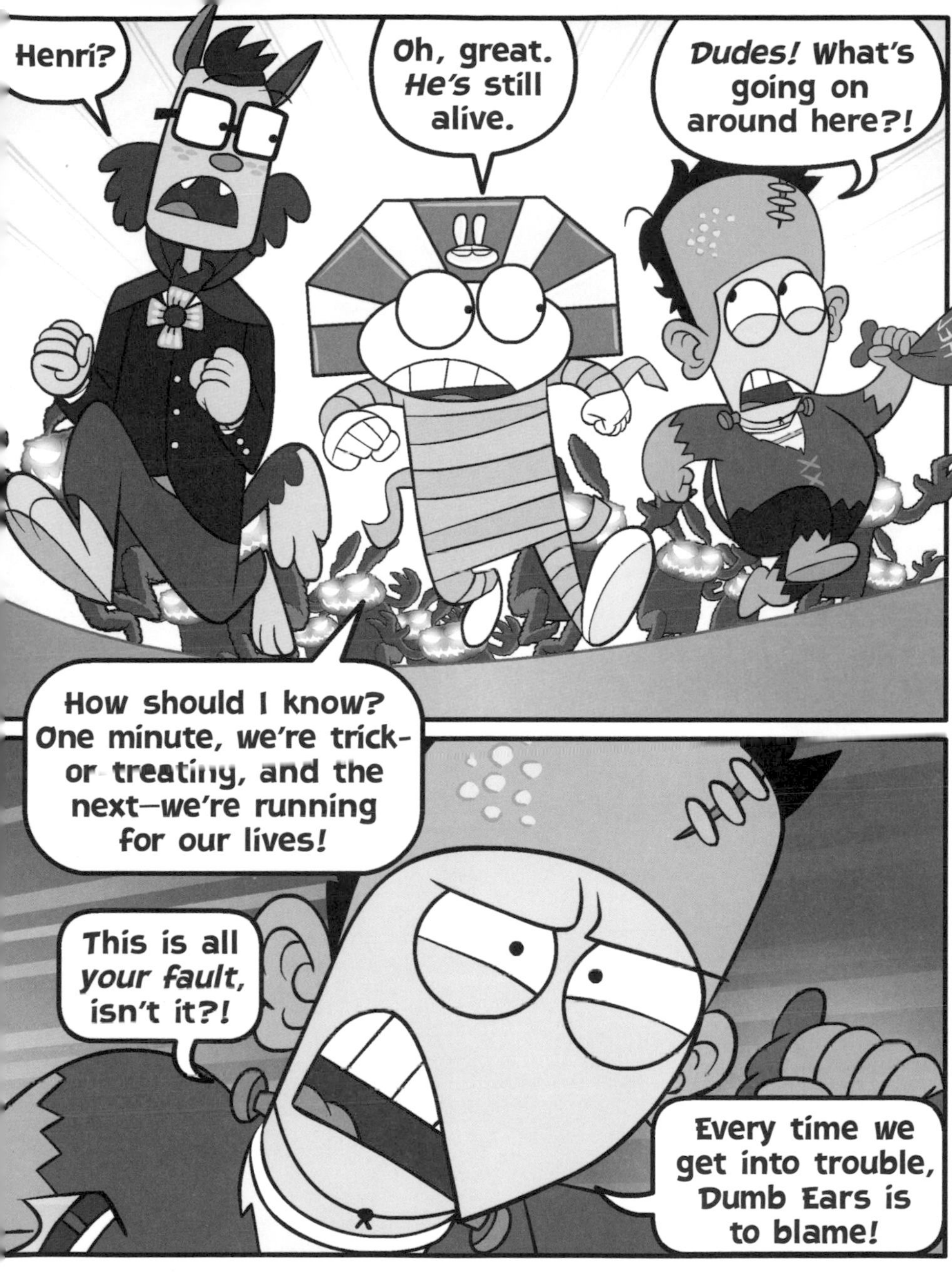
Henri?
Oh, great. *He's* still alive.
Dudes! What's going on around here?!
How should I know? One minute, we're trick-or-treating, and the next—we're running for our lives!
This is all *your fault,* isn't it?!
Every time we get into trouble, Dumb Ears is to blame!

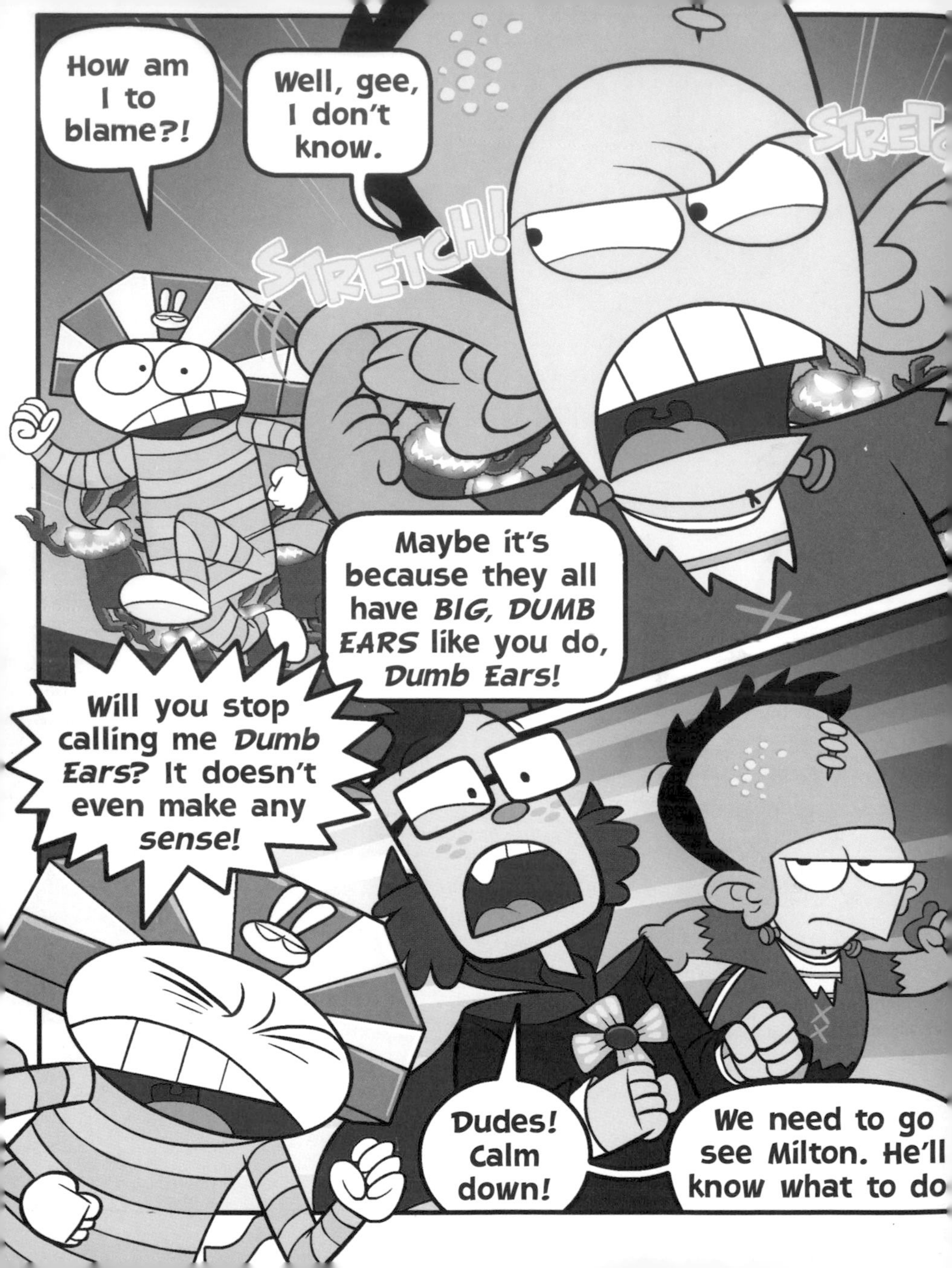
How am I to blame?!
Well, gee, I don't know.
STRETCH!
STRETC
Maybe it's because they all have *BIG, DUMB EARS* like you do, *Dumb Ears!*
Will you stop calling me *Dumb Ears?* It doesn't even make any *sense!*
Dudes! Calm down!
We need to go see Milton. He'll know what to do

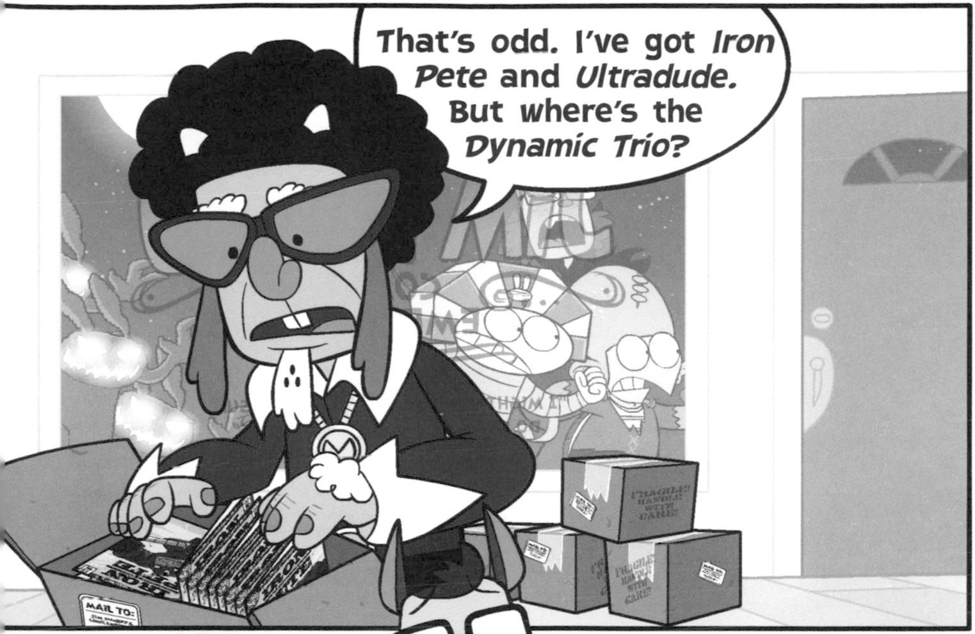
That's odd. I've got *Iron Pete* and *Ultradude.* But where's the *Dynamic Trio?*
MAIL TO:
FRAGILE! HANDLE WITH CARE!

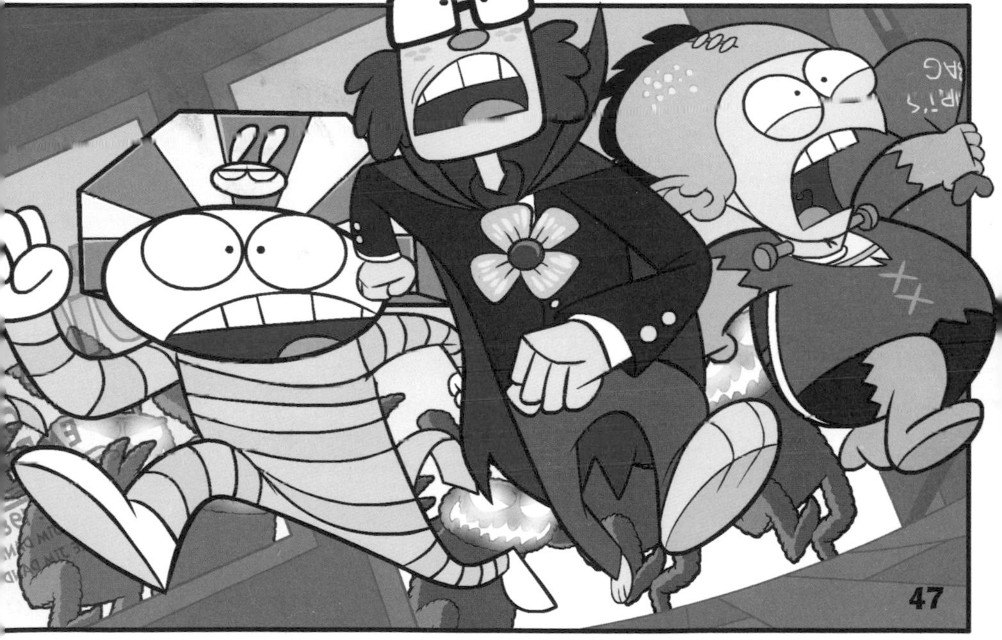

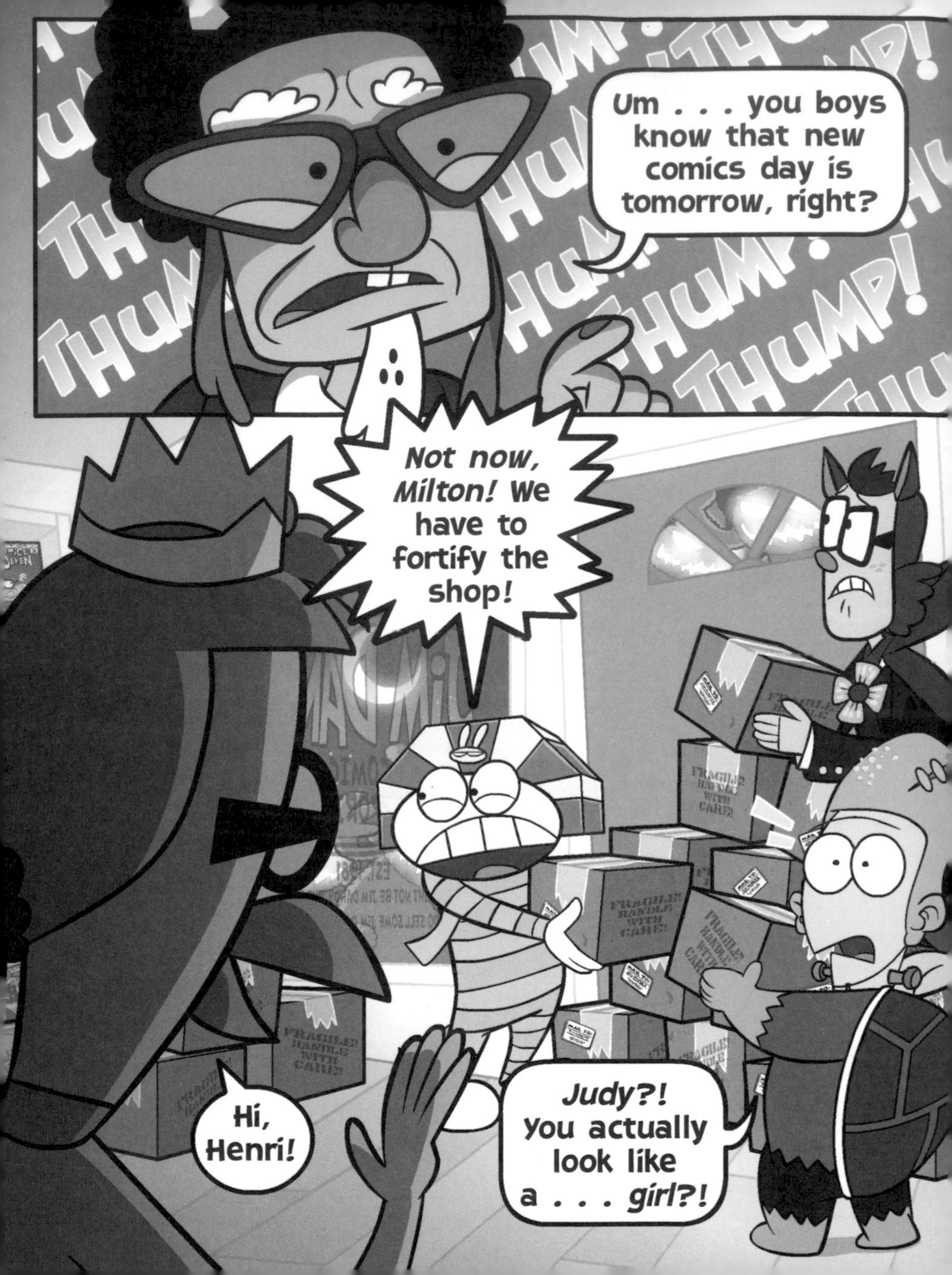
THUMP!
THUMP!
THUMP!
Um . . . you boys know that new comics day is tomorrow, right?
Not now, Milton! We have to fortify the shop!
Hi, Henri!
Judy?! You actually look like a . . . *girl*?!

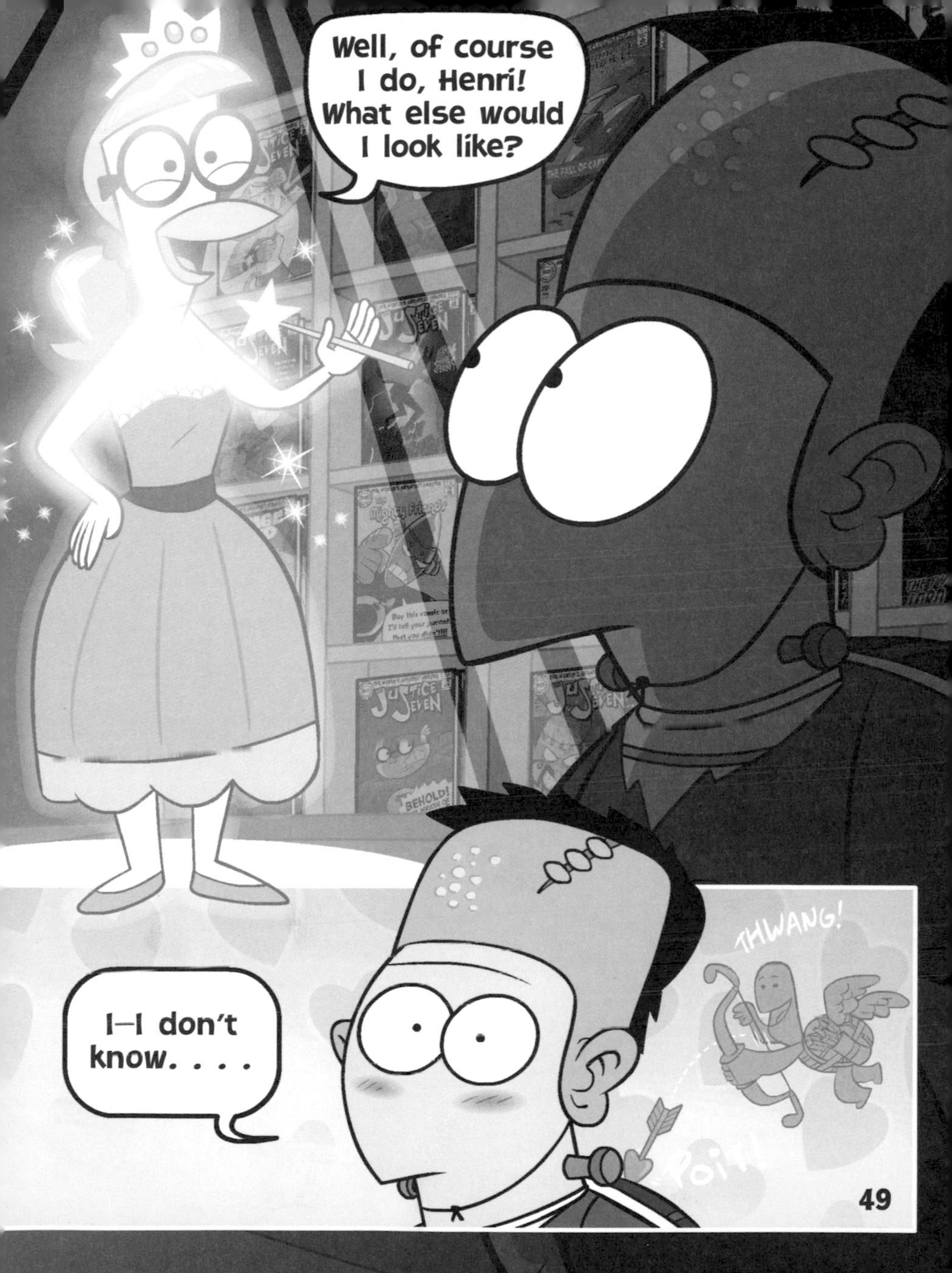
Well, of course I do, Henri! What else would I look like?
I—I don't know. . . .
THWANG!

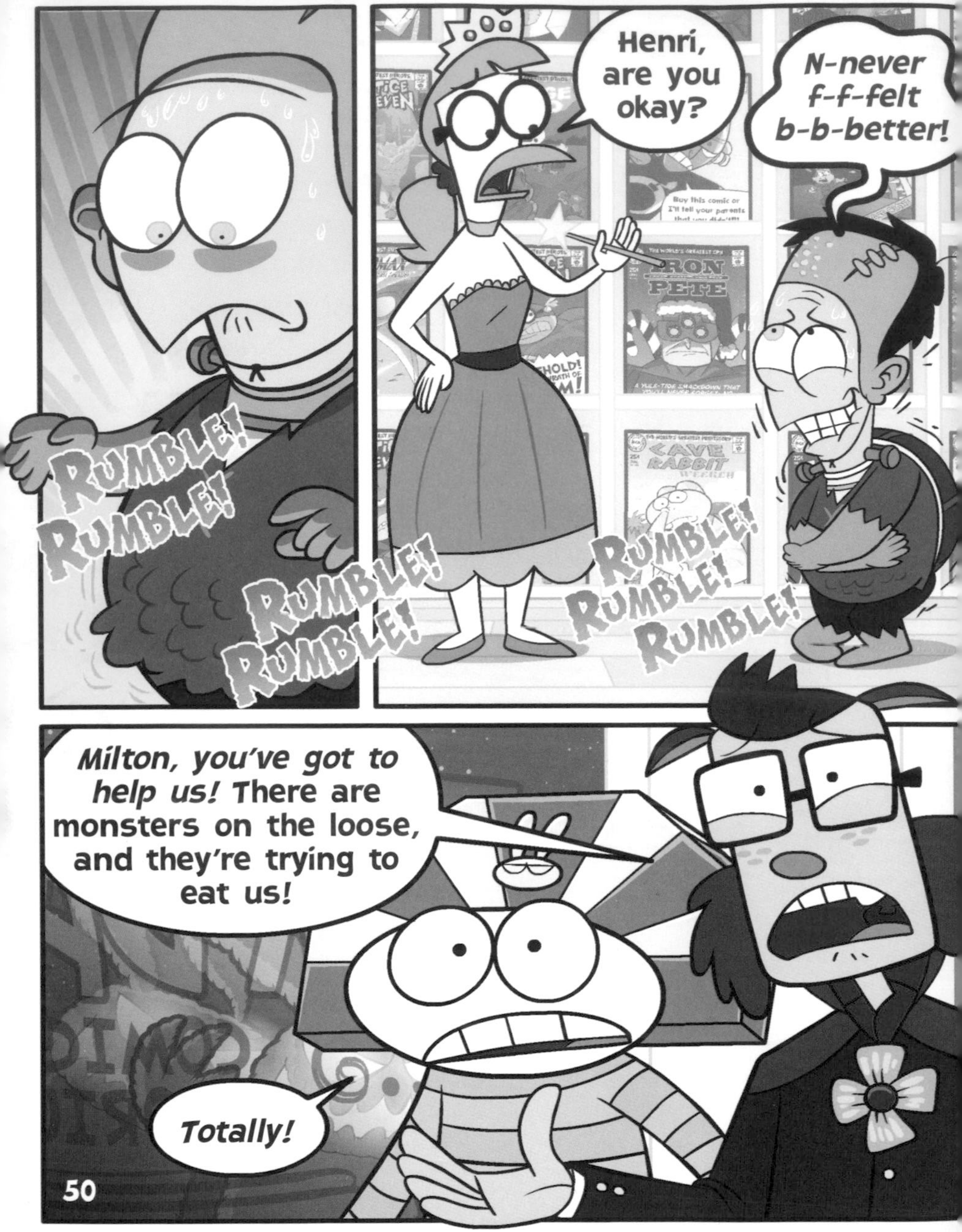
RUMBLE! RUMBLE!
Henri, are you okay?
N-never f-f-felt b-b-better!
RUMBLE! RUMBLE!
RUMBLE! RUMBLE! RUMBLE!
Milton, you've got to help us! There are monsters on the loose, and they're trying to eat us!
Totally!

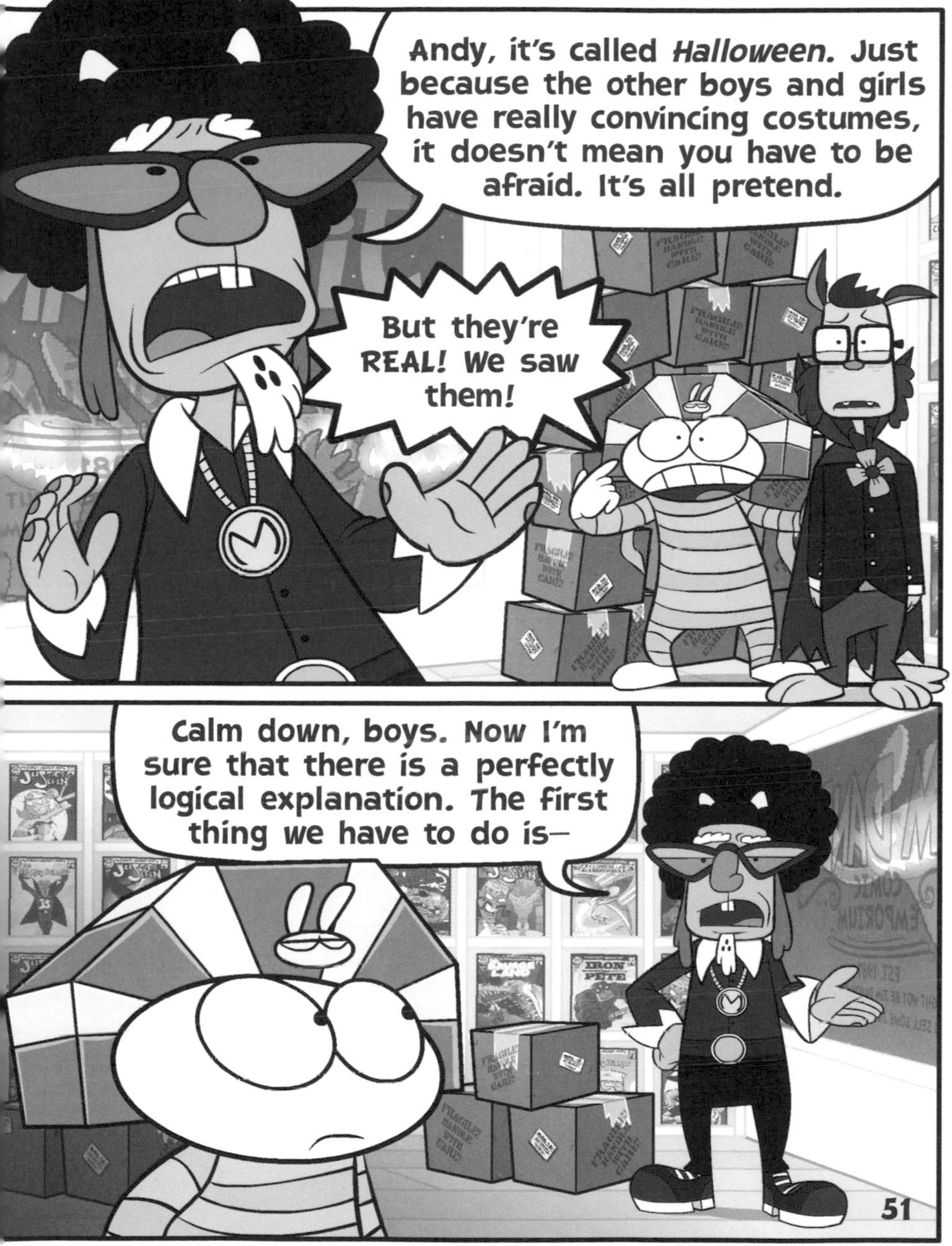
Andy, it's called *Halloween.* Just because the other boys and girls have really convincing costumes, it doesn't mean you have to be afraid. It's all pretend.
But they're REAL! We saw them!
Calm down, boys. Now I'm sure that there is a perfectly logical explanation. The first thing we have to do is—

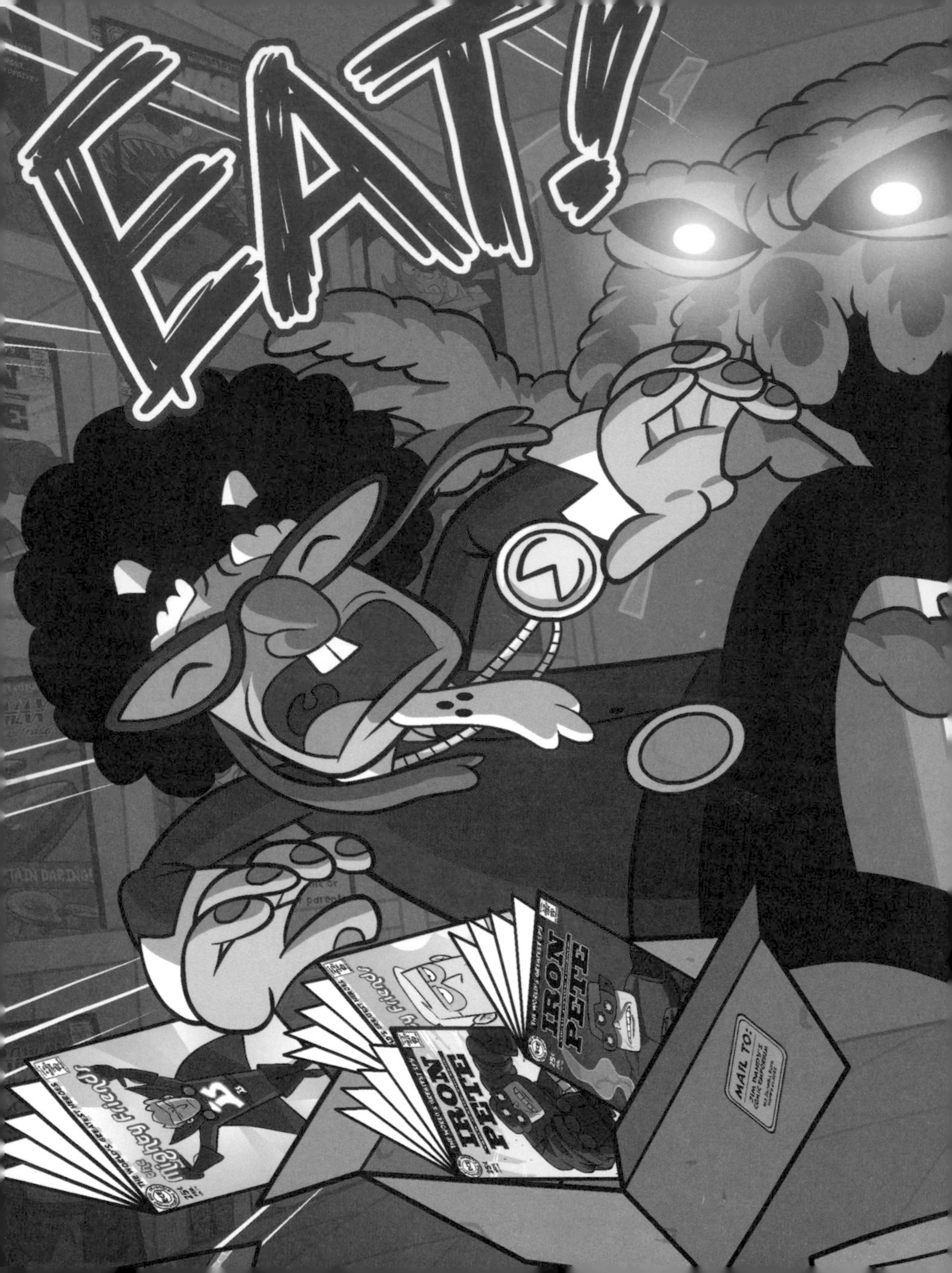
EAT!
THE WORLD'S GREATEST SPY
IRON PETE
MAIL TO:

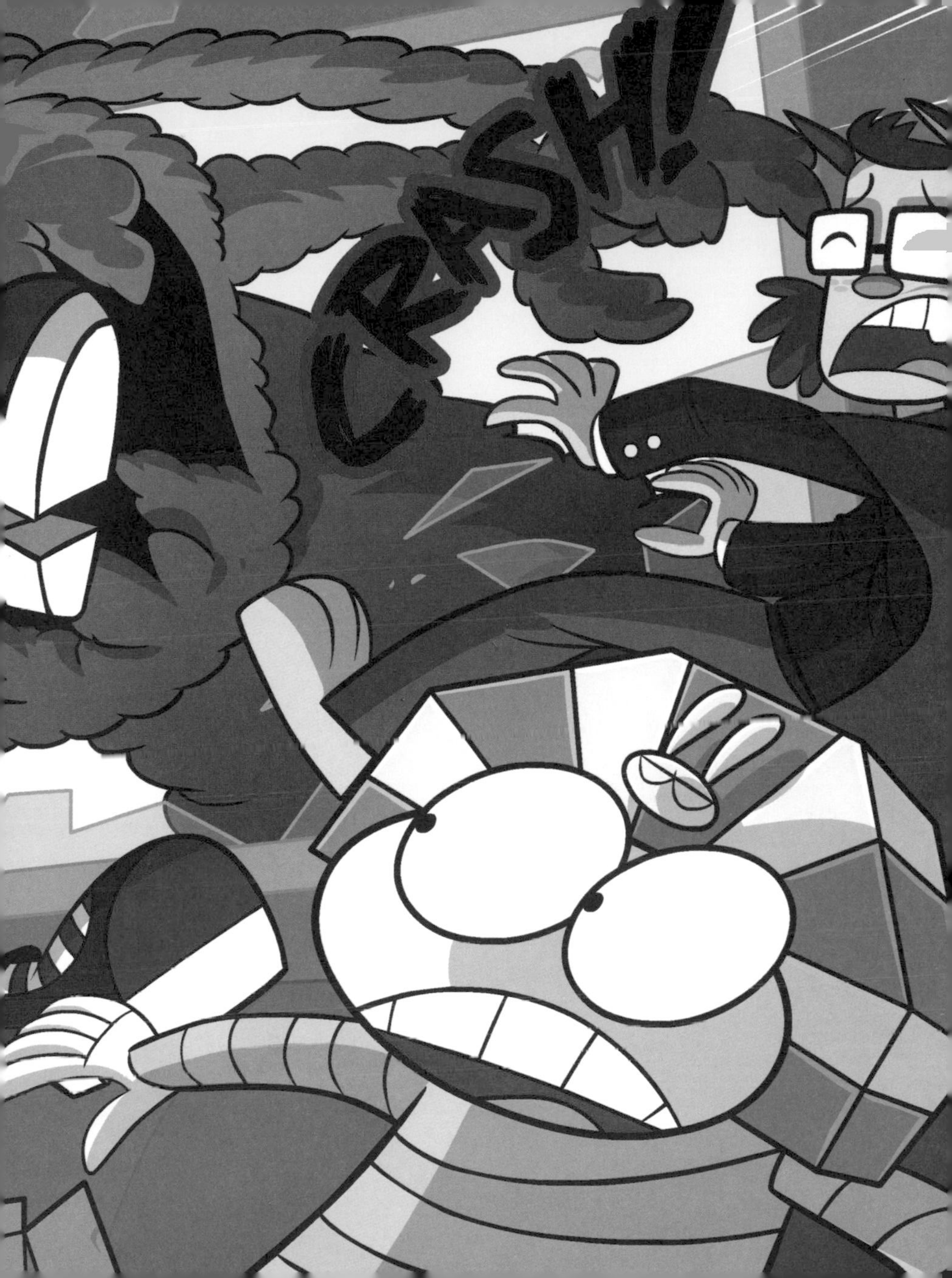
CRASH!

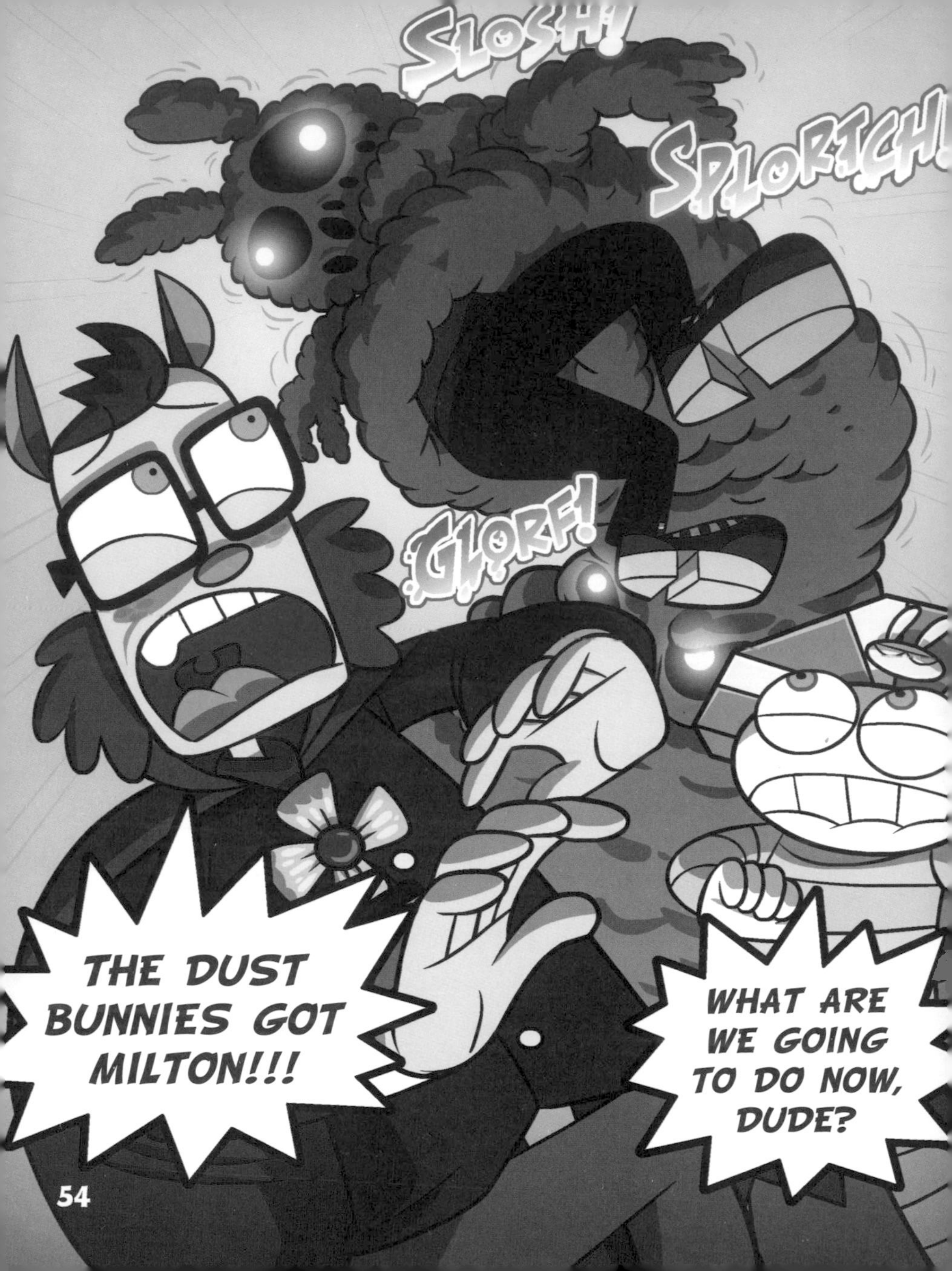
SLOSH!
SPLORTCH!
GLORF!
THE DUST BUNNIES GOT MILTON!!!
WHAT ARE WE GOING TO DO NOW, DUDE?

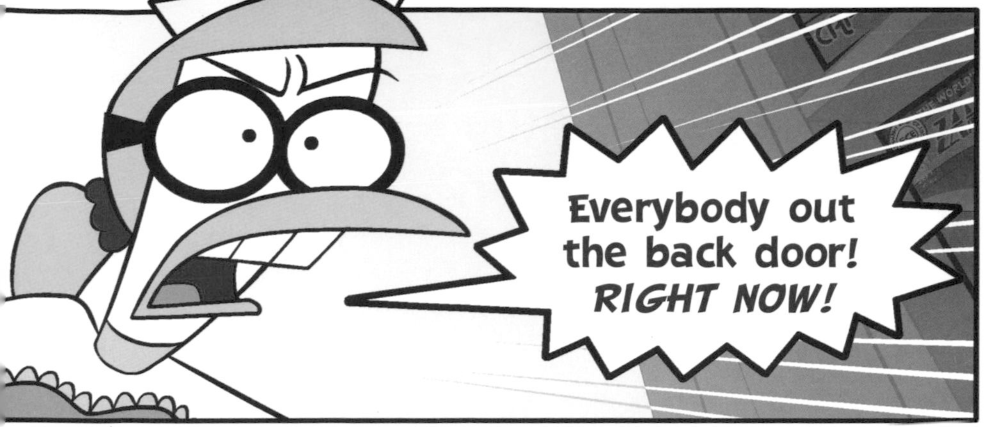
Everybody out the back door! *RIGHT NOW!*

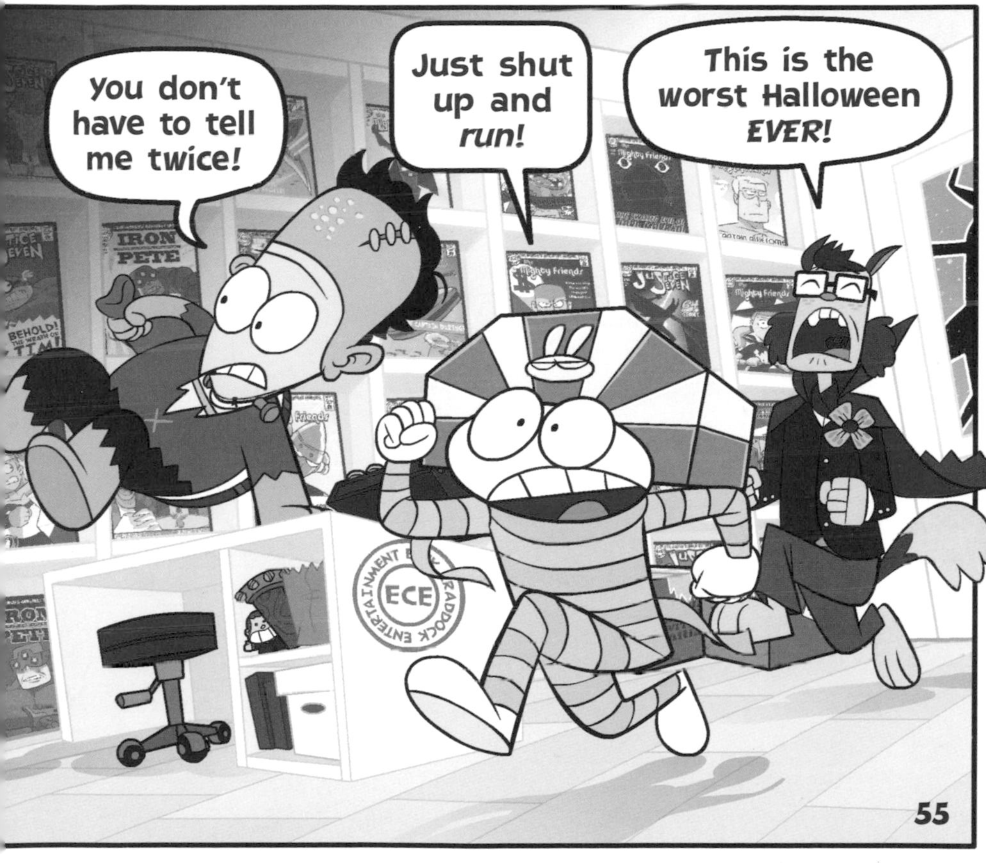
You don't have to tell me twice!
Just shut up and *run!*
This is the worst Halloween *EVER!*

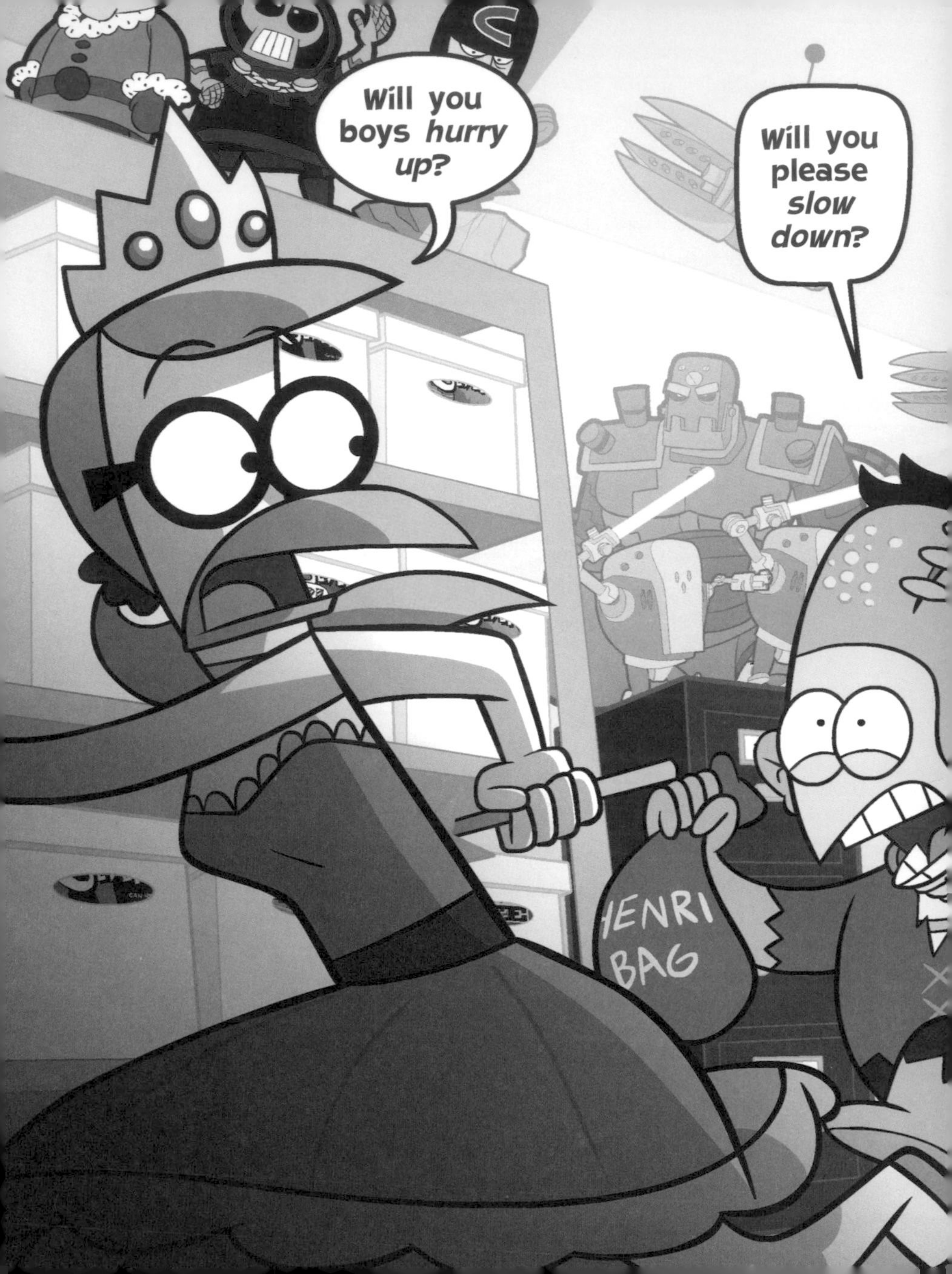
Will you boys hurry up?
Will you please slow down?
HENRI BAG

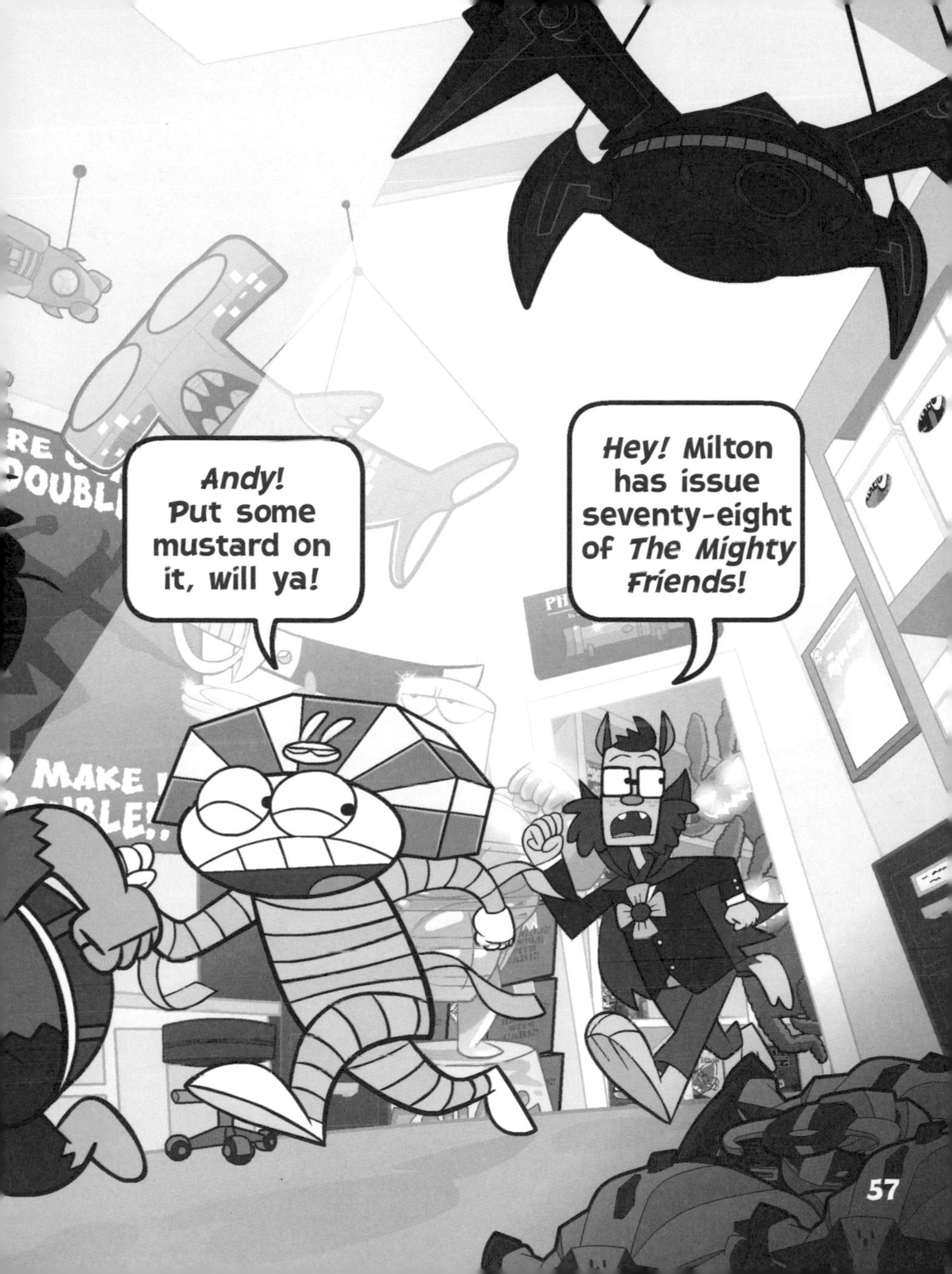
Andy! Put some mustard on it, will ya!
Hey! Milton has issue seventy-eight of The Mighty Friends!

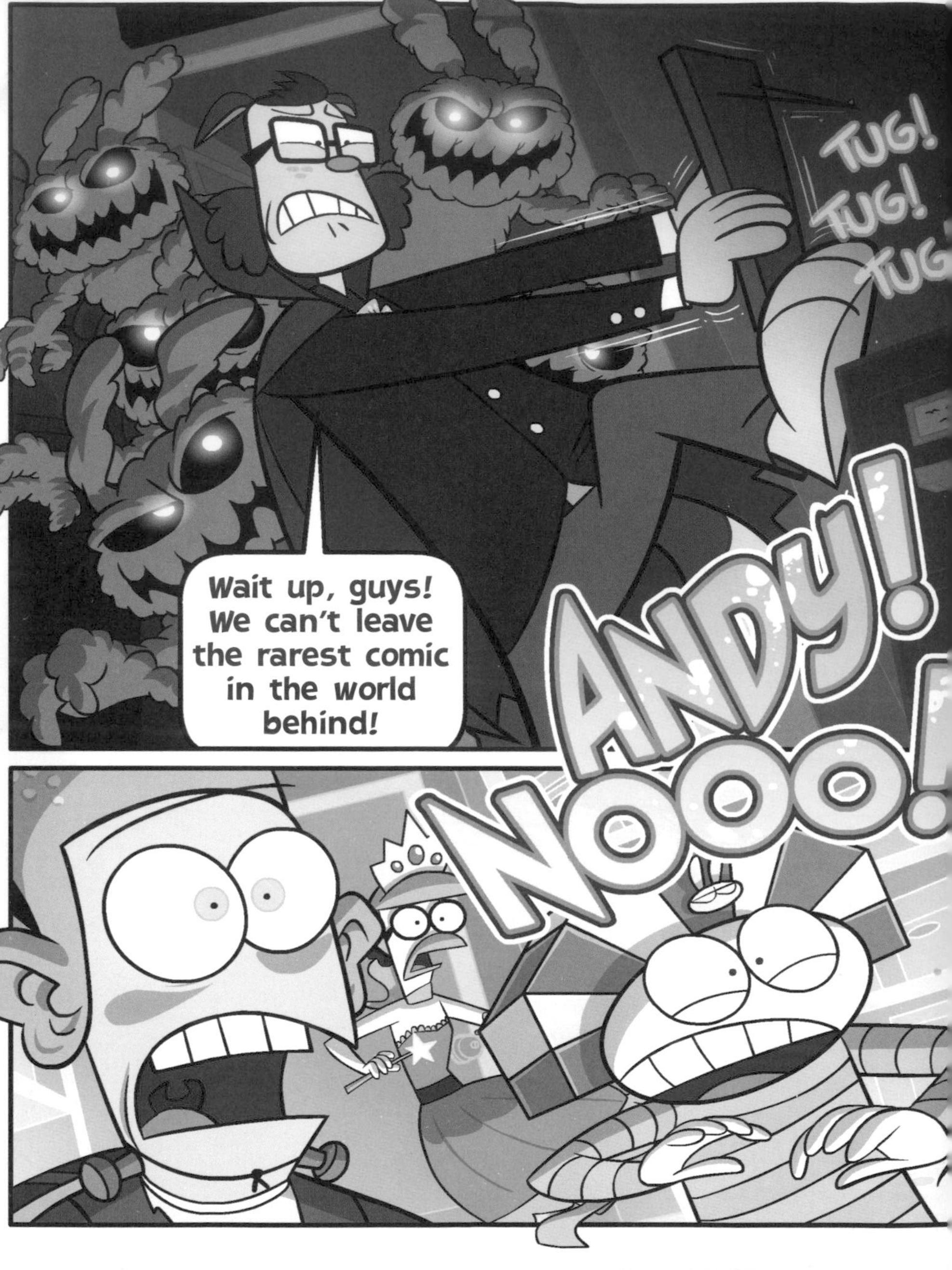
TUG! TUG! TUG
Wait up, guys! We can't leave the rarest comic in the world behind!
ANDY! NOOOO!

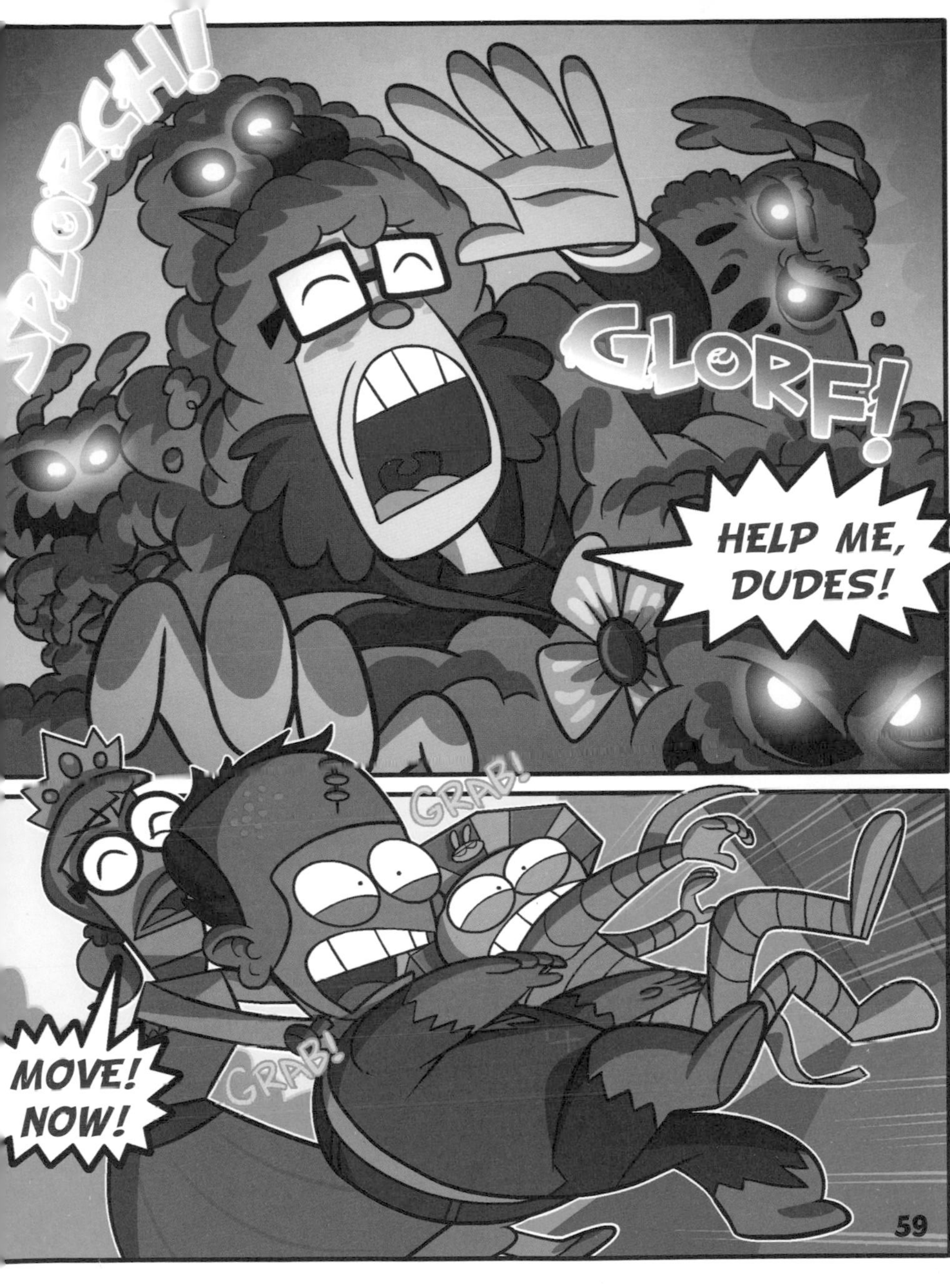
SPLORCH!
GLORF!
HELP ME, DUDES!
GRAB!
MOVE! NOW!
GRAB!

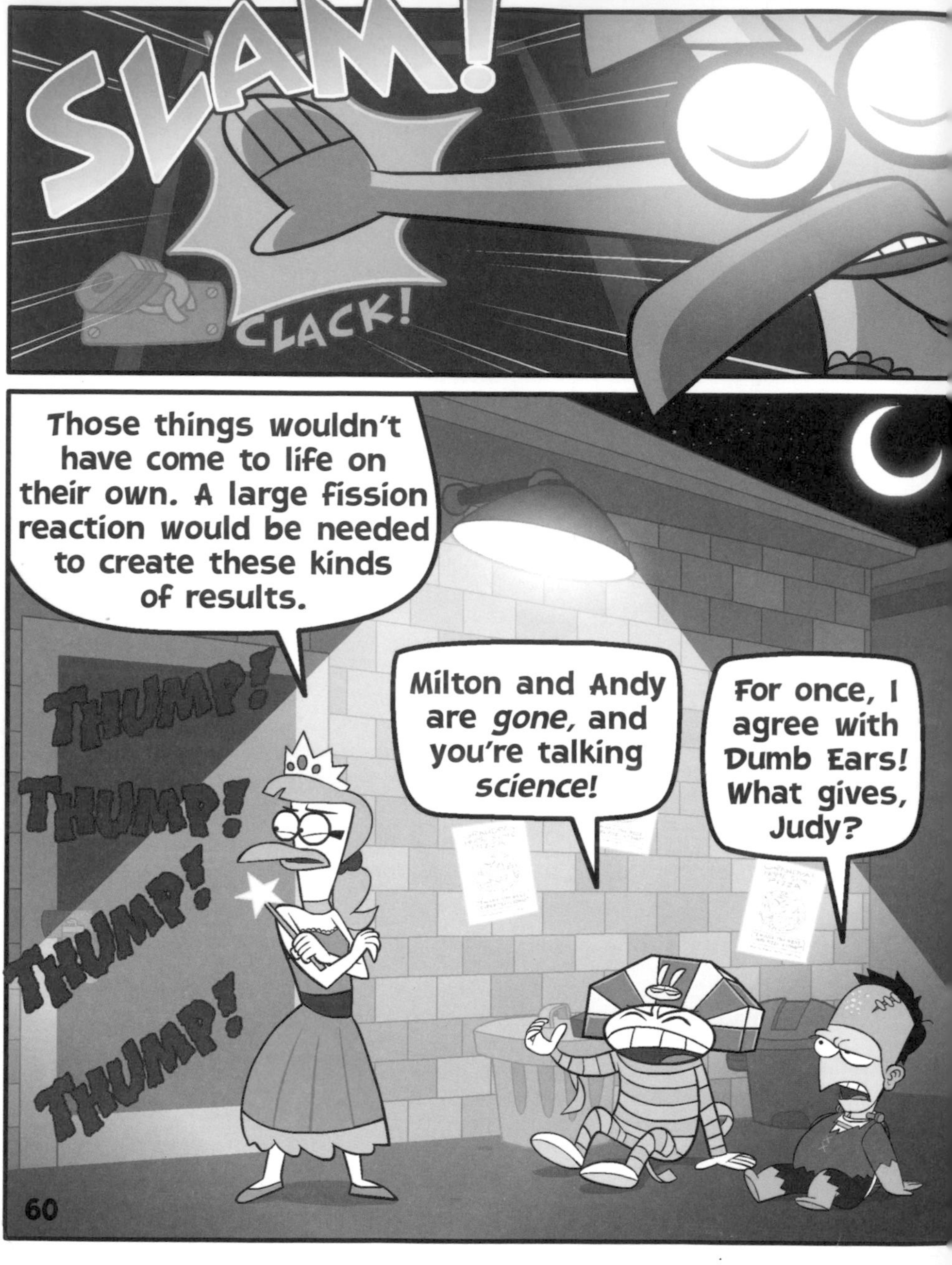
SLAM!
CLACK!
Those things wouldn't have come to life on their own. A large fission reaction would be needed to create these kinds of results.
THUMP!
THUMP!
THUMP!
THUMP!
Milton and Andy are *gone,* and you're talking *science!*
For once, I agree with Dumb Ears! What gives, Judy?

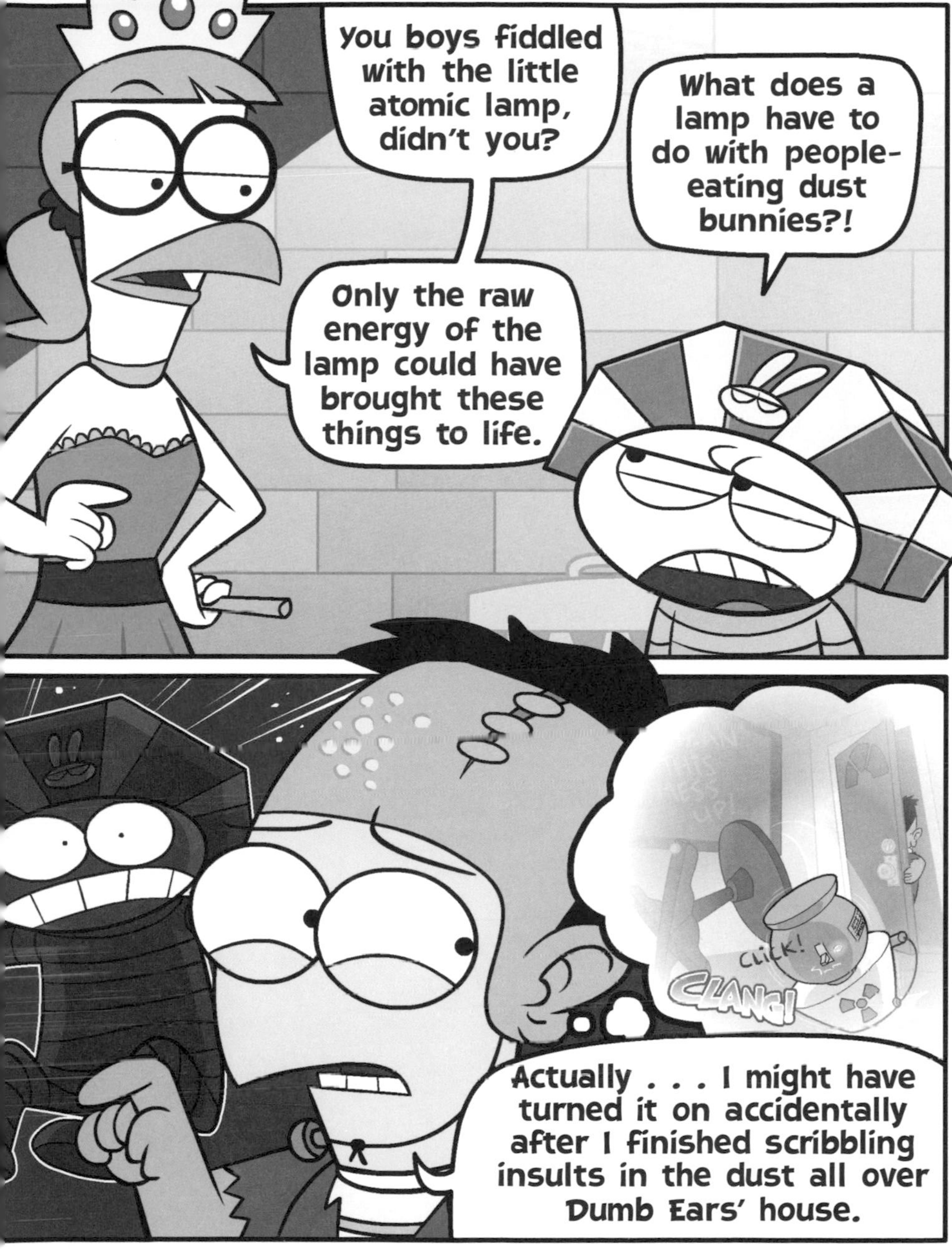
You boys fiddled with the little atomic lamp, didn't you?
What does a lamp have to do with people-eating dust bunnies?!
Only the raw energy of the lamp could have brought these things to life.
CLICK!
CLANG!
Actually . . . I might have turned it on accidentally after I finished scribbling insults in the dust all over Dumb Ears' house.

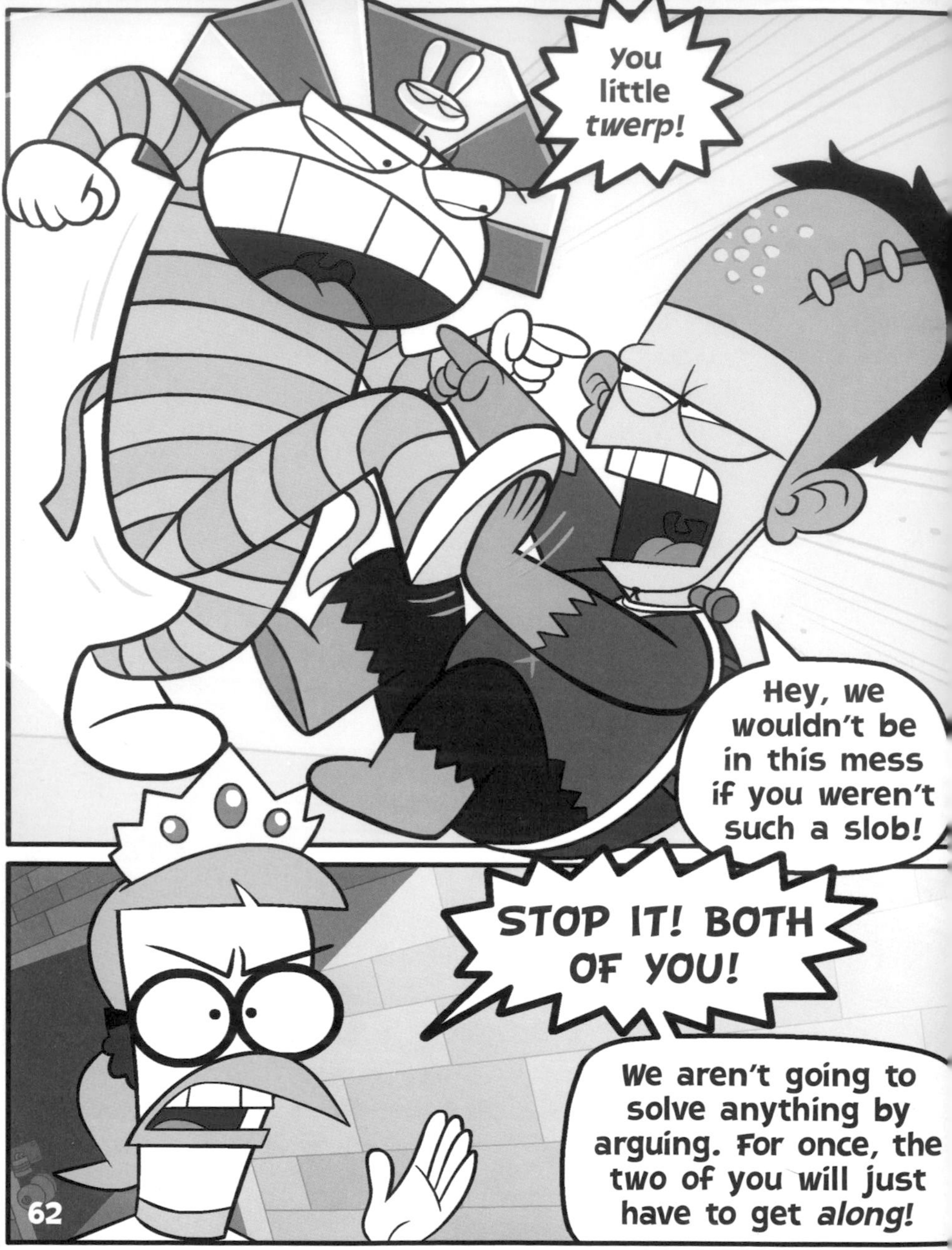
You little *twerp*!
Hey, we wouldn't be in this mess if you weren't such a slob!
STOP IT! BOTH OF YOU!
We aren't going to solve anything by arguing. For once, the two of you will just have to get *along*!

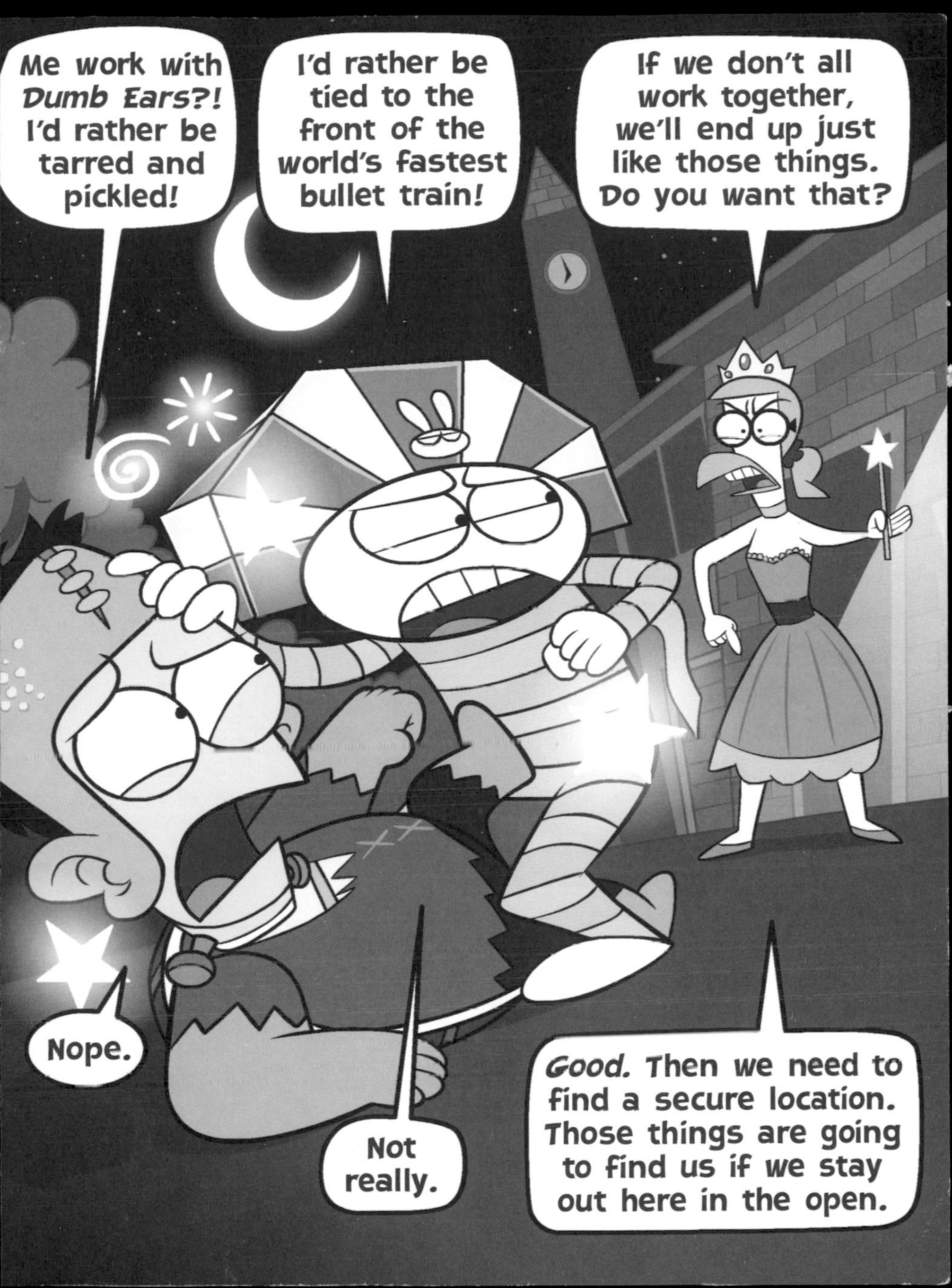

Me work with *Dumb Ears?!* I'd rather be tarred and pickled!
I'd rather be tied to the front of the world's fastest bullet train!
If we don't all work together, we'll end up just like those things. Do you want that?
Nope.
Not really.
Good. Then we need to find a secure location. Those things are going to find us if we stay out here in the open.

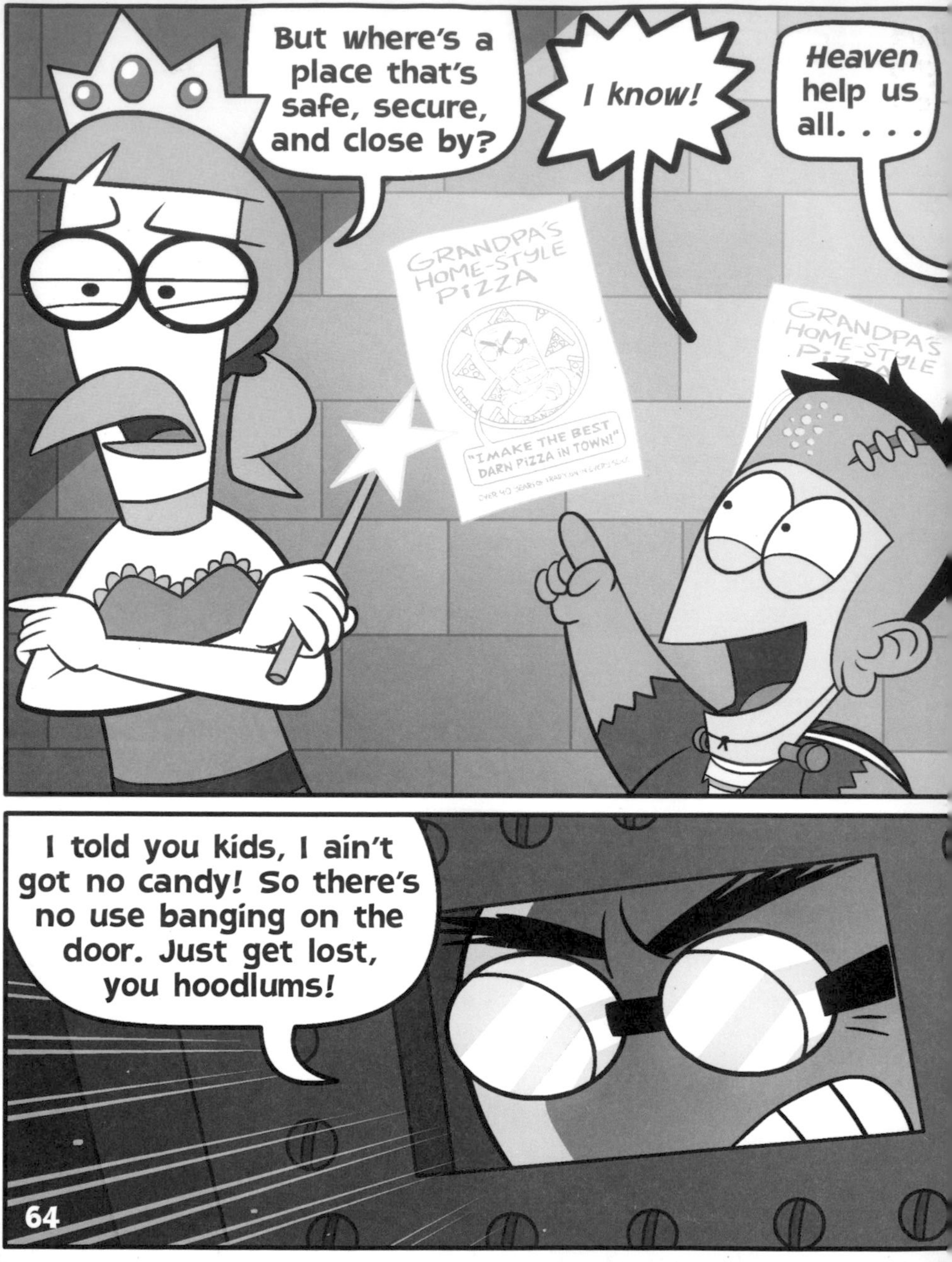
But where's a place that's safe, secure, and close by?
I know!
Heaven help us all. . . .
GRANDPA'S HOME-STYLE PIZZA
"I MAKE THE BEST DARN PIZZA IN TOWN!"
I told you kids, I ain't got no candy! So there's no use banging on the door. Just get lost, you hoodlums!

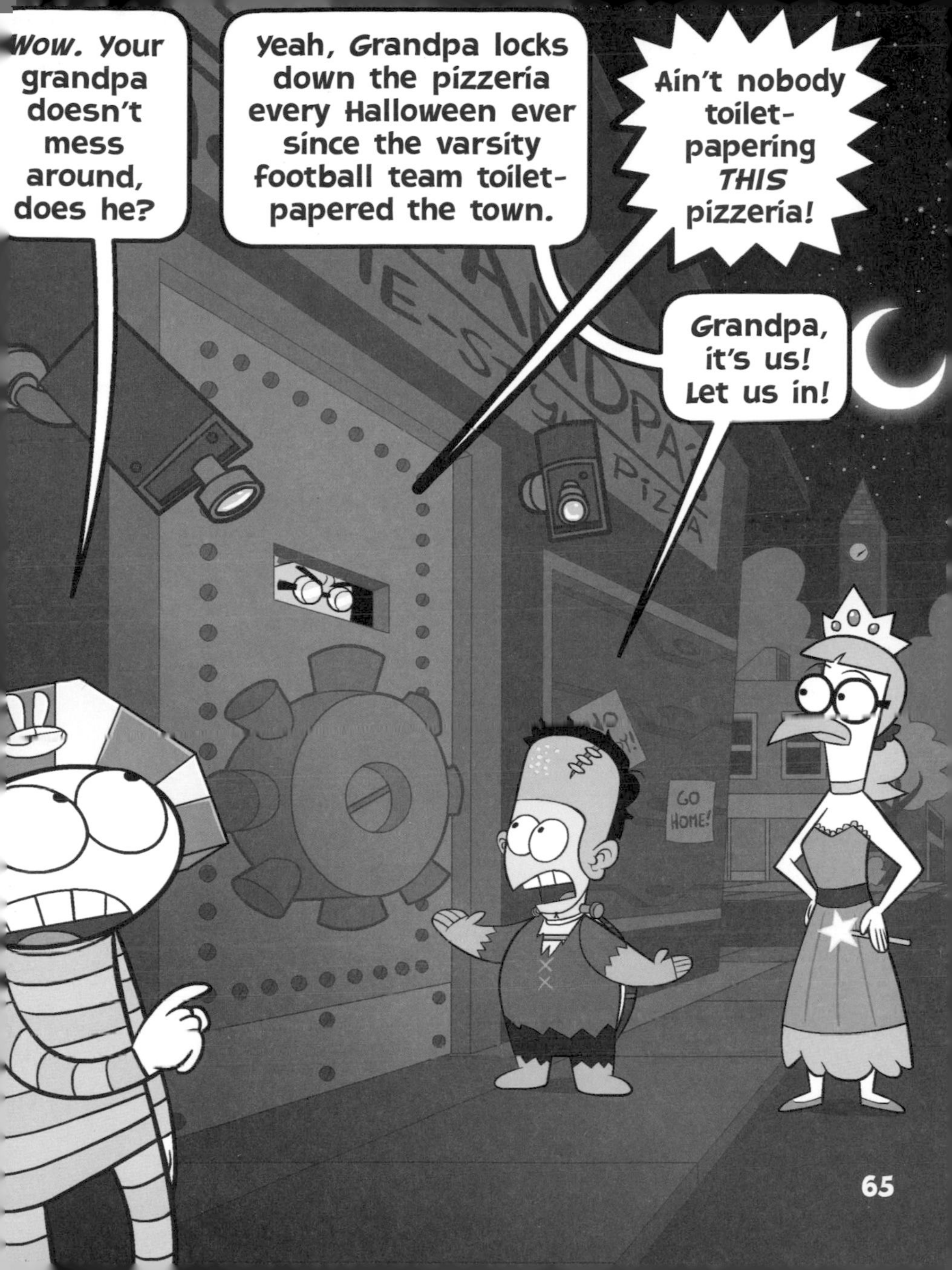
Wow. Your grandpa doesn't mess around, does he?
Yeah, Grandpa locks down the pizzeria every Halloween ever since the varsity football team toilet-papered the town.
Ain't nobody toilet-papering THIS pizzeria!
Grandpa, it's us! Let us in!
GO HOME!

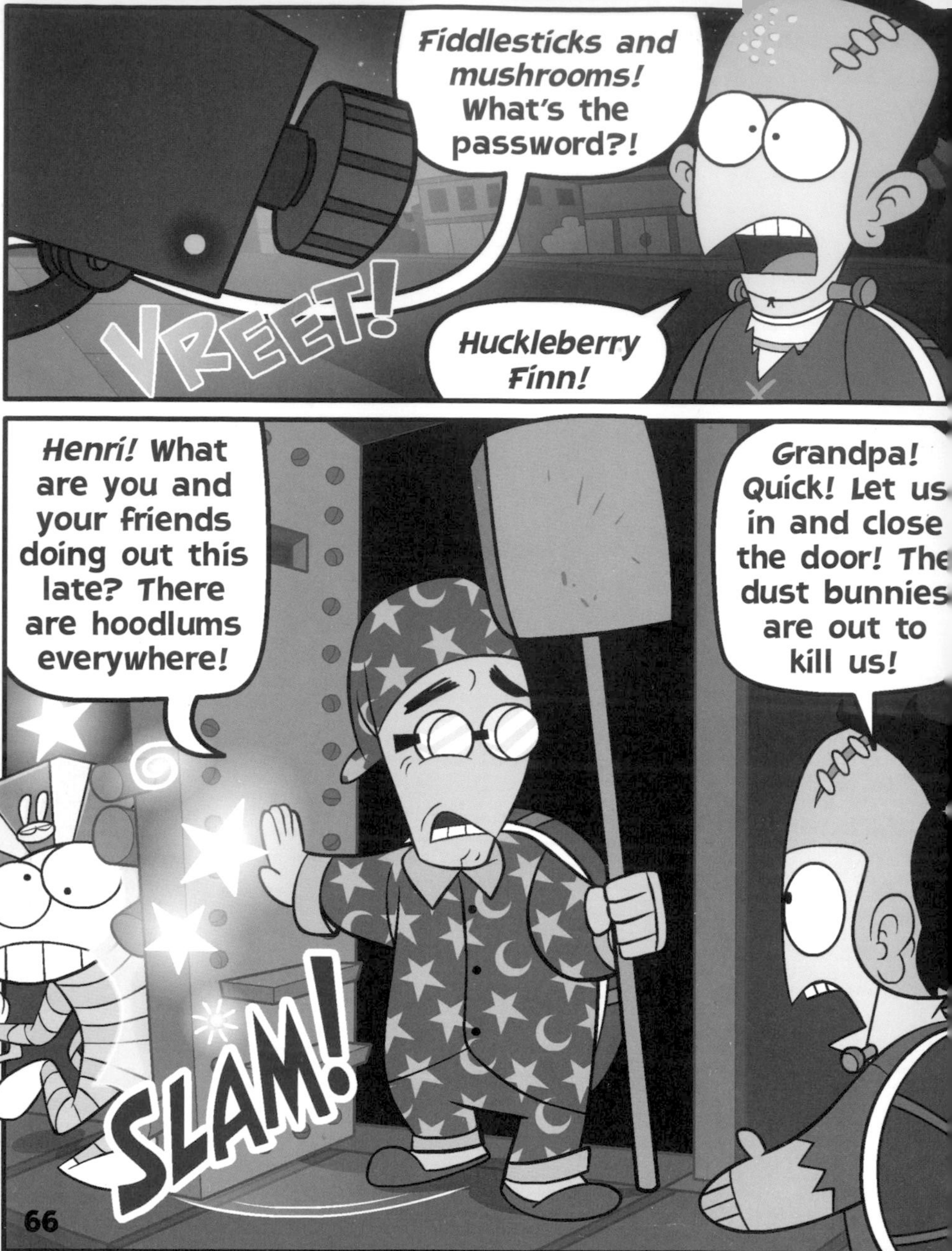
Fiddlesticks and mushrooms! What's the password?!
VREET!
Huckleberry Finn!
Henri! What are you and your friends doing out this late? There are hoodlums everywhere!
Grandpa! Quick! Let us in and close the door! The dust bunnies are out to kill us!
SLAM!

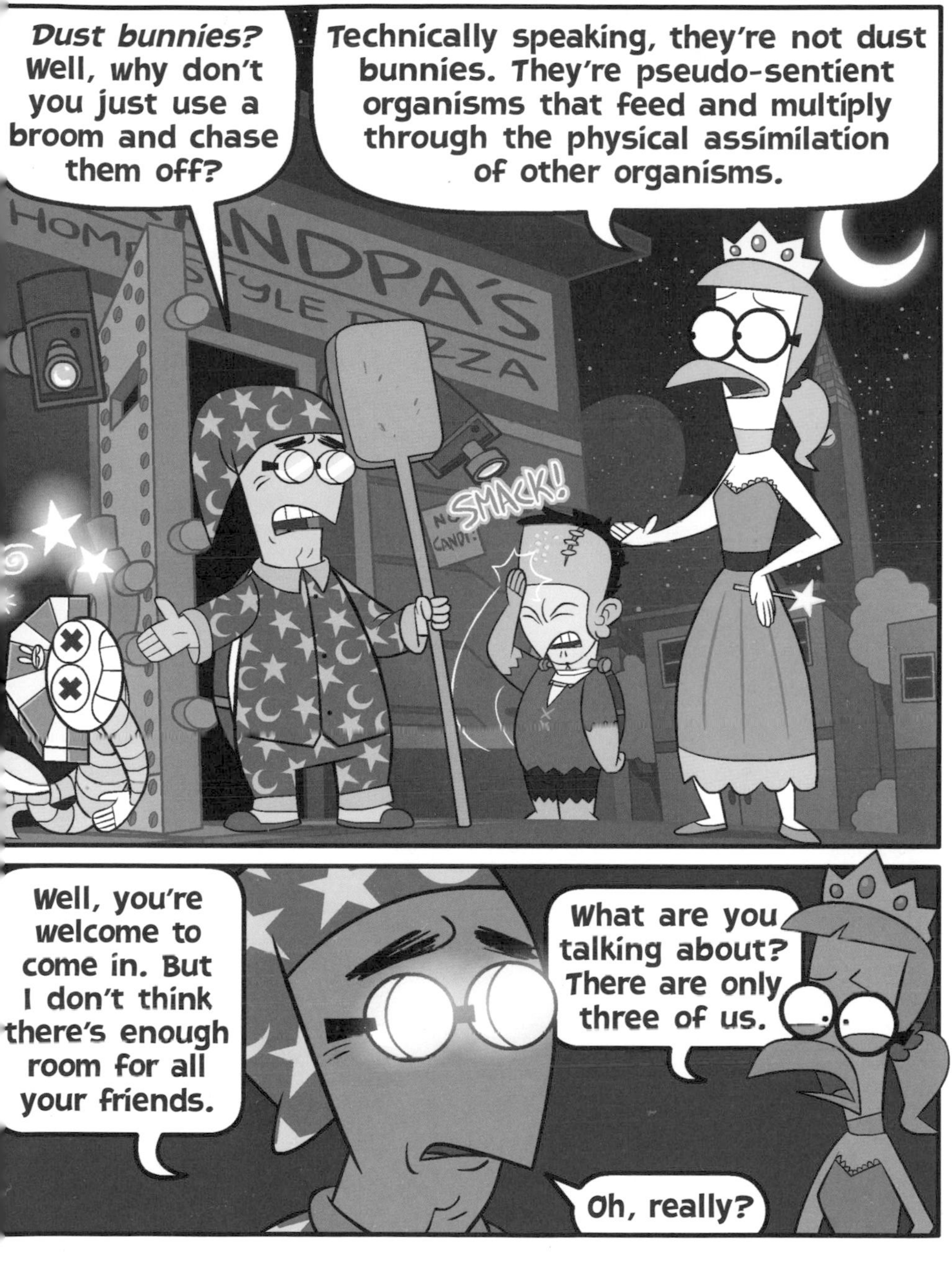
Dust bunnies? Well, why don't you just use a broom and chase them off?
Technically speaking, they're not dust bunnies. They're pseudo-sentient organisms that feed and multiply through the physical assimilation of other organisms.
SMACK!
Well, you're welcome to come in. But I don't think there's enough room for all your friends.
What are you talking about? There are only three of us.
Oh, really?

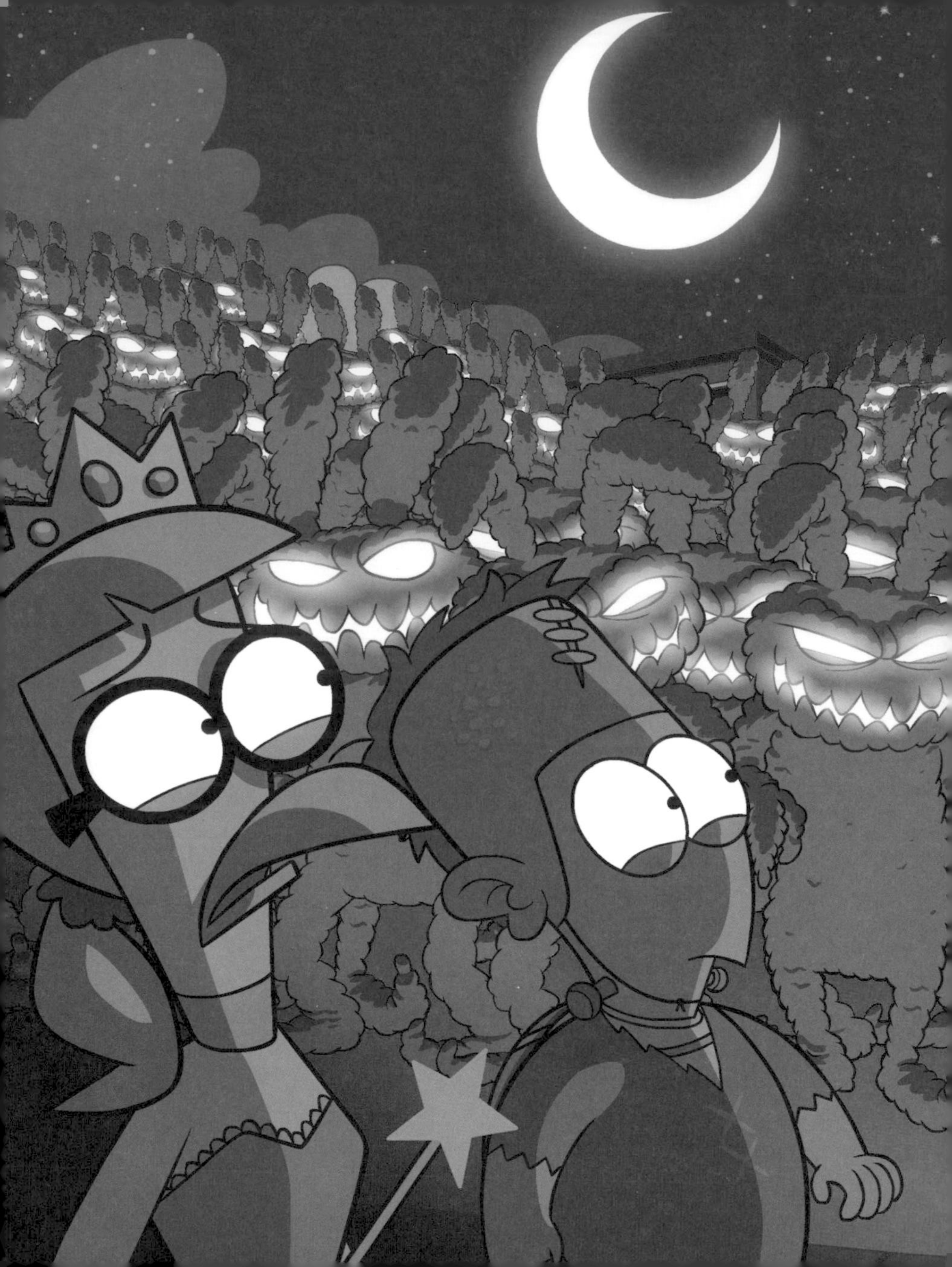

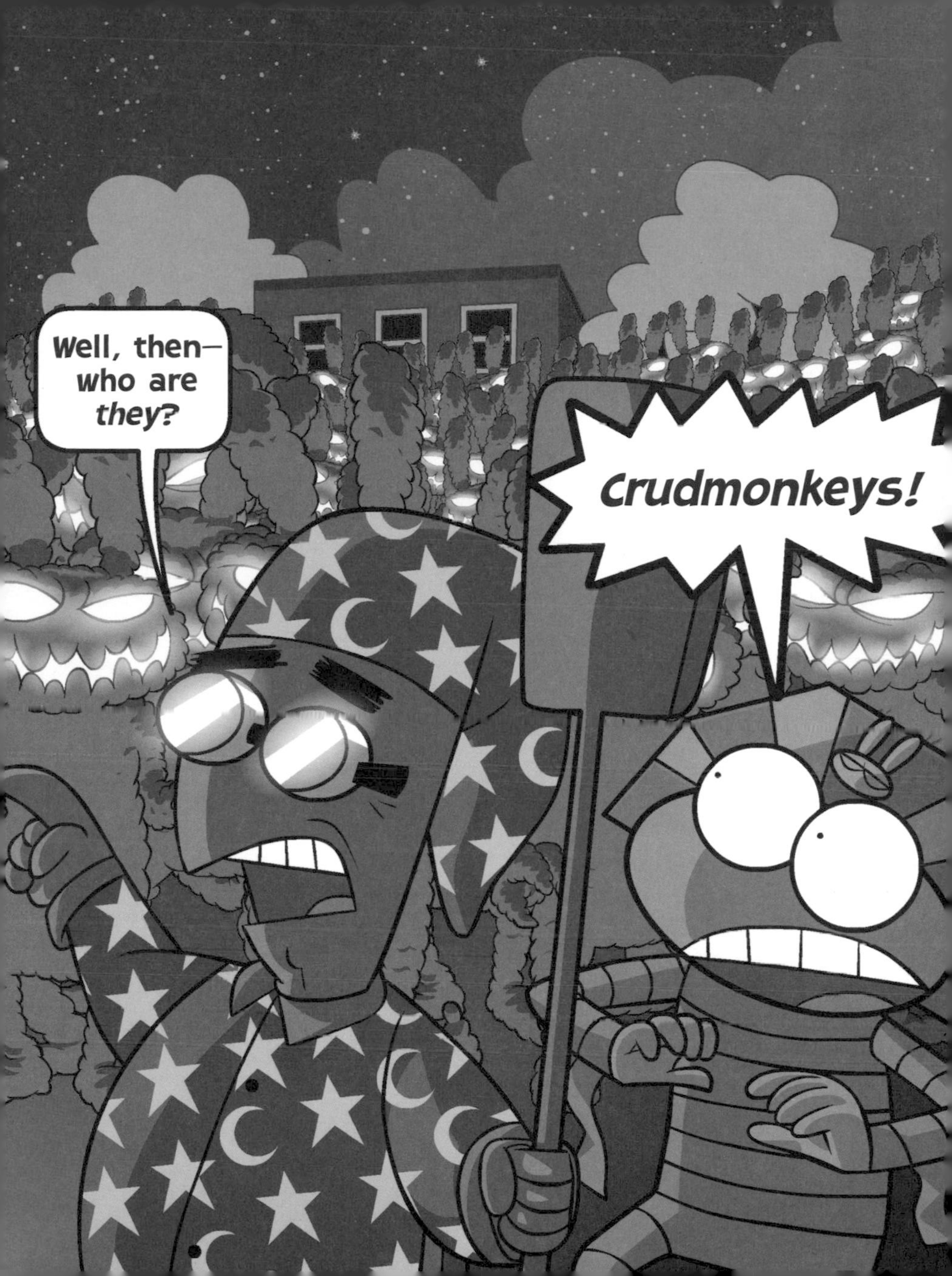
Well, then— who are *they?*
Crudmonkeys!

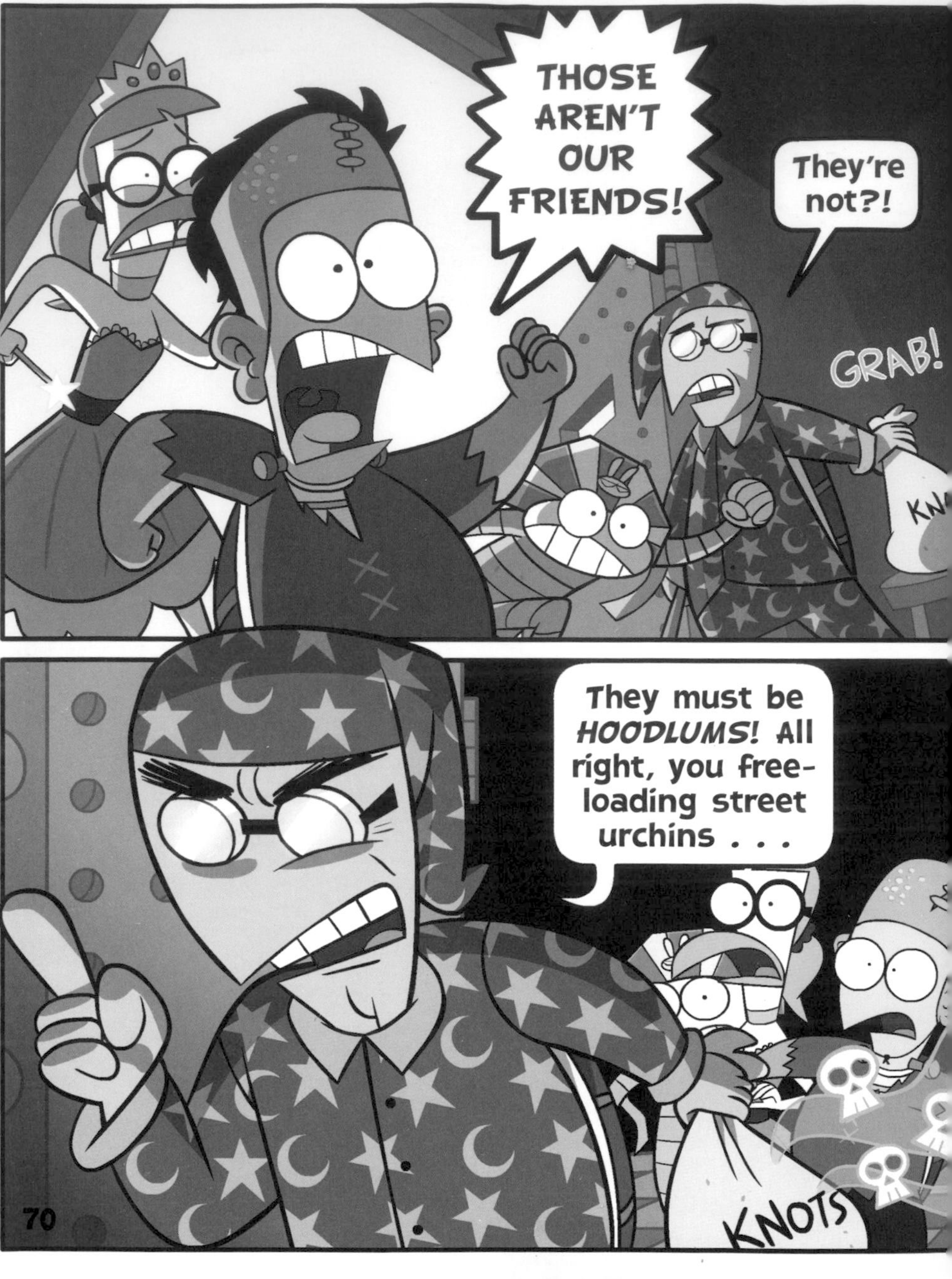
THOSE AREN'T OUR FRIENDS!
They're not?!
GRAB!
They must be *HOODLUMS!* All right, you free-loading street urchins . . .
KNOTS

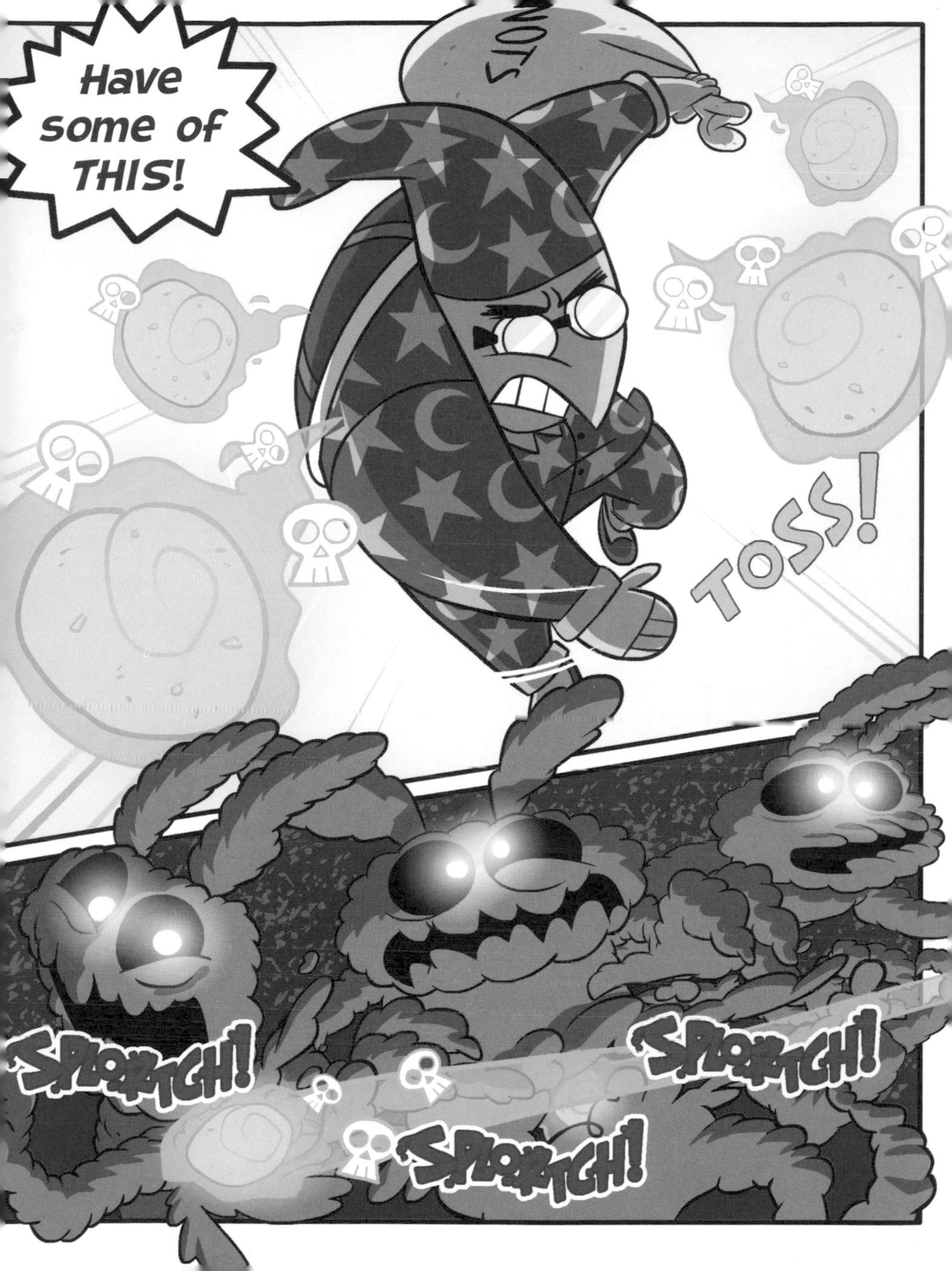
Have some of THIS!
TOSS!
SPLORTCH!
SPLORTCH!
SPLORTCH!

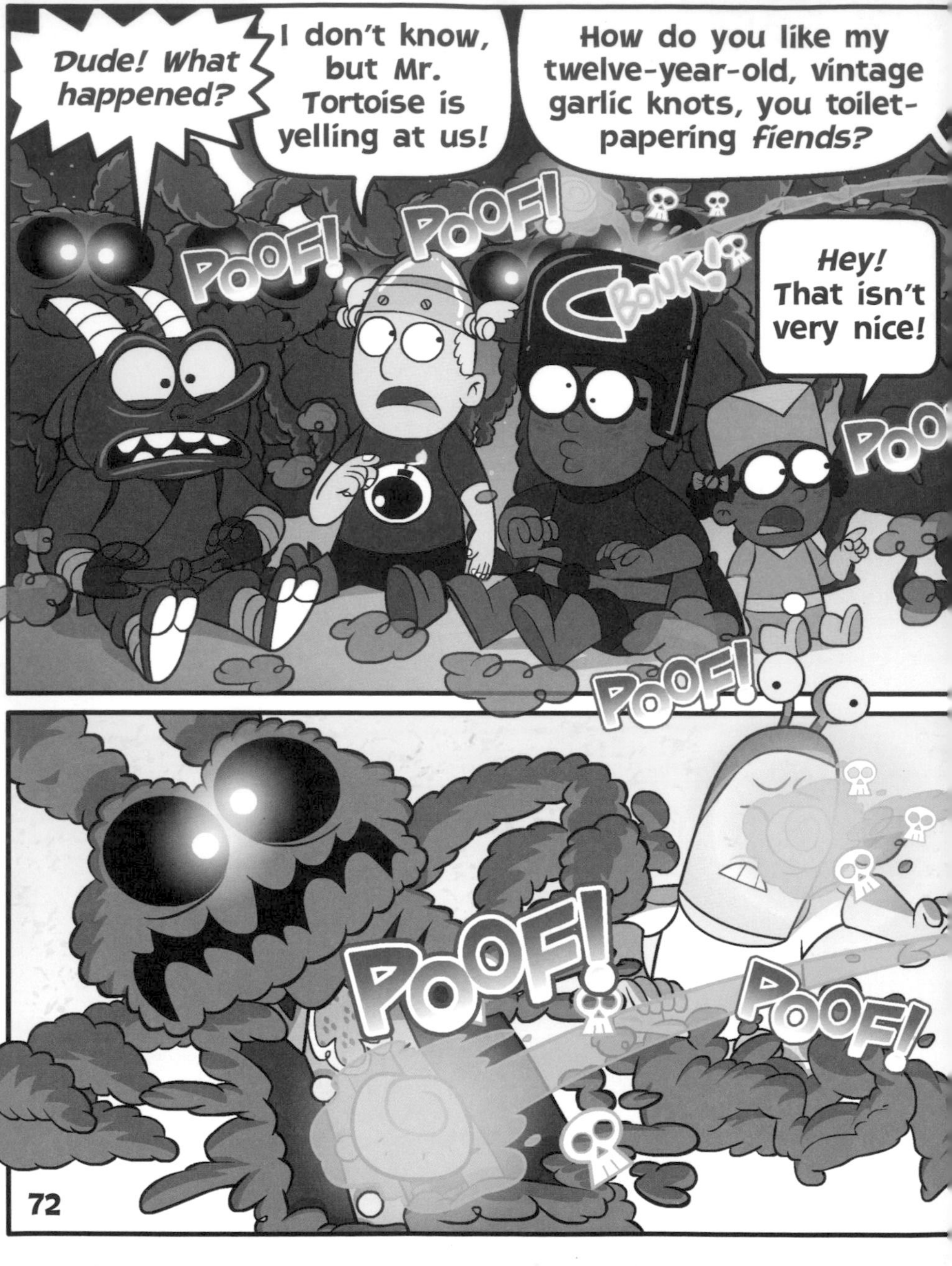
Dude! What happened?
I don't know, but Mr. Tortoise is yelling at us!
How do you like my twelve-year-old, vintage garlic knots, you toilet-papering *fiends?*
POOF!
POOF!
BONK!
Hey! That isn't very nice!
POO
POOF!
POOF!
POOF!

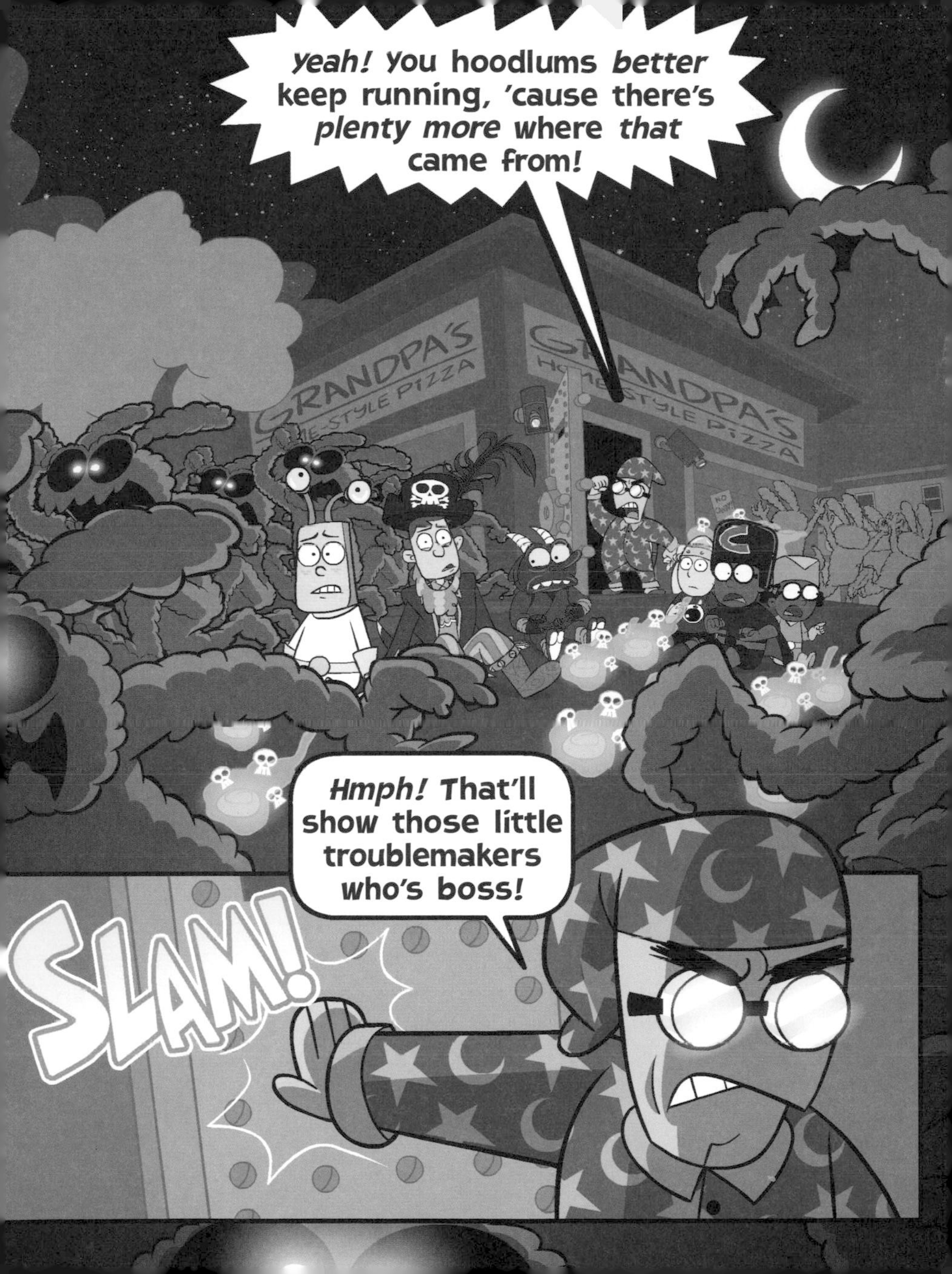
yeah! You hoodlums better keep running, 'cause there's plenty more where that came from!
GRANDPA'S HOME-STYLE PIZZA
GRANDPA'S HOME-STYLE PIZZA
Hmph! That'll show those little troublemakers who's boss!
SLAM!

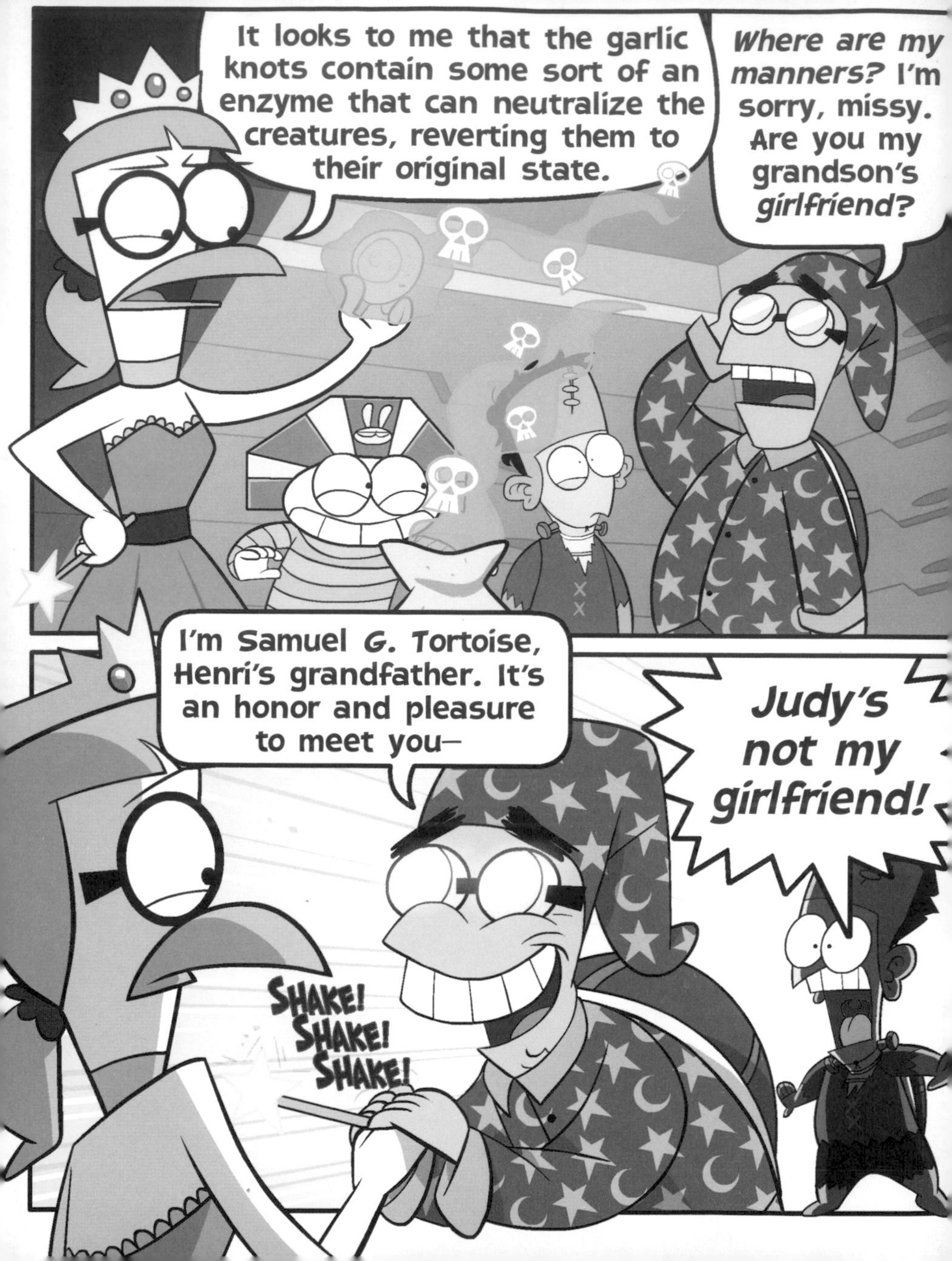
It looks to me that the garlic knots contain some sort of an enzyme that can neutralize the creatures, reverting them to their original state.
Where are my manners? I'm sorry, missy. Are you my grandson's *girlfriend?*
I'm Samuel *G.* Tortoise, Henri's grandfather. It's an honor and pleasure to meet you—
Judy's not my girlfriend!
SHAKE! SHAKE! SHAKE!

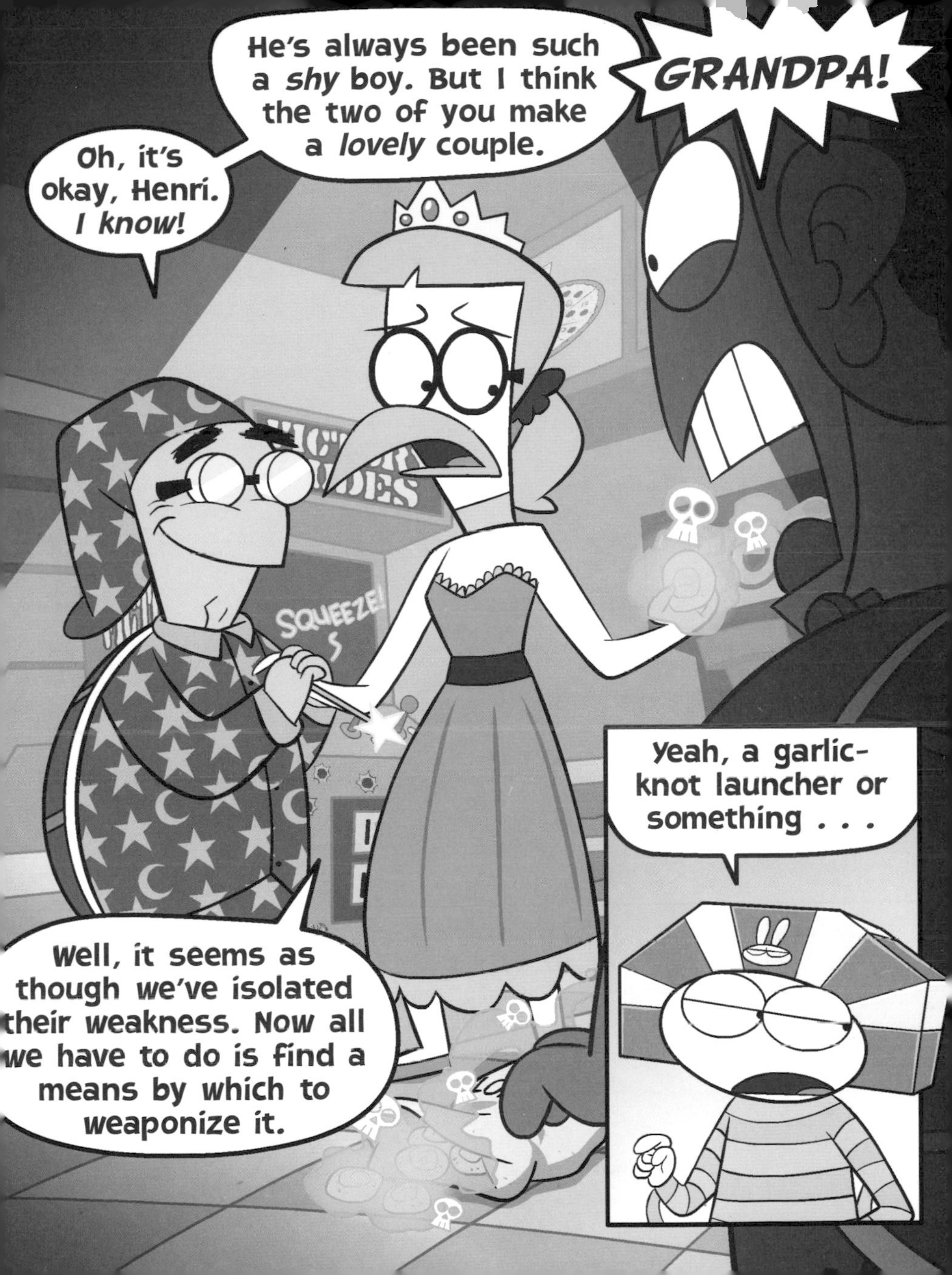

Oh, it's okay, Henri. *I know!*
He's always been such a *shy* boy. But I think the two of you make a *lovely* couple.
GRANDPA!
SQUEEZE!
Well, it seems as though we've isolated their weakness. Now all we have to do is find a means by which to weaponize it.
Yeah, a garlic-knot launcher or something . . .

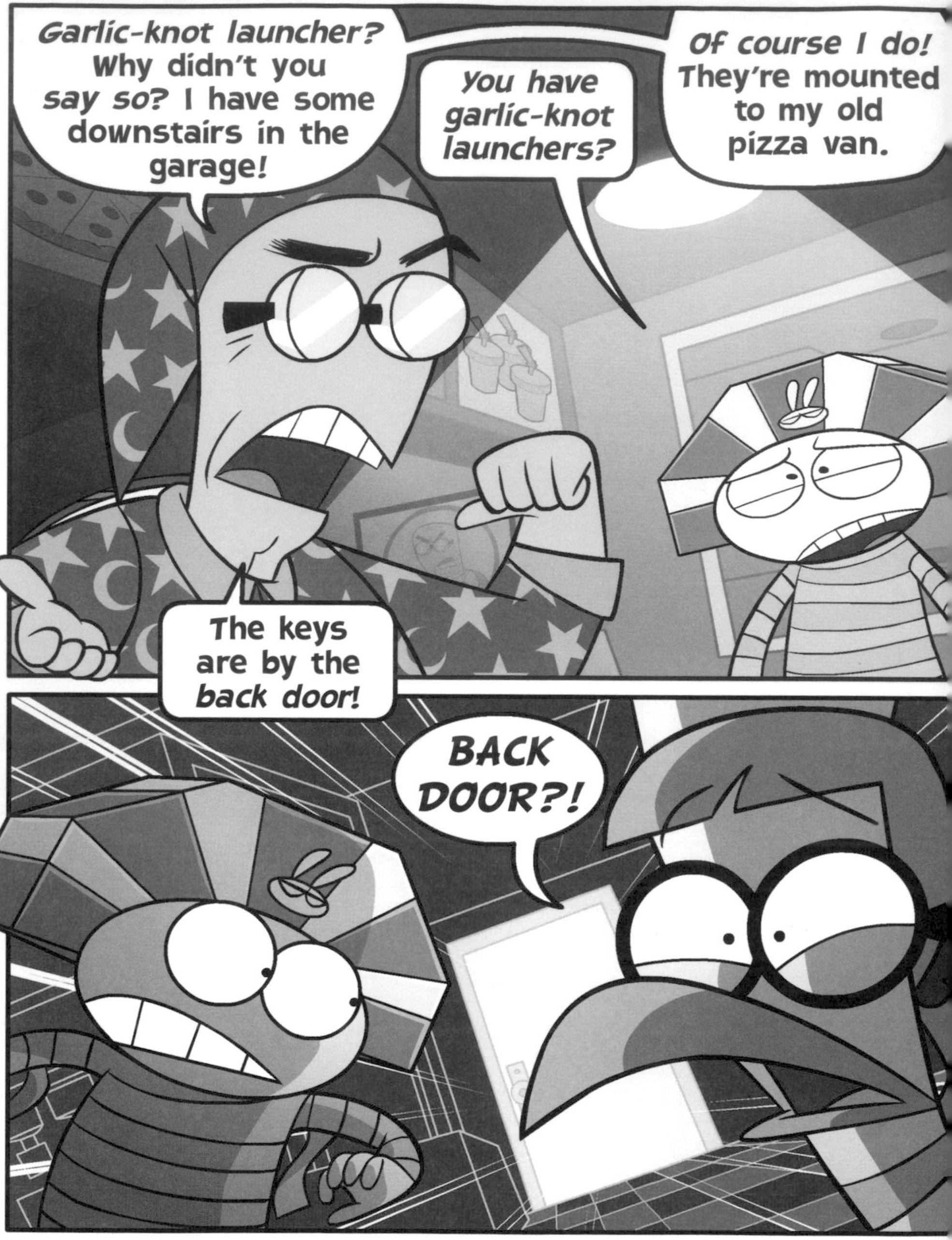
Garlic-knot launcher? Why didn't you say so? I have some downstairs in the garage!
You have garlic-knot launchers?
Of course I do! They're mounted to my old pizza van.
The keys are by the back door!
BACK DOOR?!

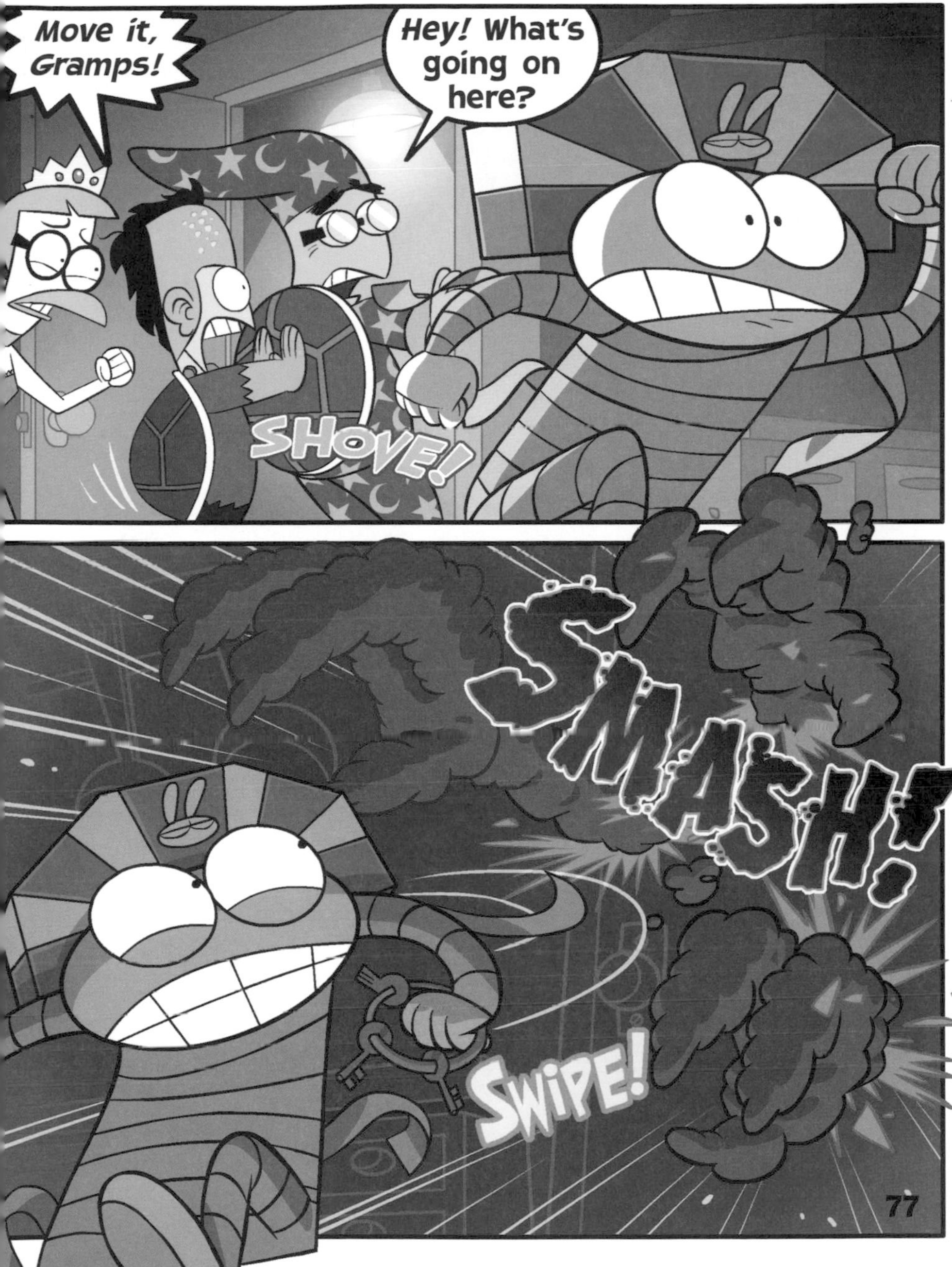
Move it, Gramps!
Hey! What's going on here?
SHOVE!
SMASH!
SWIPE!

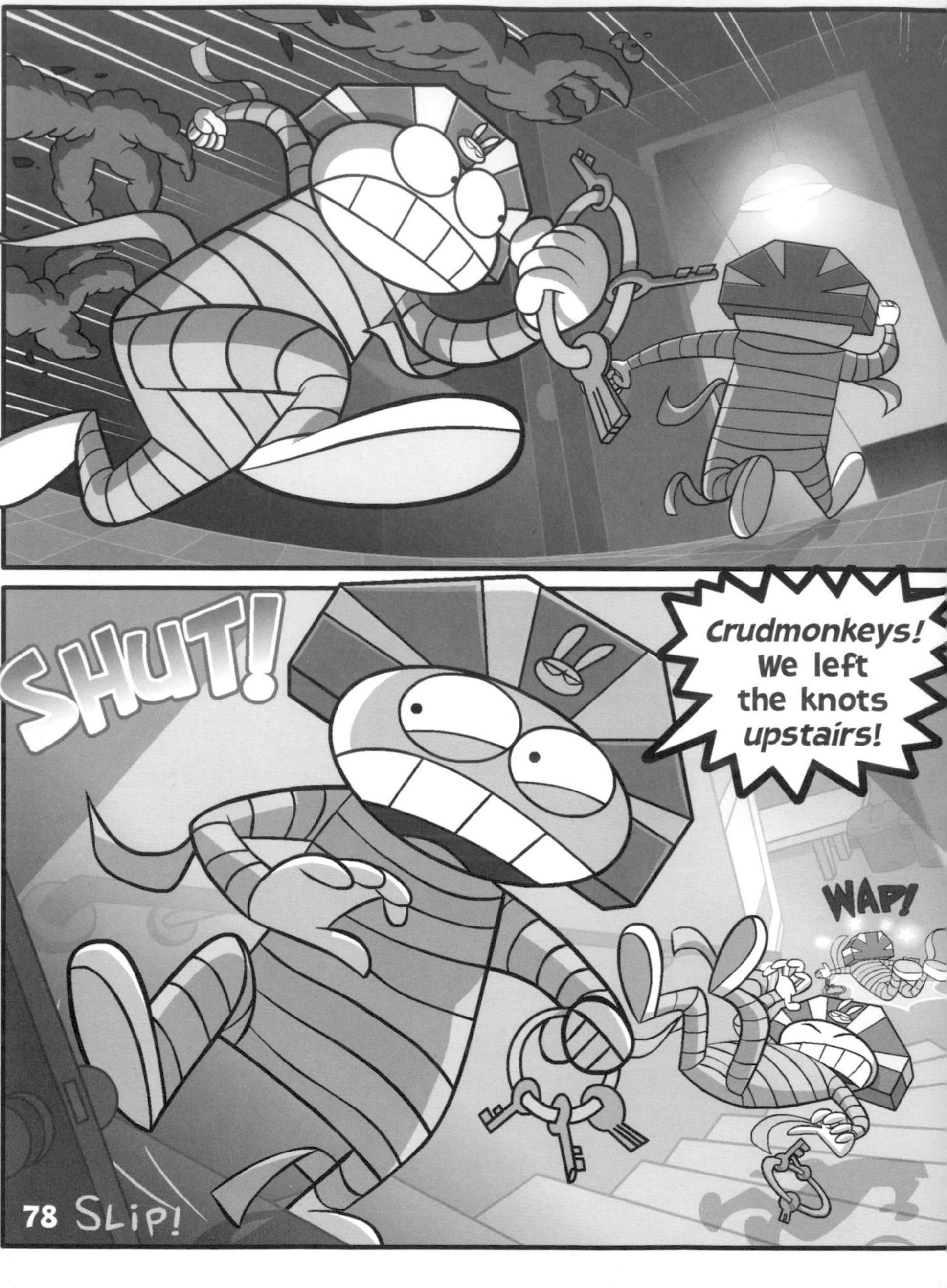
SHUT!
Crudmonkeys! We left the knots upstairs!
WAP!
SLIP!

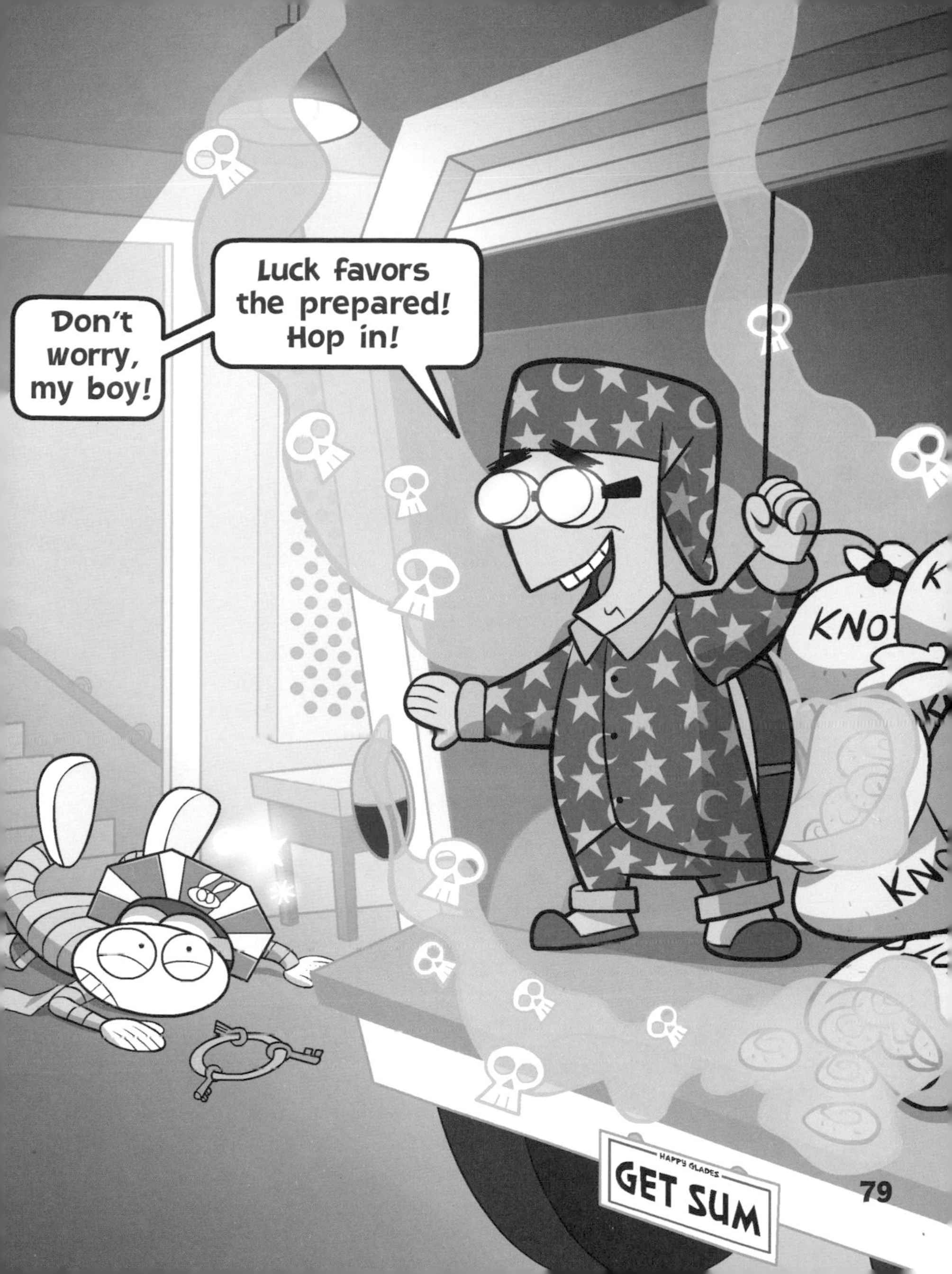
Don't worry, my boy!
Luck favors the prepared! Hop in!
HAPPY GLADES
GET SUM

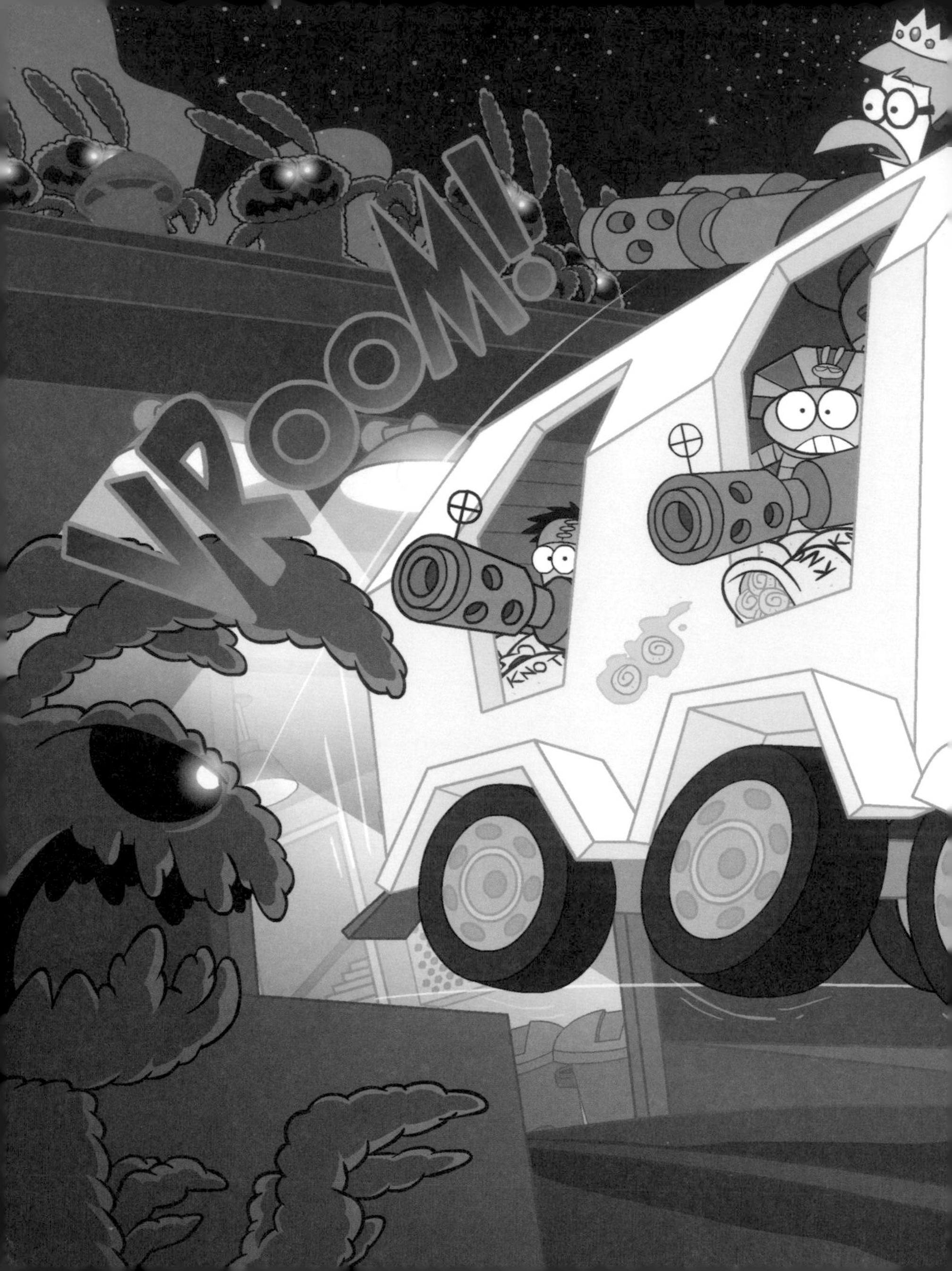
VROOM!
KNOT

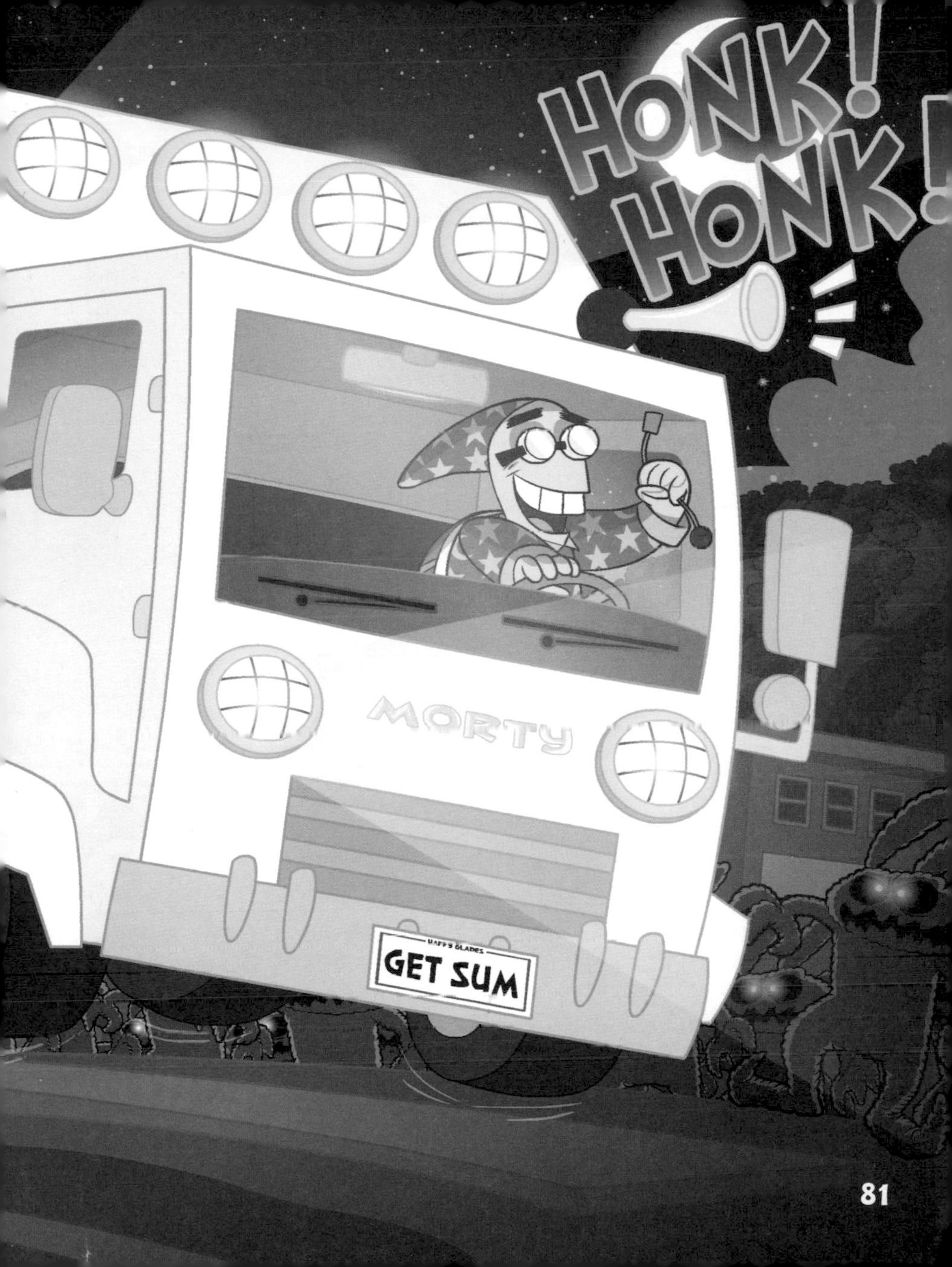
HONK!
HONK!
MORTY
GET SUM

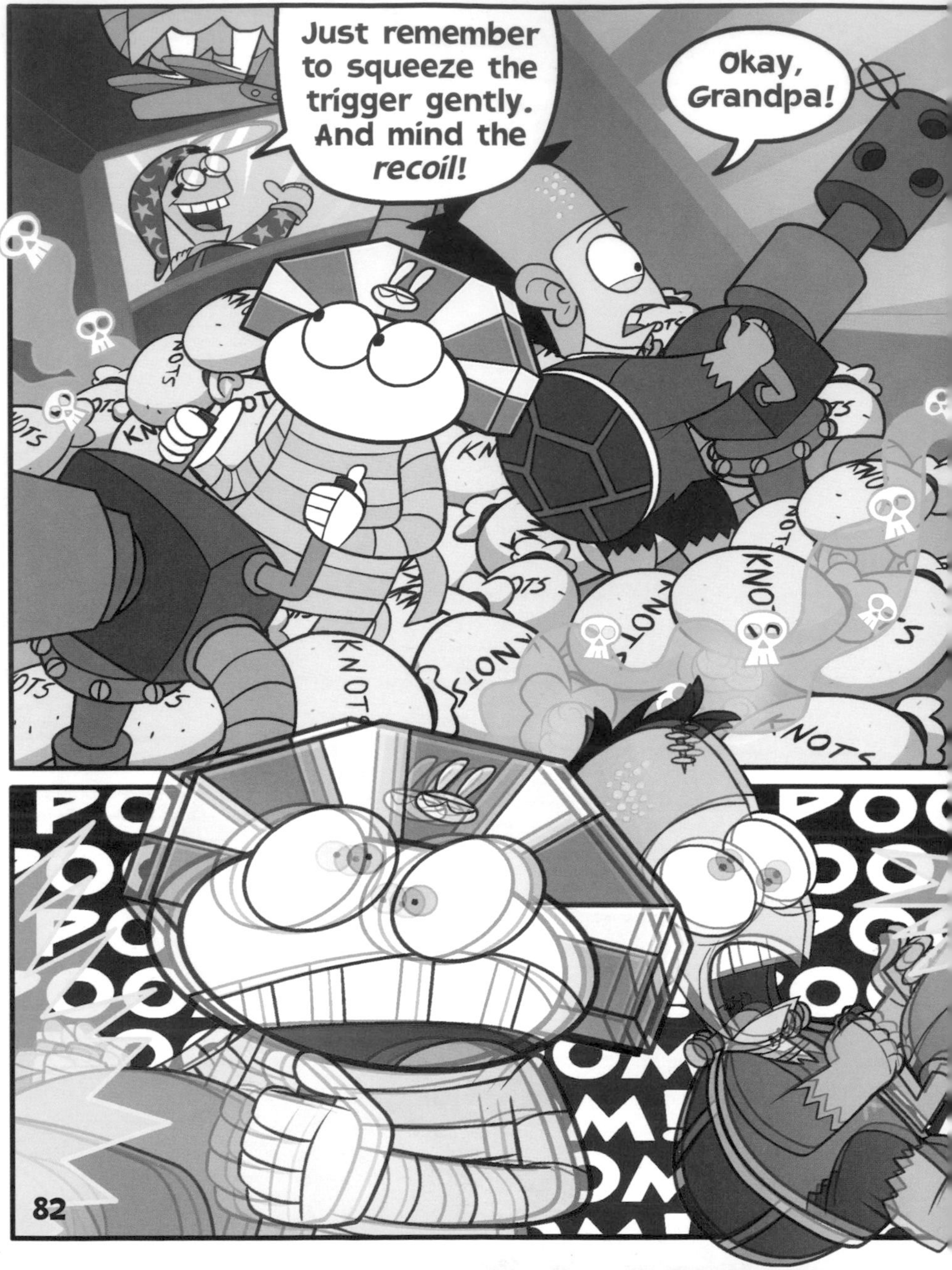
Just remember to squeeze the trigger gently. And mind the *recoil*!
Okay, Grandpa!

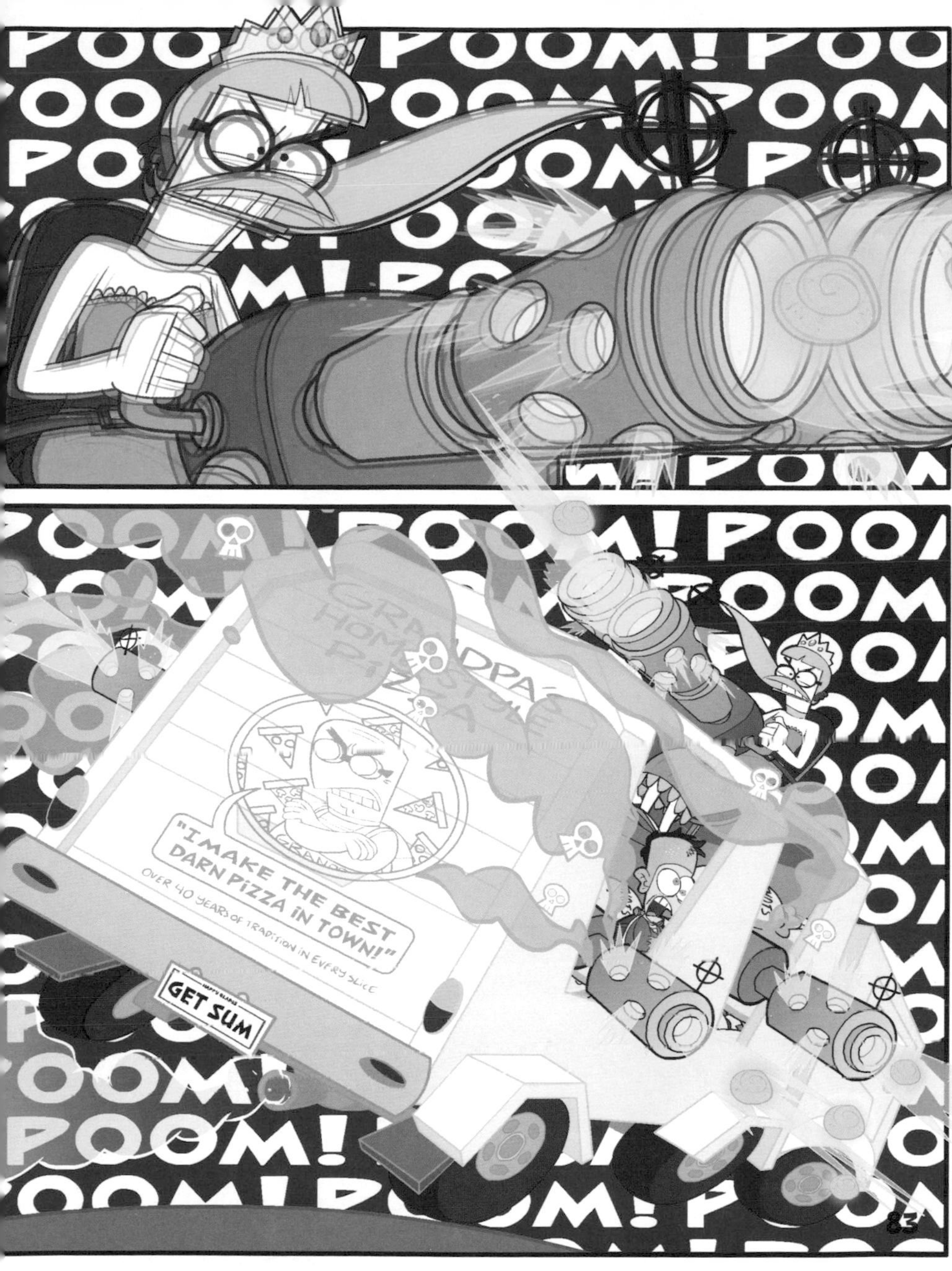
POOM! POOM!
POOM! POOM!
"I MAKE THE BEST DARN PIZZA IN TOWN!"
OVER 40 YEARS OF TRADITION IN EVERY SLICE
GET SUM

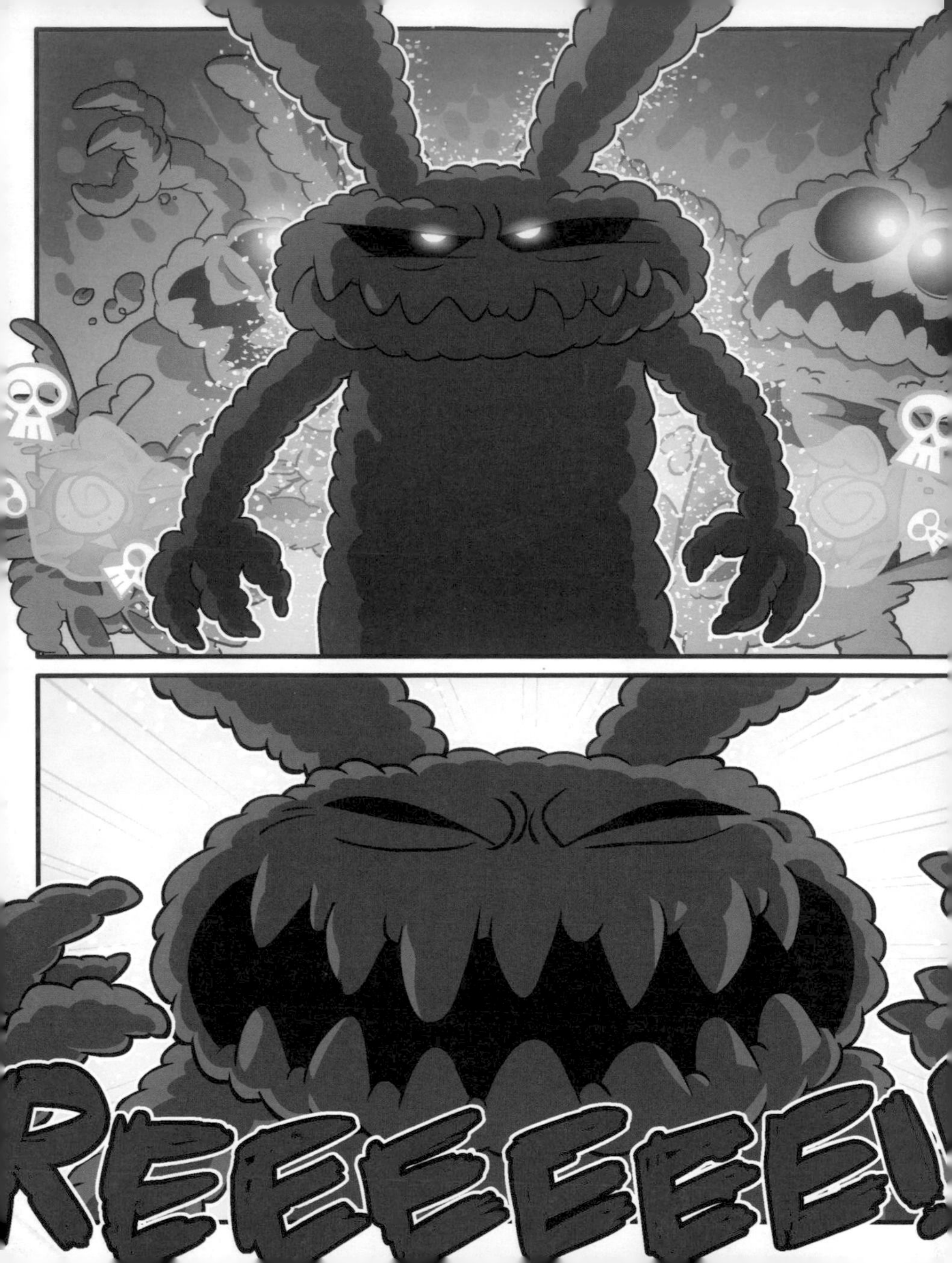
REEEEEE!

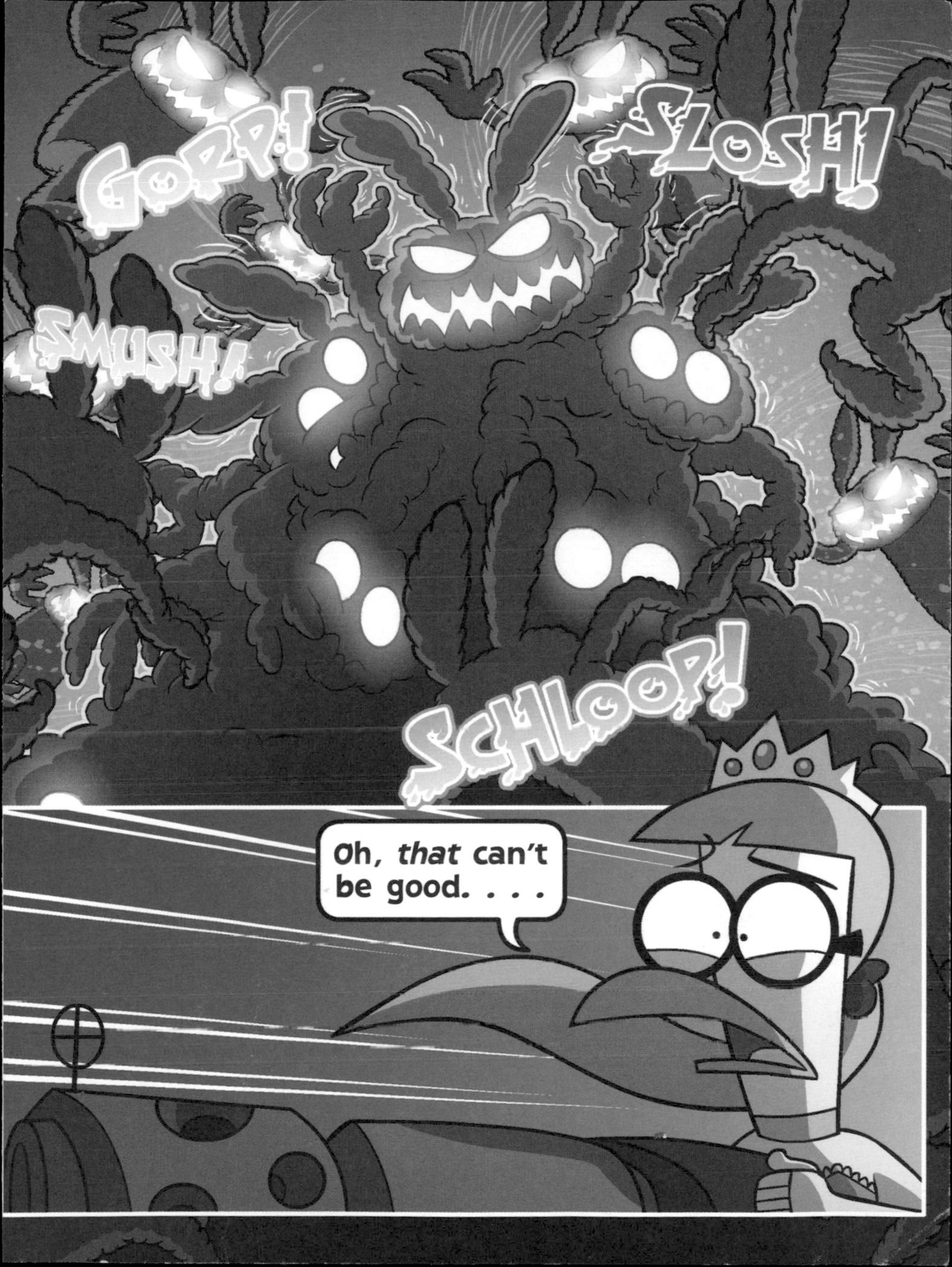
GORP!
SLOSH!
SMUSH!
SCHLOOP!
Oh, *that* can't be good. . . .

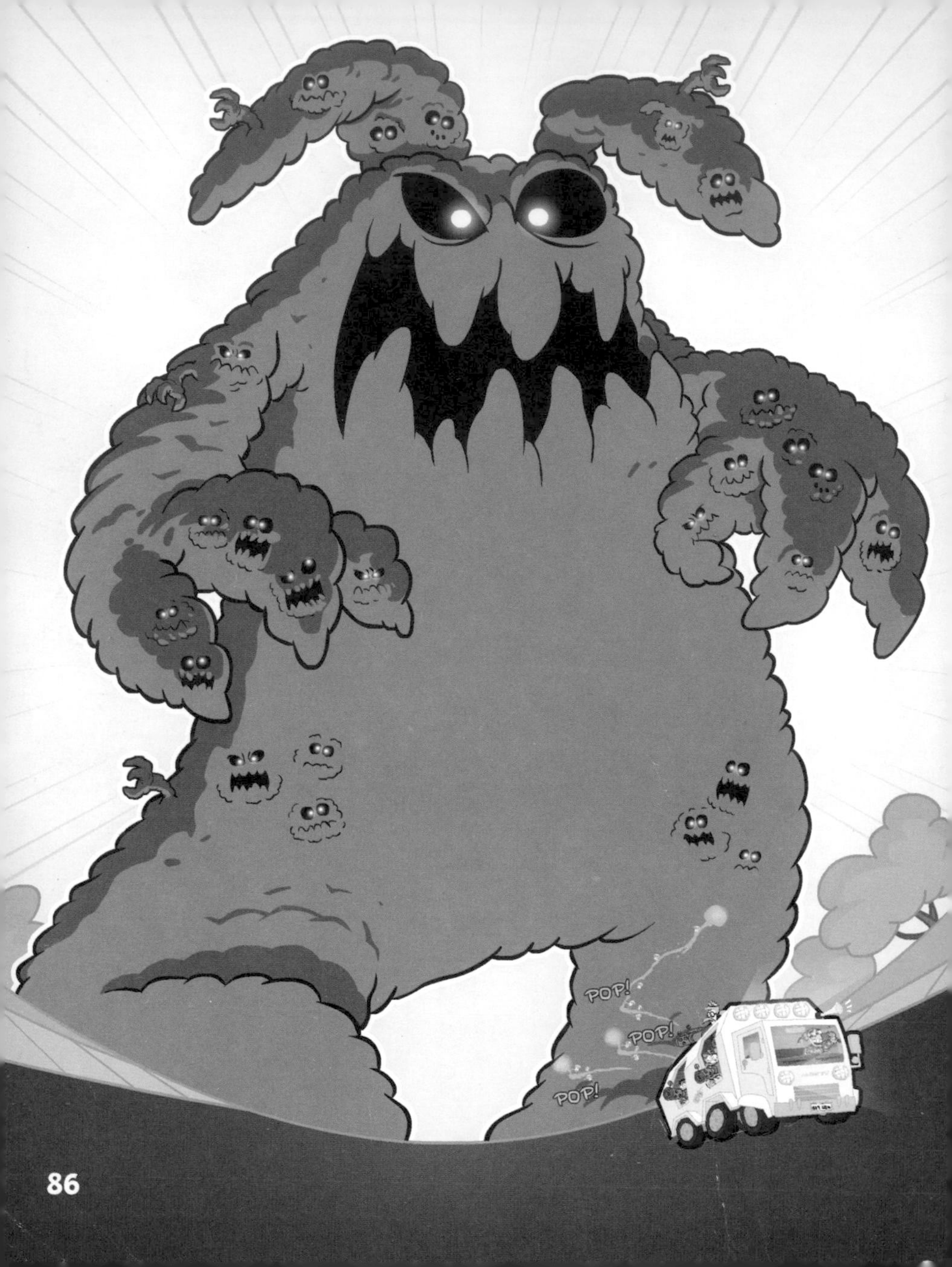
POP!
POP!
POP!

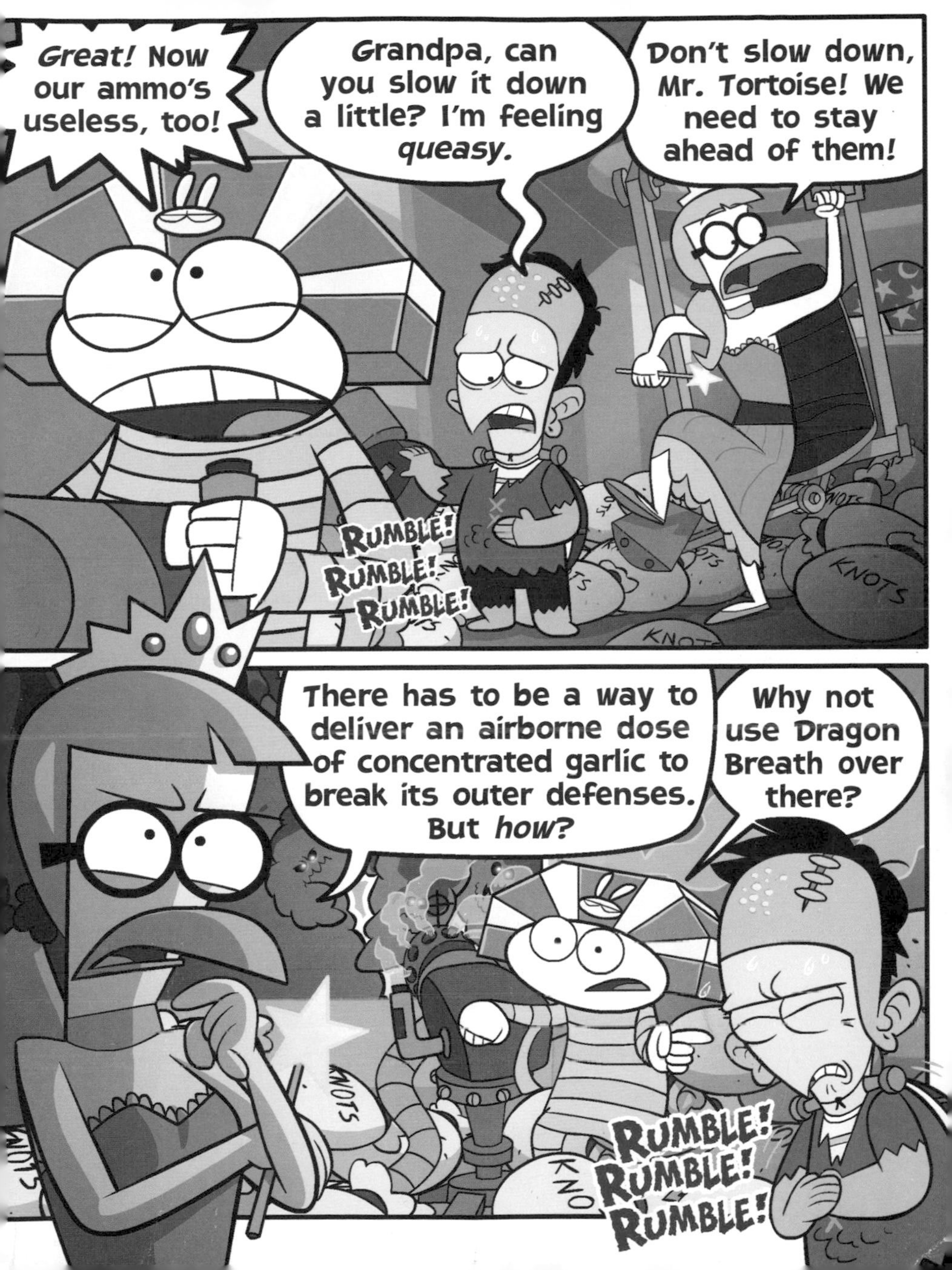

Great! Now our ammo's useless, too!
Grandpa, can you slow it down a little? I'm feeling *queasy.*
Don't slow down, Mr. Tortoise! We need to stay ahead of them!
RUMBLE! RUMBLE! RUMBLE!
KNOTS
There has to be a way to deliver an airborne dose of concentrated garlic to break its outer defenses. But *how?*
Why not use Dragon Breath over there?
KNOTS
RUMBLE! RUMBLE! RUMBLE!

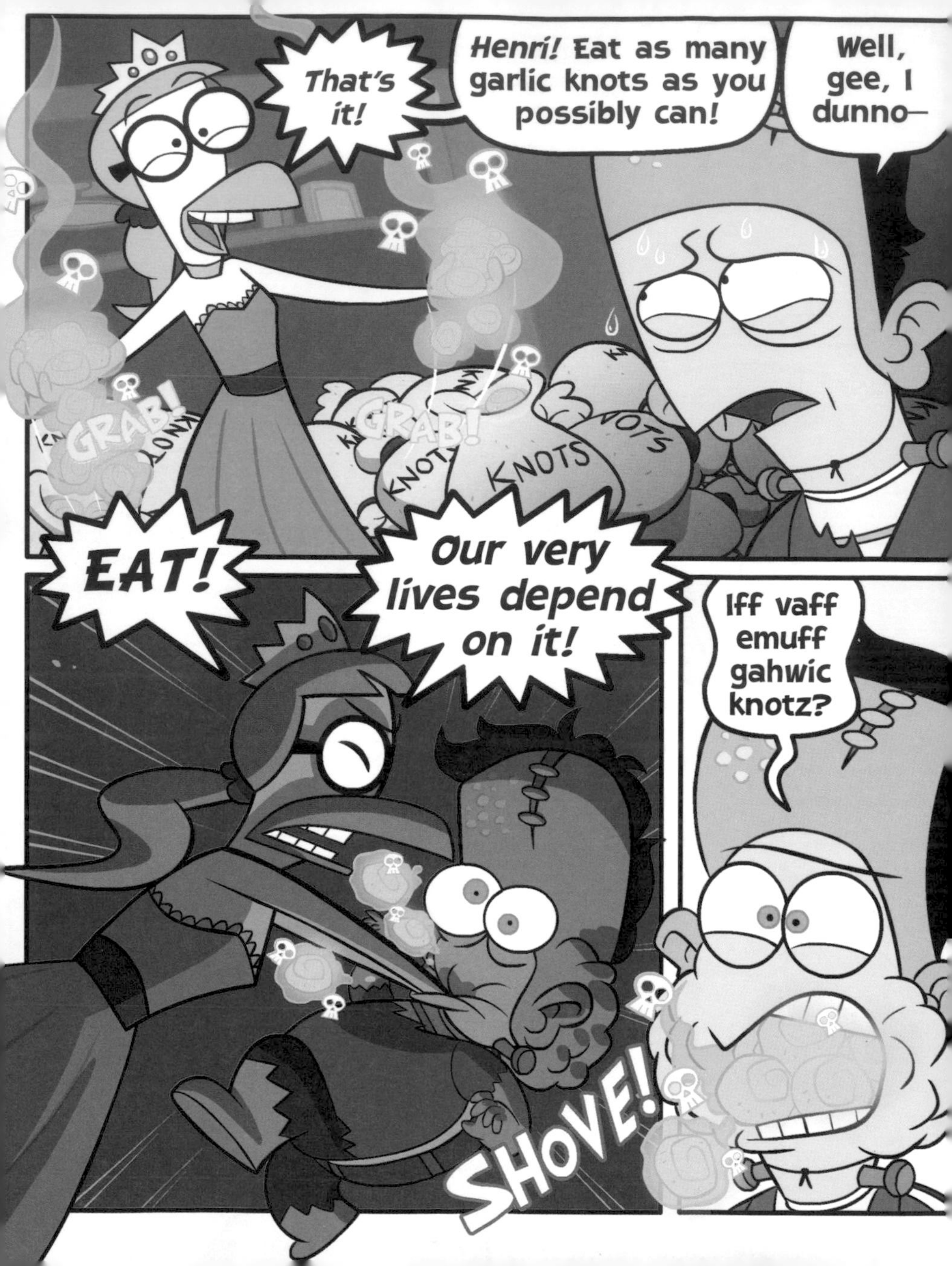
That's it!
Henri! Eat as many garlic knots as you possibly can!
Well, gee, I dunno—
GRAB!
KNOTS
GRAB!
KNOTS
KNOTS
KNOTS
EAT!
Our very lives depend on it!
Iff vaff emuff gahwic knotz?
SHOVE!

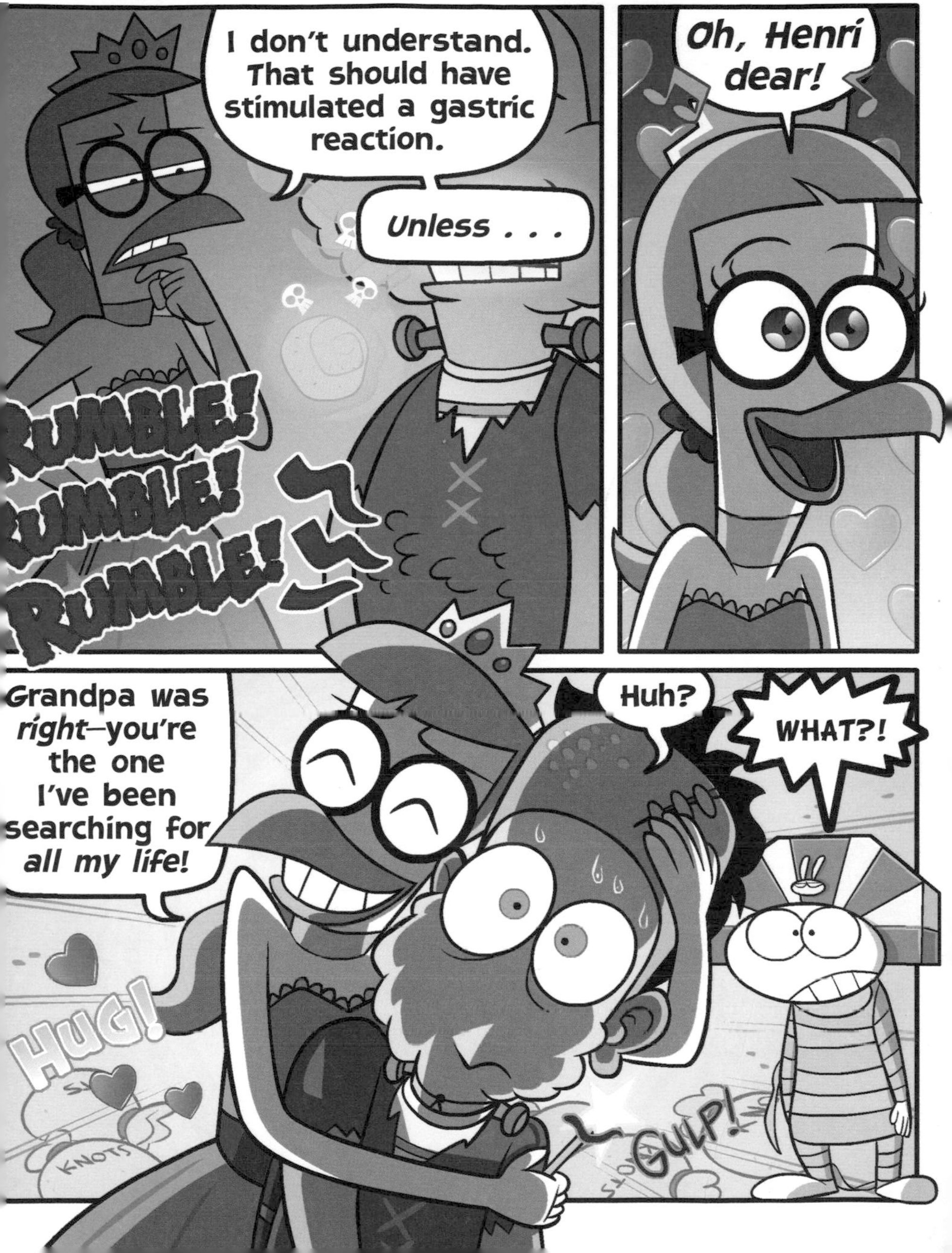
I don't understand. That should have stimulated a gastric reaction.
Unless . . .
RUMBLE! RUMBLE! RUMBLE!
Oh, Henri dear!
Grandpa was *right*—you're the one I've been searching for *all my life!*
Huh?
WHAT?!
HUG!
GULP!
KNOTS

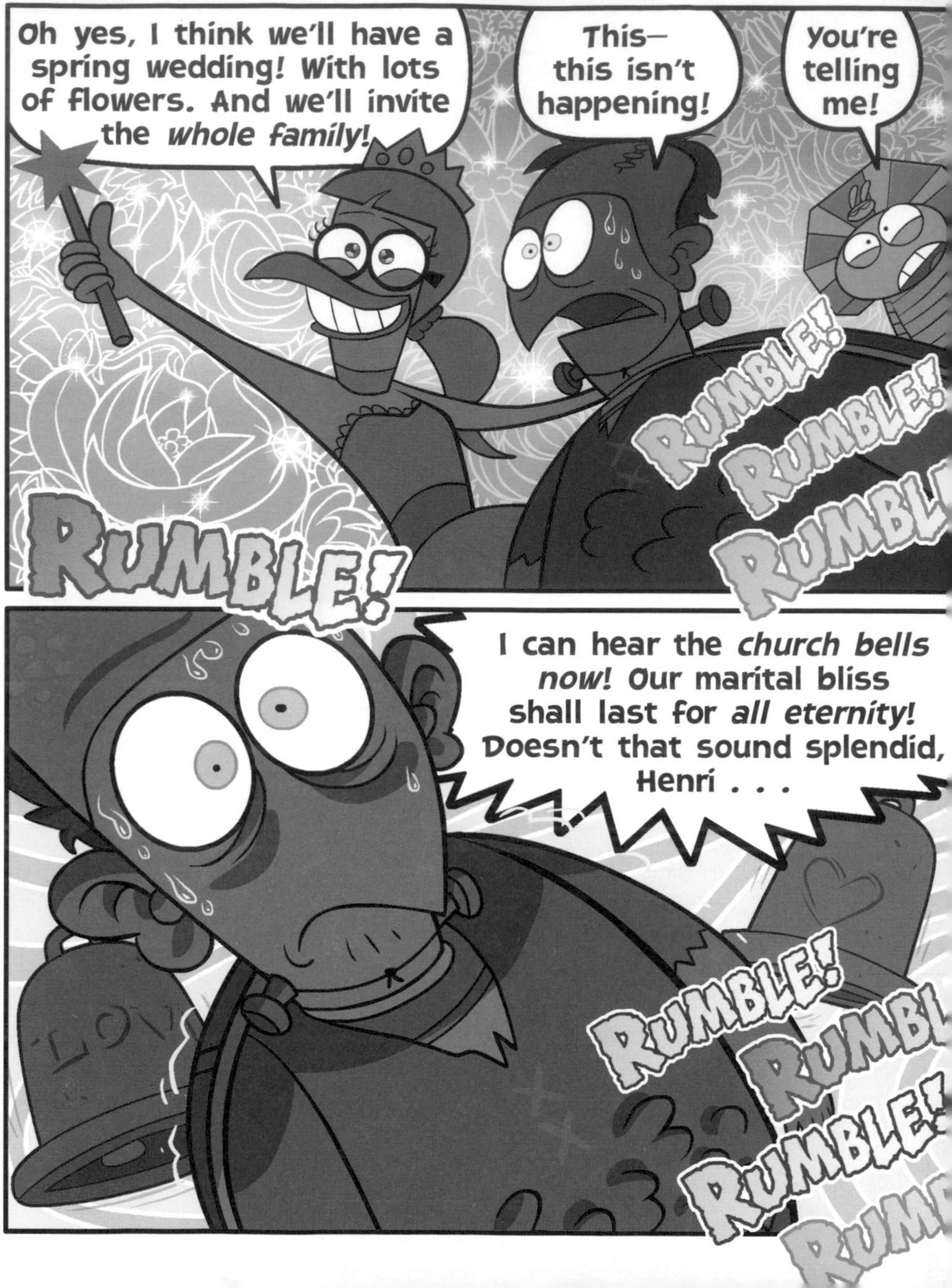
Oh yes, I think we'll have a spring wedding! With lots of flowers. And we'll invite the *whole family*!
This— this isn't happening!
You're telling me!
RUMBLE!
RUMBLE!
RUMBLE!
RUMBL
I can hear the *church bells now*! Our marital bliss shall last for *all eternity*! Doesn't that sound splendid, Henri . . .
RUMBLE!
RUMBL
RUMBLE!
RUM

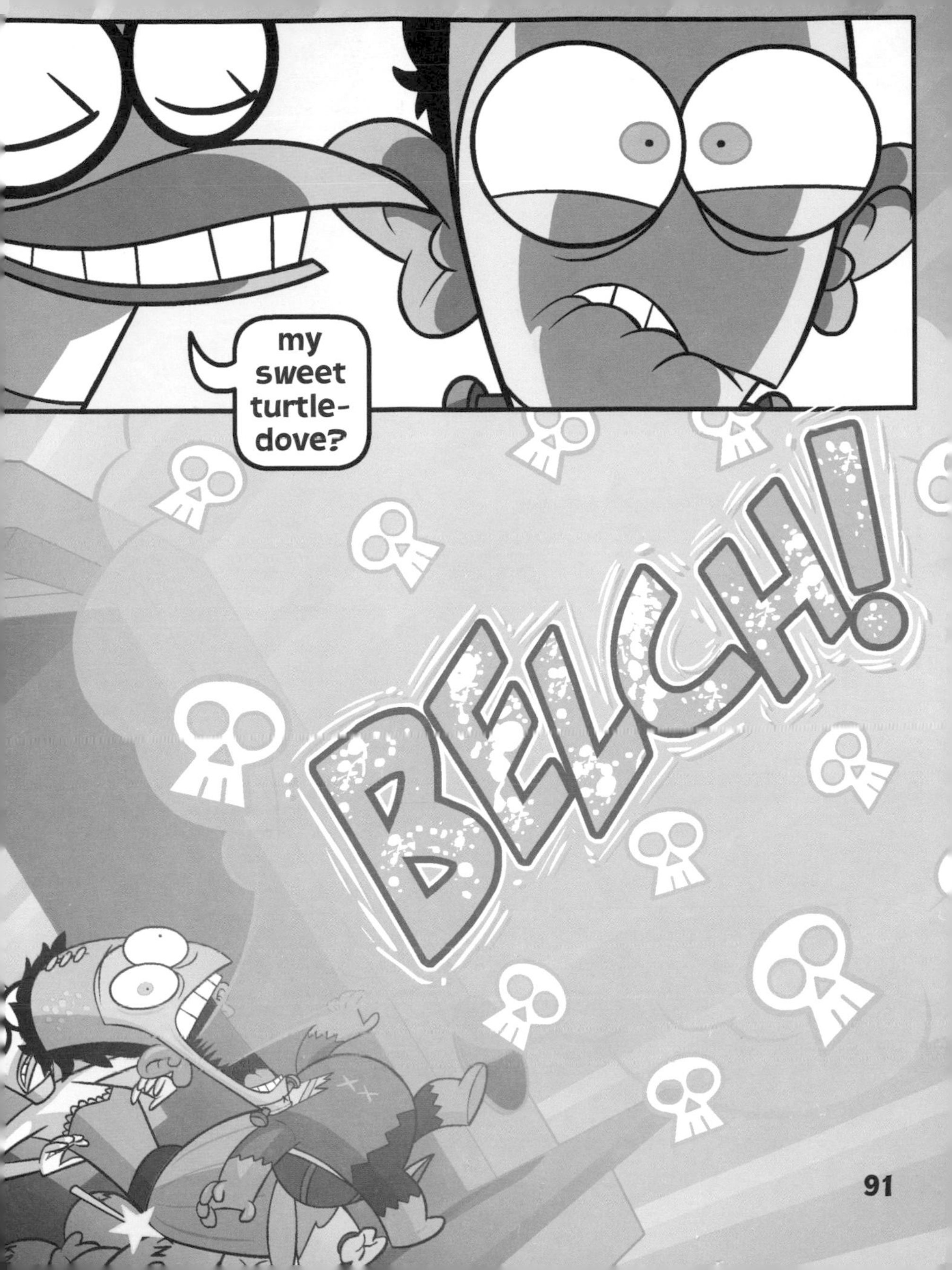
my sweet turtle-dove?
BELCH!!

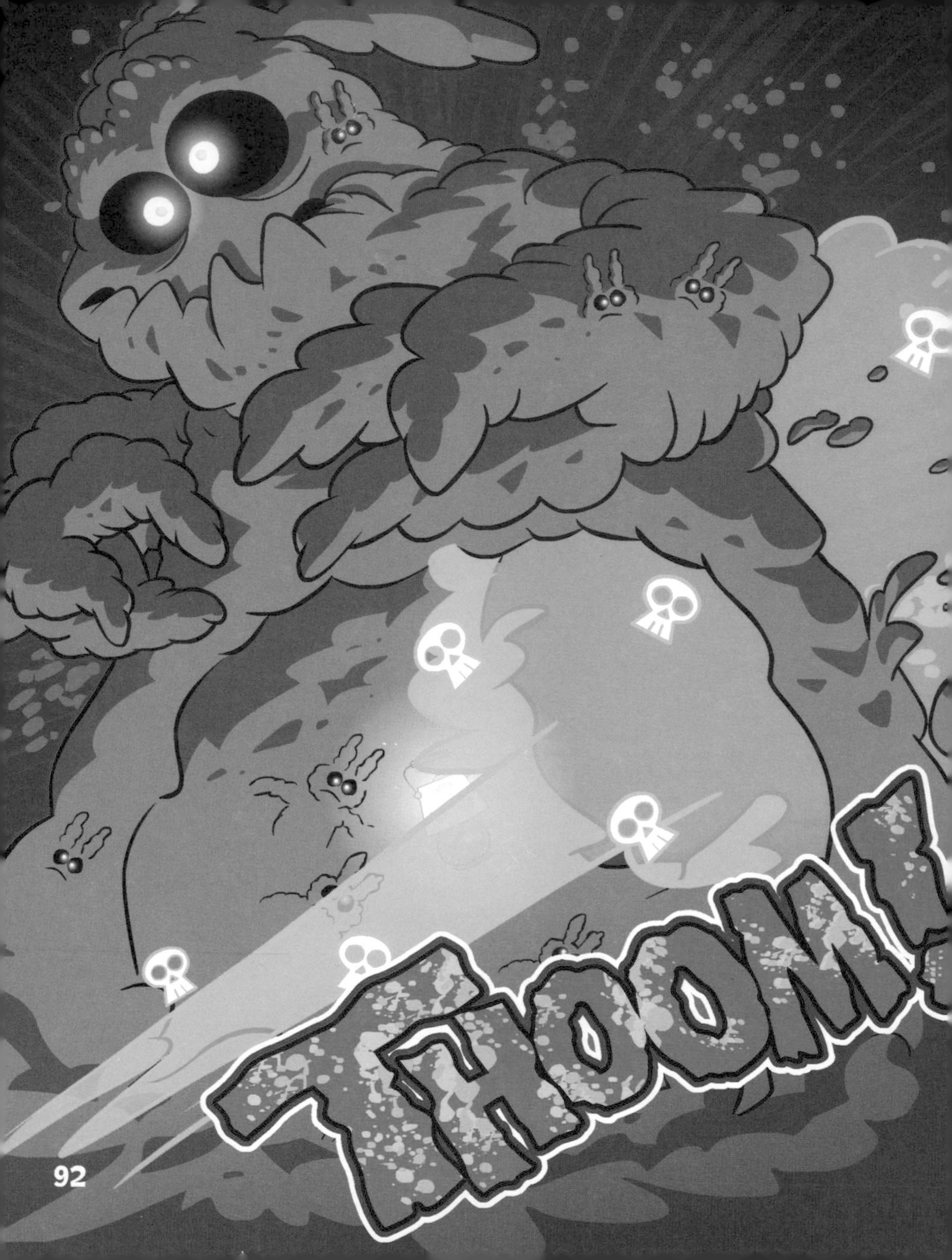
THOOM!

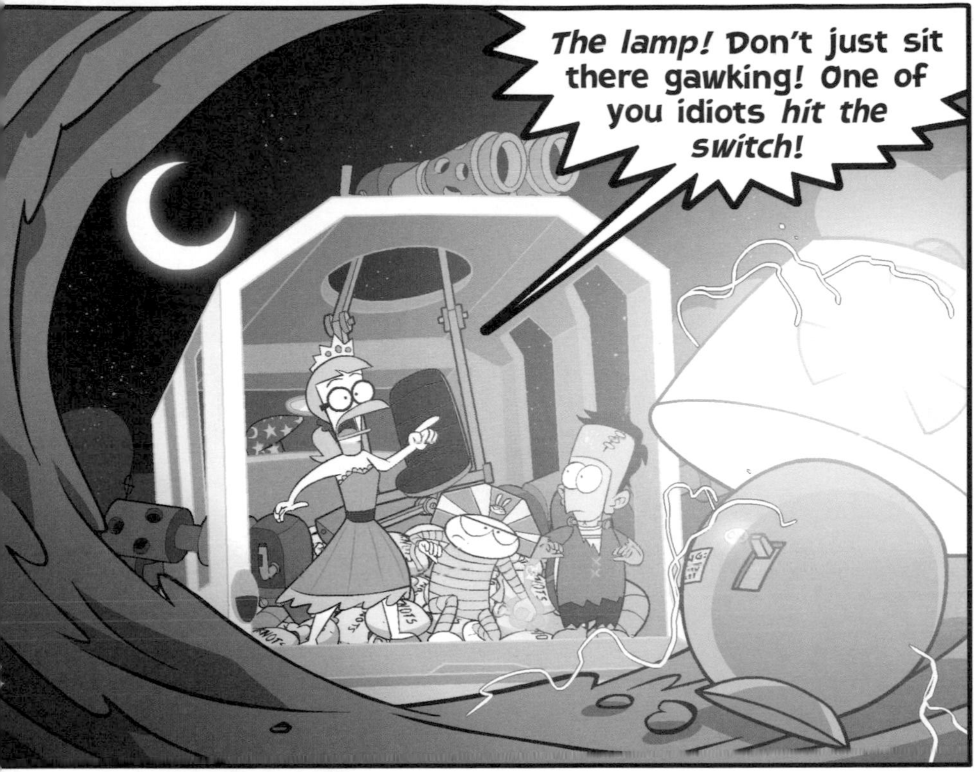
The lamp! Don't just sit there gawking! One of you idiots *hit the switch!*

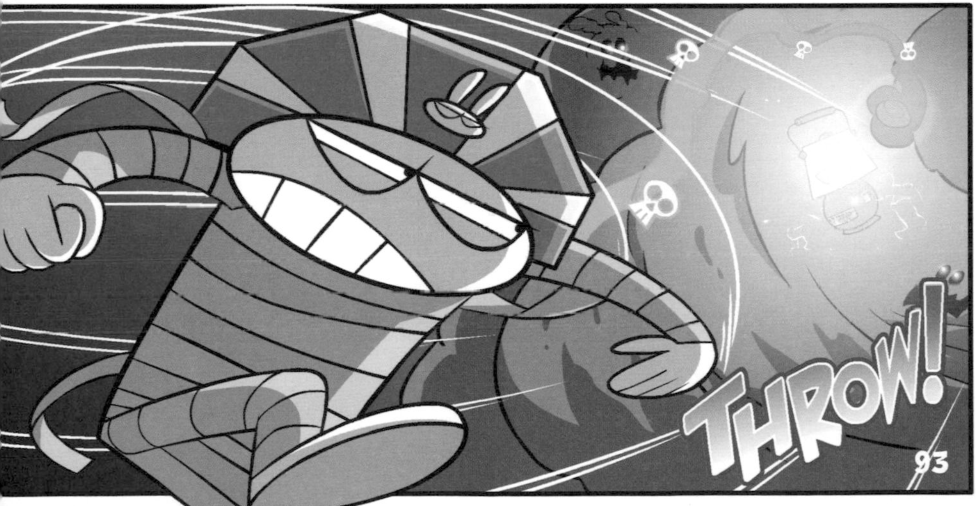
THROW!

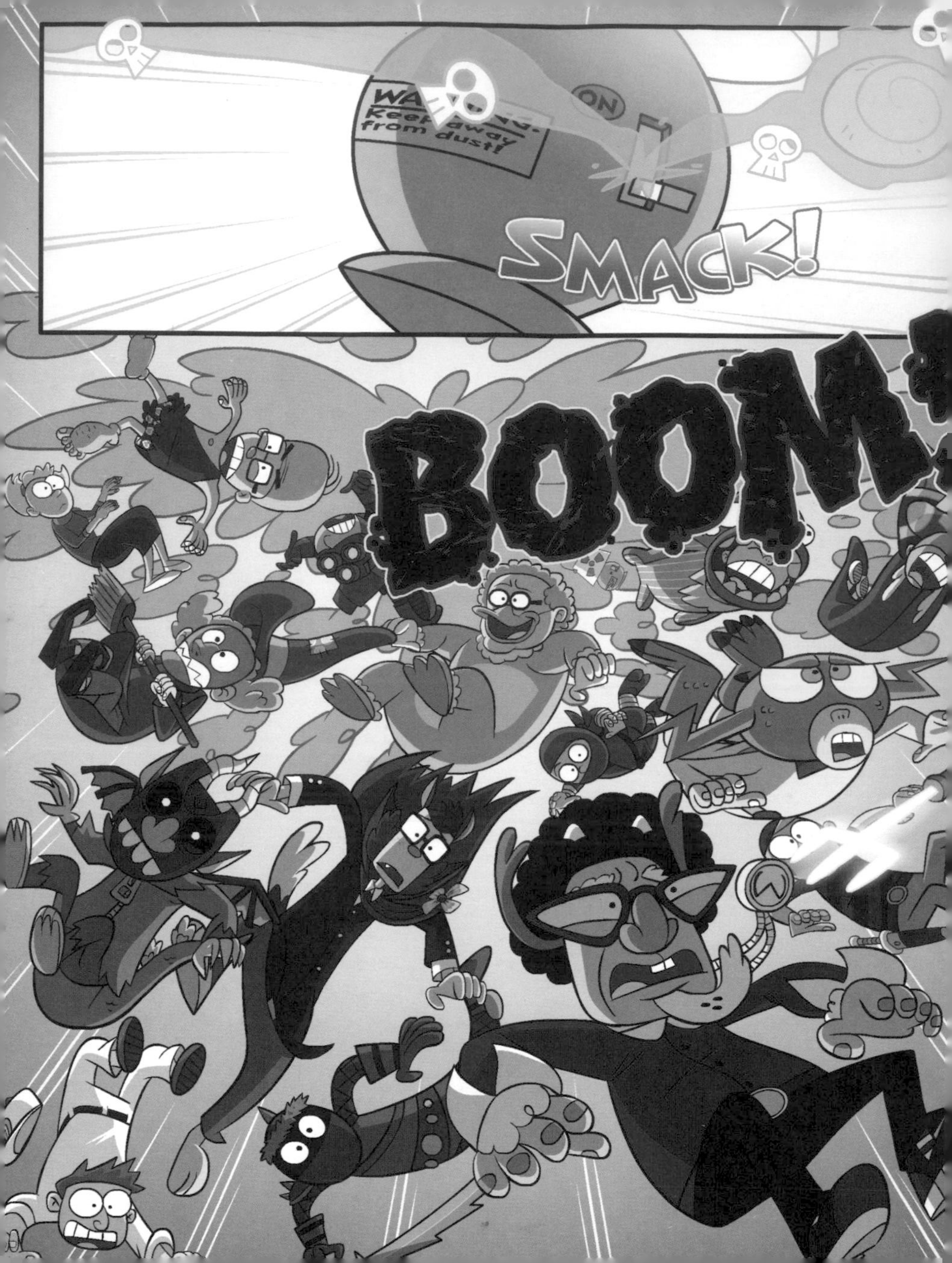

Keep away from dust!
ON
SMACK!
BOOM

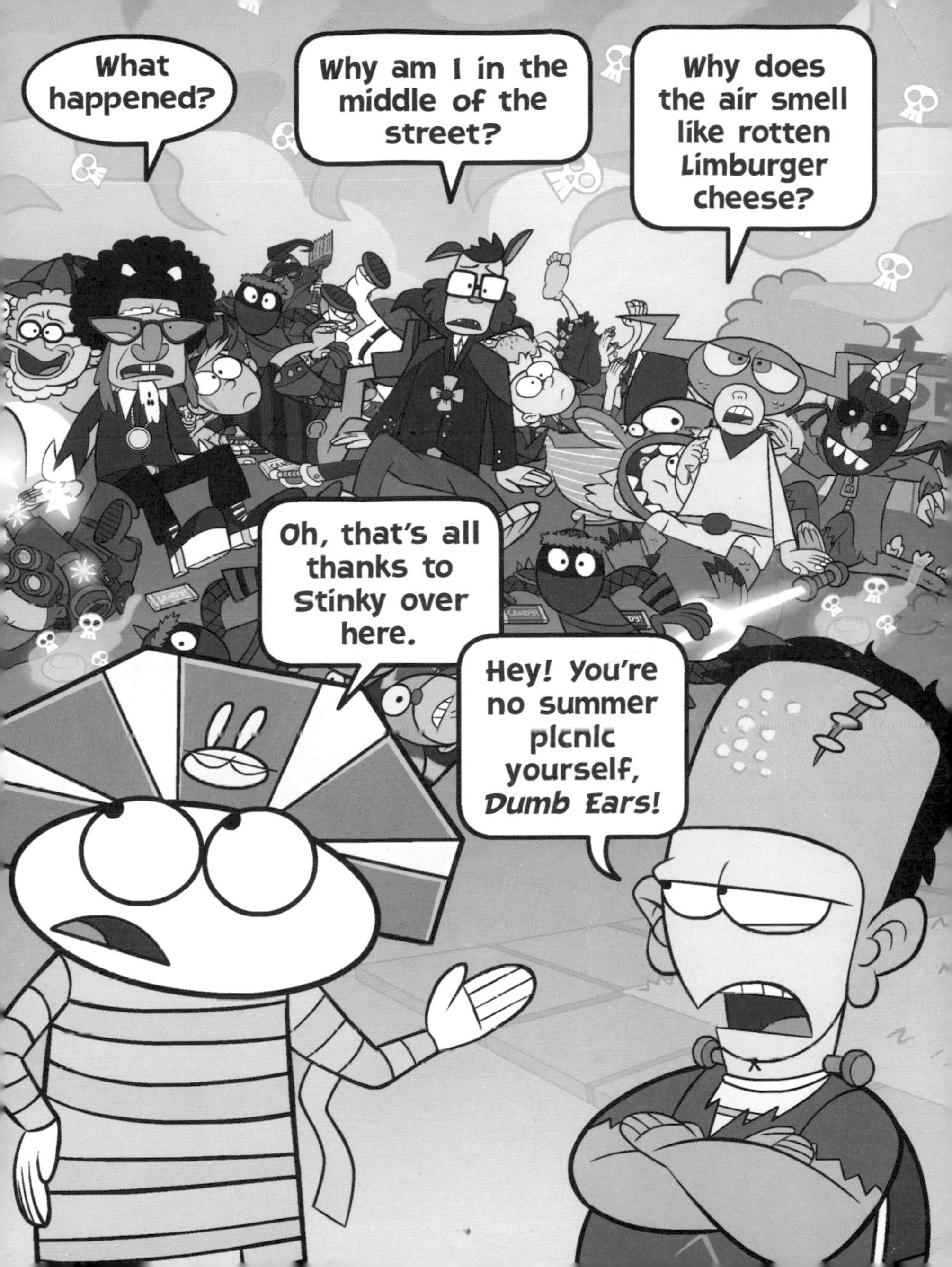
What happened?
Why am I in the middle of the street?
Why does the air smell like rotten Limburger cheese?
CANDY!
Oh, that's all thanks to Stinky over here.
Hey! You're no summer picnic yourself, Dumb Ears!

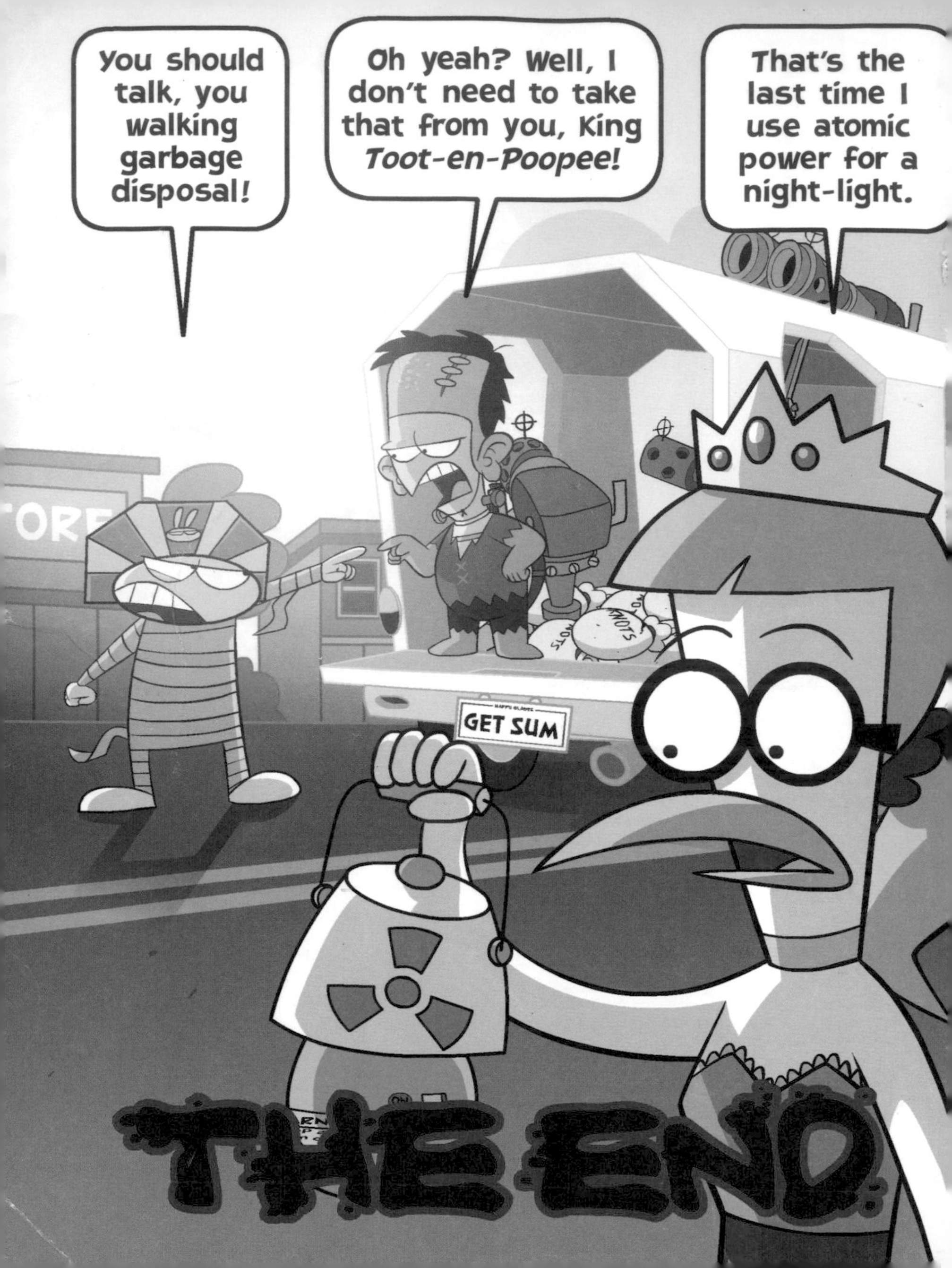
You should talk, you walking garbage disposal!
Oh yeah? Well, I don't need to take that from you, King *Toot-en-Poopee!*
That's the last time I use atomic power for a night-light.
GET SUM
THE END